ECHO
UNBOUND

ECHO UNBOUND

Echo Power Trilogy, Book Three

ANNA DURAND

JACOBSVILLE BOOKS • MARIETTA, OHIO

ECHO UNBOUND

The characters and events in this book are fictional. No portion of this book may be copied, reproduced, or transmitted in any form or by any means, electronic or otherwise, including recording, photocopying, or inclusion in any information storage and retrieval system, without the express written permission of the publisher and author, except for brief excerpts quoted in published reviews.

ISBN: 979-8-9852412-7-3 (paperback)
ISBN: 979-8-9852412-6-6 (ebook)
ISBN: 979-8-9852412-8-0 (audiobook)

Jacobsville Books
www.JacobsvilleBooks.com

Publisher's Cataloging-in-Publication Data
provided by Five Rainbows Cataloging Services

Names: Durand, Anna.
Title: Echo unbound / Anna Durand.
Description: Marietta, OH : Jacobsville Books, 2022. | Series: Echo power trilogy, bk. 3.
Identifiers:ISBN 979-8-9852412-7-3 (paperback) | ISBN 979-8-9852412-6-6 (ebook) | ISBN 979-8-9852412-8-0 (audiobook)
Subjects: LCSH: Magic--Fiction. | Survival--Fiction. | Amnesia--Fiction. | End of the world--Fiction. | Man-woman relationships--Fiction. | Romance fiction. | Paranormal romance stories. | BISAC: FICTION / Romance / Paranormal / General. | FICTION / Romance / Fantasy. | FICTION / Romance / Suspense. | GSAFD: Love stories. | Occult fiction. | Romantic suspense fiction.
Classification: LCC PS3604.U723 E25 2022 (print) | LCC PS3604.U724 (ebook) | DDC 813/.6--dc23.

CHAPTER ONE

Gabriel

KEEP CLIMBING! WE'RE ALMOST THERE." I LATCH ON TO A HANDHOLD in the cliff and pull myself up another a few feet, then repeat the process again and again as I inch upward. Sweat pours down my face and soaks my shirt. Damn, this is taking too long. The monsters below us will catch up soon. "Faster! No time to waste, people, keep moving."

I risk a glance downward. My friends are still climbing, but some have begun to fall back. I know they can't help it. None of us trained for climbing up a sheer cliff in the dark. Doing this in the daytime would test the best climber's skills. We are not the best of the best. We're only the best this world has got right now. At least the cliff offers a ton of natural handholds. But our job is still a damn hard one.

A scream echoes below me, receding swiftly.

No, no, no. I glance down, and my heart thuds.

Below me, a figure tumbles toward the ground.

I catch a glimpse of Rafiq's terrified face, and though my first impulse is to look away, I refuse to do that. My team, my friends, followed me onto this cliff without reservations. Losing even one person hurts like a knife driven into my heart, but I can't stop to grieve. Not right now. My friends have stopped climbing, frozen in place as they stare at the ground far below us. That's the last thing they should do right now.

"No gawking," I shout. "We have to keep climbing."

Everyone starts moving again, one handhold at a time, slowly making our way toward the summit. Fog shrouds it, but we know what lies on top of the cliff.

The castle created by Sefton Stainthorpe, the architect of the apocalypse.

I reach up, feeling for anything I can grip, and my palm lands on a flat surface. Peering up through the fog, I can just make out the ground. I've done it. I've reached the summit.

"Come on, guys!" I holler. "I'm at the top. You can make it too."

I find a foothold and push my body up, over the edge, landing face-first on flat ground. For a moment, I just lie here, catching my breath. My pulse pounds in my ears, but gradually, it slows down and becomes almost normal. I roll onto my back, wiping sweat off my face with my shirt. Just as I sit up, my friends begin to pour onto the summit.

Kai crawls toward me on hands and knees. Though he looks exhausted, he manages to grin. "We're here. We made it, sir."

I can't respond, not yet, not until I know the rest of my crew has reached the summit. I rattle off their names in my head as each one climbs over the edge, onto flat ground. Once they've all arrived, I relax a little. Can't relax all the way. We lost a member of our family tonight.

And the battle hasn't even begun yet.

Despite several hundred feet separating us from the street below, I can hear our enemies clamoring at ground level, desperate to reach the summit. They've only just arrived at the cliff's base, though.

"What now?" Kai asks.

"Let's go inside. That's what we came here for—to seize control of the castle. Sefton's palace belongs to us."

I get up and offer Kai my hand, helping him rise too. The rest of our friends lie on the ground or slump on their knees. I'd like to give them time to recover from that climb, but I can't do it. The monsters below will not give us a chance to catch our breath.

"Time to get moving again," I shout. "Into the castle. Now."

Nobody complains. They all get up and follow me and Kai as we approach the castle. The structure hunkers on the summit like an abandoned castle from a fairy tale, with sloping lines and rounded turrets. The whole thing feels off, though, like a painting with another picture hidden under the surface paint.

The wooden gates hang open.

Yeah, that's just creepy enough to give me pause. I've fought more battles with Echo creatures than I can count, and I've walked into some of the freakiest quadrants in this world. Yet the fact the castle doors are open, as if they were waiting for us, makes me uneasy.

But we have no choice. We can't turn back now.

I slowly walk through the open doors and into a large, empty entryway. A staircase winds its way up to the second floor. Doors on either side of the entryway stand closed. Light that seems to come from nowhere illuminates the interior of Sefton's palace. It's a castle, really, but apparently the mad architect of doomsday labeled it a palace.

The man who created it is dead. Even his Echo is dead. Sefton cannot ever return to reclaim this place.

Do I have an Echo? If I do, I haven't met him. All humans on Earth supposedly have twisted copies of themselves running around in the Echo or in the normal world, beings who have scaly skin, horns, or a thousand other aberrations.

And yes, that includes my friends.

"We need to search the castle," I announce. "Look for anything that might help us understand what this building was created to do."

Yeah, I don't buy that Sefton just wanted a throne to rest his maniacal ass on, or that he wanted to flaunt his power by creating a "palace" in the sky that everyone would see.

Kai sticks close to me as we explore the ground floor.

Outside, the cries of our enemies have died away. That seems like a bad sign.

"Stay here," I tell Kai. "I need to take a look outside."

"I should come with you, sir. No one works alone, that's what you tell us.'"

Suddenly, I wish I had never said that. I meant that none of them should ever do anything alone. I can handle myself.

I grasp Kai's shoulders and stare straight into his eyes. "Just stay here."

His shoulders flag, and his expression falls. But he does what I told him. He stays in the castle while I hurry outside to check on what's happening. Silence is never a good thing in an Echo battle. It means the enemy is plotting something.

As I cross the open space in front of the castle, I hear faint growling noises. I pull out my longest, sharpest serrated knife and grip it tightly. The noises draw closer and closer. I slow my pace as I approach the cliff's edge and halt a few yards away, tilting my head to the side to listen.

Grunting. Growling. Scrabbling.

That doesn't sound like an army climbing up the cliff.

I inch toward the edge, leaning forward, peering into the darkness below.

An Echo creature vaults over the edge to land inches away from me. The beast charges me, and I thrust my knife at its chest, aiming for the heart. The blade sinks into the creature's flesh to the hilt. Blood oozes from the wound—until I yank the blade free. Then blood pours out, and the beast collapses to the ground. I've heard rumors that some creatures can be killed by piercing the exact center of the heart, but I hadn't tried it until tonight. Did I hit the exact center? Can't be sure.

I punch the knife into the beast's heart again, just to be safe. Since the strike doesn't trigger a new rush of blood, I assume the creature is dead.

Where are this guy's friends? I scuffle up to the very edge of the cliff and peer down into the darkness. I don't see any shapes climbing toward the summit. The moon provides just enough light for me to tell that absolutely no creatures are scaling the cliff.

A chill shivers up my spine, lifting every hair.

Screams erupt inside the castle.

I whirl around and race back inside.

But I'm too late. The screams have ended, and the deepest silence I've ever heard suffuses the entire castle. Bodies lie strewn across the floor of the entryway. The bodies of my friends. I grip my knife so hard that my fingers ache. Where are the monsters who did this? I scurry from body to body, verifying that they're actually dead and not just injured.

I don't find anyone still alive. My people are all accounted for, along with quite a few of our enemies. I find Kai last and pick him up to hold him for a moment. My throat goes thick. The kid had followed me around like a lost puppy, and he became my best ally and battle partner.

Shuffling noises originate from another part of the castle.

My people are dead. Those noises must be the enemy.

I grab my knife and the machine gun Kai had liked to carry, then I stalk toward the noises. It sounds like someone is rifling through stuff, searching for who knows what. I clench my jaw and shove my knife into its scabbard. The machine gun works better—and faster, for sure. Whatever creatures are left in the castle, they will die tonight.

When I stalk into the room from where the noises originated, I find myself inside Sefton's throne room. A single creature hustles around, hunting for something to steal but finding nothing. The room is empty, except for the throne.

The monster faces away from me.

"Hey, turn around," I holler.

Slowly, the beast shuffles around to look at me. "Mm, I am hungry. Maybe I should eat you, human."

"You and your friends murdered my family."

"But you fight alongside my kind."

"No. I fight with my family." I raise the machine gun. "You murdered them. I believe in the eye-for-an-eye approach to justice."

"You want to swap eyes with me?"

These creatures can be incredibly stupid, but they also have a vicious type of cunning. Vicious and gruesome.

"I prefer to eat human eyes," the monster says. "But hearts taste the best."

Fury rises inside me, searing and sharp, and I can't hold back any longer. I roar as I bolt for the beast, pulling the trigger to spray round after round at the thing that murdered my surrogate family. I don't stop firing until the beast hits the floor with a thud that vibrates the entire castle. When the bullets run out, I get my knife and stab it straight into the creature's heart.

He lies dead, his eyes open and vacant.

It's over. The Echo has won. The only decent beings living in this world have died while following my orders. The family I cultivated here no longer exists. I am alone.

The weight of the loss envelops me, and the bitter taste of it seeps into my soul. I trudge over to the marble throne Sefton had erected and drop onto it. Every muscle in my body slackens. The gun falls from my hand, clattering on the floor. I let my head fall back against the throne and shut my eyes.

"You grieve for your friends, but you cannot give up yet."

The female voice that spoke those words makes me crack one eye open. A pretty Echo creature with scaly flesh and small spikes on her head stands several yards away, watching me with a bland expression. When she blinks, her inner lids flick across her eyes, and her green eyes have an iridescent quality that makes them almost seem to glow.

I leap off the throne and rip my knife out of its scabbard, wielding it at the pretty beast. "Your buddies killed my family."

"They were not my friends. I serve no master."

"Who are you?"

She moves closer. "I am Aldith, guardian of the Echo's Heart and Lifeblood. I also protect the Brain."

"What brain?"

"The Echo is a living thing composed of magics. It cannot think or act like a human or an Echo creature. It has no sentience of its own, thus it requires another being to keep the Brain working properly." She steps even closer, seemingly unfazed by the big knife in my hand. "I have waited for you. I had no knowledge of who you might be, but I sensed you would come."

"If you live in this castle, you are not my ally."

She scans the throne room, though she seems only faintly interested in it. "I don't live here. The castle belongs to the one who claimed it. That would be you."

"You think I want to live here?" I shake my head. "You're insane. And I'm out of here."

I stomp toward the doorway.

"Don't you wish to know why I came here?" Aldith asks. "Or would you prefer never to know your true destiny?"

"Don't believe in that shit."

"You, Gabriel Merchant, cannot escape your destiny. Belief is not required, but cooperation is mandatory."

I glance back at her. "Sorry, I'm fresh out of cooperation."

She sighs. "I regret the need to force your compliance. But you leave me no choice. The fate of two worlds depends on you, and I know of only one way to convince you of that. I'm sending you to Sanctuary."

"To where? You're nuts, lady."

I walk out of the throne room—and straight into the entryway, where my friends lie dead, their blood staining the floor. My feet won't move. My eyes force me to look at their faces. They stare at me with the starkness of death.

My friends. My family. Every one of them was murdered by the monsters who inhabit this world. What made me believe I could protect them and bring them to a place where no one could find us? I'd been so arrogant.

Outside, the footfalls of a gigantic beast detonate like synchronized bomb blasts. Then the racket stops.

Aldith appears in front of me. "Your ride is here."

"My ride to where?"

"Sanctuary." She turns to the side, gesturing for me to exit the building. "Jarek doesn't like to be kept waiting."

Why not do what she says? I've got nothing now, except the responsibility for getting my friends killed. Whether Aldith intends to send me to a nice place or the hell I deserve, it doesn't matter anymore. I walk outside and stop a few feet from the cliff's edge.

A gigantic creature made of flesh and metal stands there, his eyes at my chest level. He offers me his enormous hand.

I guess I'm supposed to sit on his palm. "Are you my taxi to Sanctuary?"

The behemoth nods.

He looks familiar, but I know I've never met this creature before. I think I heard stories about him.

"Are you the golem?" I ask. "The creature Sefton created out of magics?"

He nods.

With a heavy sigh, I climb onto the golem's hand. Aldith had called him Jarek.

The golem walks through the city, and no one dares to get in his way or question him about where he's going or what he's doing. Maybe he can't talk, but I wouldn't be surprised if he can write. Eventually, we leave the Capital City behind, heading out into the ravaged wasteland beyond it. The Echo destroyed both worlds, but I have no idea what Earth looks like now.

Jarek takes me to the gateway that joins the two worlds, a spinning black disk high in the sky. For Jarek, reaching that height proves no obstacle at all. He raises his hand just as the gateway spirals open, then stretches his hand through it to set me down on the cracked pavement of a city street.

I turn around just in time to see the golem's hand retreating into the Echo. The gateway shuts.

Where am I? It looks like a city. But which one? The destruction wrought by the Echo might have made it impossible to tell, or at least very difficult to figure out. I don't get why Aldith wanted to drop me here. Sanctuary? I don't think so. But I have nowhere else to go. Might as well explore my new environment.

And pray I haven't been tricked into walking into hell.

Chapter Two

Sarah

LIE ON THE BEACH, STRETCHED OUT ON MY TUMMY ON A SOFT TOWEL, and let the warmth of the sun penetrate my skin and warm me from the inside out. The apocalypse might have destroyed the world, but I've found a lovely new home here on the Lost Coast, in what used to be called Northern California. I don't remember the day the Echo struck, or what happened after that. But oddly, I do remember where California is.

Yeah, amnesia can be totally confusing.

My new friends here at Sanctuary took me in, despite having no idea who I am or how I got here. I woke up on this very beach two months ago, dressed in ragged clothes and with no memory of who I am or how I came to be here. Months and still nothing. My life before I found Sanctuary remains a gaping black hole.

A few days after I turned up here, Allison, one of my new friends, asked me what I'd like to be called. The name Sarah popped out of my mouth. Is that my real name? I still don't know. How old am I? Everybody took a poll and decided I must be twenty-eight. Works for me.

I roll over onto my back and slip on my sunglasses. I'm glad my friends have the ability to teleport to basically anywhere they want, because they bring home a lot more than food. They grab fun things too. Like Allison says, "Everybody needs to feel normal, even if it's only for a little while." My towel and my shades came from a partially destroyed department store in Yuma, Arizona. Or what used to be Yuma. Echo creatures took control of the city not long after the gang came home.

Ahhh, the sun feels so good on my skin. I asked if I could sunbathe in the nude, and Allison said sure. Dax, her grumpy British husband, threatened to "knock the bloody daylights" out of anyone who might spy on me. But

"

that was unnecessary. The Sanctuary gang obeys the rules of etiquette in our camp. No Echo creatures have come here in months, which is the only reason I'm allowed to sunbathe alone.

Maybe I used to love nude sunbathing before the apocalypse. I definitely love it today. With the trees providing privacy, I feel totally relaxed for the first time since I woke up here.

An angry yell echoes from high above me and further down the beach. It draws closer every second, almost as if the person doing the yelling has been launched through the air.

Whump.

Sand sprays up and rains down on my body.

I jerk into a sitting position, my eyes flying open, and gape at the man lying near my feet. The shock of what just happened ensures that I don't do the smart thing. No, I just sit here staring at the man.

He pushes up onto his straight arms, seeming dazed. He blinks rapidly several times, then his attention lands on me. On my breasts.

I still can't move. While he stares at my body, I can't stop myself from admiring him too. The man has a muscular physique, and his clothes have gotten torn. Only a few scraps cling to his torso, and his pants have been ripped in various places. His hair is a mess.

Suddenly, I realize I'm still naked.

I scurry backward and snatch my towel up to cover my front side. "Who are you? What are you doing here?"

The man rises to his knees and brushes sand off himself. "Where am I?"

"California."

He surveys the beach, seeming satisfied. "Well, that's better than where I just came from."

"You haven't answered my questions."

"Maybe I don't feel like answering."

I glance to my right, where I'd left my clothes in a neat little pile.

"Want your clothes?" the man asks. "Or would you rather fuck right here on the beach?"

"Excuse me? I do not have sex with strangers." Well, maybe I used to be like that, but I don't remember. I hope not.

He licks his lips as he gazes at my bare thighs. "I haven't been with a woman in such a long time."

I leap up and grab my clothes, then bolt for the path that leads up and over the mountain, to where Sanctuary lies. I only make it halfway there before the stranger throws his arms around me from behind and hoists me off my feet.

"Don't run," he growls into my ear. "Tell me one thing, and I'll consider letting you go."

"Gee, thanks."

He rubs his stubbly cheek against my face. "Guess you don't want me to let go yet."

"Just ask your damn question."

"Is this Sanctuary?"

His question stops me for a moment. Sure, people find us here and often join our camp. But they don't know what name we gave it until we tell them. This man already knows. That realization sweeps a shiver up my spine.

My captor gives me a quick, hard squeeze. "Answer my question."

"I can't. Need to talk to my friends first."

"Wrong answer." He rips the towel away, leaving me naked and holding on to my lump of clothes. "Guess it's fucking on the beach, then."

"Threatening me with sexual assault won't convince me to give you information."

For a moment, he doesn't move or speak. I hear only the whispering of his breaths and the pounding of my own heart. Then he releases me. "Go on. Run to your friends, Lady Godiva."

I race for the camp, running faster than I ever have before, and crest the mountain in a few minutes. I stop there. Needing to rest is only part of the reason. I glance around but don't see that vile man. So I take the time to quickly yank my clothes on before I sprint down the mountainside. By the time I reach the camp, everyone is busy preparing for lunch. They've started a small fire to roast over a spit what looks like a chicken. As I draw closer, slowing to a jog, I can tell they have another spit set up on the other side of the fire, and that one seems to have a pig roasting on it.

I approach Grant Larson and Erin Harding, the people who found me on the beach two months ago. They've become my friends, just like Dax and Allison Stainthorpe and their adopted daughter, Willow. Dax's brother was the lunatic who created the apocalypse, but nobody brings up that subject without a really good reason.

Erin smiles and waves for me to go to her. "Did you have a good time sunbathing?"

"Uh, yeah. Until some guy fell out of the sky and grabbed me."

"What? Are you okay?"

I shrug. "Sure, fine. He let me go, and I ran back here."

"You're awfully calm, considering what happened."

Why don't I feel panicky? It's weird.

Erin throws an arm around my shoulders. "If that creep comes within two hundred yards of the camp, we'll know about it—and we'll eighty-six that guy. So just relax and eat some lunch."

The guards positioned discreetly around the camp will never let that jerk past the perimeter. They're armed and well-trained by Grant and Erin, who both have military experience.

"Don't worry," Grant says. "No one in this camp will ever let anyone hurt you."

I wish they wouldn't treat me differently than everyone else in Sanctuary. Amnesia doesn't make me special. All the residents of Sanctuary have a story of loss, the gut-wrenching kind. I have no idea if I've lost anyone, or if somebody out there is looking for me.

"Please, just treat me like everyone else," I say. "And I really wish you guys would let me do something. I can help with the cooking or sewing, or anything."

"Do you remember how to sew?" Erin asks.

"Well, no. But I can't keep sitting around doing nothing." I suddenly remember that maniac on the beach. "Erin, would you teach me how to defend myself? I'd love to know how to shoot arrows like you do."

"Allison can show you self-defense techniques. Dax taught her. But if you really want to learn about archery, I'd be happy to teach you."

"Thank you." I try to restrain myself, but I fail. "When can we start? Today?"

Erin smiles and shakes her head. "You might not remember your past, but you sure know what you want. Yes, we can get started later this afternoon. I need to help Grant with something after lunch, then I'll come find you."

Well, that's a start. I need to feel useful, and after my encounter earlier, I need to develop some fighting skills.

"Maybe you shouldn't go out by yourself anymore," Grant says. "Just to be safe."

No more nude sunbathing. He's right, of course. But I wish he were wrong.

"I should check around," Grant says, "to see if anybody has seen that creature."

"He wasn't an Echo creature," I say. "He was a man."

"Oh. Well, we should send a few people to search the beach and the woods along our favorite trails to make sure that guy has left the vicinity."

"Lunch," Dax hollers. "Come and get it."

Hearing a British man speak those words always strikes me as kind of funny. Shouldn't he announce that lunch will be served in the dining room? But we don't have a dining room, or any type of rooms. Just tents. Grant, Erin, and I head for the fire and the nicely roasted meat waiting for us there. As I eat a hunk of white meat chicken, I can't help wondering for the thousandth time if I used to like meat or if I might've been a vegetarian, maybe even a vegan.

Will I ever find out the truth about myself?

I say goodbye to Grant and Erin, who are going off to do whatever they need to do that I'm not allowed to know about. Despite the fact they've welcomed me into Sanctuary and treat me like family, I often wonder if their secret discussions revolve around me and who or what they think I am.

Someone screams.

We all freeze. I glance at Grant and Erin, who have barely walked halfway to Dax and Allison's tent.

"Out of my way, you moron!" a man shouts.

I recognize that growly, nasty voice. But no, it can't be him. We have look-outs who watch for anyone or anything that might waltz into our camp.

"Hey! Don't push my wife. Who do you think you are, anyway?"

That sounds like Stan Woodruff. He and his wife, Miriam, are the oldest residents of Sanctuary, though they're only in their sixties.

Dax and Allison rush out of their tent and race toward the ruckus, but Dax waves for her to stay away. She is pregnant, so I get why she needs to stay back. Grant and Erin hurry after Dax.

Will I just stand here? That's what I usually do. But I refuse to keep letting everyone treat me like the fairy-tale princess who can't stand to lie on a pea. So I race after my friends, heading straight for the ruckus on the other side of the camp. Halfway there, we stop.

A figure stumbles out from between two tents.

My heart thuds, and a wave of ice floods through me. Oh yes, I know that man. He saw me naked, and I tried to get away from him. I only succeeded because he let me.

The man still wears torn and tattered clothes, but grass stains have joined the dirt stains. "Is this Sanctuary?"

Dax approaches the man. "Who are you? And why have you frightened our friends?"

"Not my fault if they're pansies who screech every time they see a stranger."

"Perhaps you should try a less violent approach to entering a new place."

The man squints at Dax. "Is this Sanctuary or not? Aldith sent me here, and I want to know why."

Dax goes perfectly still, his expression blank. He glances at Allison, who hovers just outside their tent. She shrugs. Grant and Erin shrug too.

"Tell us what you know about Sanctuary and Aldith," Dax demands. "And how you got past our sentries."

The stranger clenches his fists, then loosens them. "What the hell. Aldith is an Echo creature, who must live in the Echo since that's where I met her. She told me I needed to come here. Then she got a golem to dump me on Earth, but nowhere near this place, as far as I can tell."

"Where did Aldith send you?"

"Some city. I didn't get the chance to do any sightseeing. Creatures attacked me."

Dax folds his arms over his chest. "Hmm. If you were in 'some city,' how did you reach this place? There are no metropolitan areas anywhere near the Lost Coast."

"Something threw me here, and I landed on the beach with that naked girl." He glances at me. "Figured she must know where she's going, so I followed her."

I jog over to Dax and the stranger, focusing on the man who threatened to assault me on the beach. "If you followed me, why did it take an hour for you to get here?"

"Reconnaissance, Lady Godiva. I never walk into a strange place without scouting the area first."

"My name is not Lady Godiva."

The maniac smirks. "What is it, then?"

"Like I would ever tell you."

Dax inserts himself between me and the stranger. "Start by telling us your name, and we'll go from there."

The man keeps his focus on me as he speaks to Dax. "Gabriel Merchant. Who are you, mountain man?"

"You may call me Dax. Now, you will follow me. We need to have a discussion."

Dax grasps Gabriel's arm and drags him away to the tent where we store our food. I experience a bizarre impulse to follow them, but I ignore it. The last thing I want to do is spend more time in Gabriel's presence. That man is evil.

I return to my tent and try to read a book, but I can't concentrate on it even though I love detective stories from the nineteen forties. My mind keeps forcing me to wonder what Dax and Gabriel are talking about and whether it has anything to do with me. That's narcissistic, though. Not everything strange in this place revolves around the amnesia girl. But Gabriel did seem extremely interested in me.

After chewing on my bottom lip for a moment, I shut the book and sneak out of my tent. I slip out the back way, so nobody will see me, and tiptoe past half a dozen other tents to reach the one where Dax took Gabriel. I can hear them talking.

"Who the bloody hell are you?" Dax snarls. "I want to know the truth. All of it. Right now."

"And I should cooperate, why?"

"Because I will snap your neck if you don't."

Gabriel chuckles. "I've fought with much worse things than you."

A rustling sound originates from the other side of the tent. "Mind if I come in?"

That's Grant.

"Yes, of course," Dax tells him.

"Maybe I should talk to the new guy," Grant says. "Use my Zen powers on him. After a little forced meditation, he might be more open to talking."

Gabriel chuckles again. "Forced meditation? You guys are nuts."

I really want to see what's going on in there, instead of just hearing it. So I skulk along the backside of the tent until I find a seam where the tent has been held together with snaps. I carefully push two fingers into the seam and spread them. That gives me a partial view of the interior.

Gabriel sits on a folding canvas chair with his wrists bound behind it with duct tape. He keeps smiling with smug satisfaction while Dax glares and Grant just gazes at the man placidly.

"We're not bad people," Grant says. "If you tell us about you, maybe we can help each other."

"I don't trust anyone."

"That's too bad. Trust is a beautiful thing—when it's earned."

Gabriel grunts. "Why should I give a shit about earning your trust? You haven't earned mine."

"Hey, man, we're just trying to keep our family safe. I'm sure you can understand that. Besides, you did assault our friend."

"No, I didn't. I detained her briefly."

Grant clucks his tongue. "Lying won't help us trust you."

"Screw your trust."

Gabriel swivels his head toward the rear of the tent—toward me—and his lips kink into a sly smile.

A shiver races up my spine.

No, I don't like this at all. A stranger with ulterior motives has invaded our Sanctuary, and nothing good can come of that.

CHAPTER THREE

Gabriel

I SIT HERE INSIDE A TENT, WITH MY WRISTS SECURED WITH DUCT TAPE, AND try to figure out if I should trust these people. They haven't made me feel welcome, that's for sure. I haven't given them reason to, so there's that. After months of scrabbling to survive post-apocalypse, I'd finally found a group of allies I could trust. Friends. A new kind of family. But I got them all killed.

Why did Aldith send me here? She claimed it's my destiny or some bullshit like that. I've never bought into the idea of fate. The Echo didn't change my mind about that.

The big guy who has a beard, tattoos, and a British accent walks up beside me and leans in. "You should start answering our questions, mate. Give us a reason to trust you, or we will toss you back to wherever you came from."

"Dial it back a little, Dax, would you?" the other man says. "We're trying to be nice."

The man who just spoke is American, which doesn't surprise me. The British Hulk seems out of place here, though. How many Brits lived in Northern California before the Echo hit? Not many, I'd bet. Of course, this is my first visit to California.

I glance toward the rear of the tent. The blonde sunbather is still peeking through a slit in the tent to watch us. So, she's a nudist and a voyeur.

"What should we do with him, Grant?" the British Hulk says. He told me I could call him Dax, but I prefer my nickname for him.

"Try to make peace," Grant says.

What do I have to lose? Everyone I cared about is gone. I sigh and slump in my chair. "Look, I don't want to hurt anybody. But I don't know you guys, and I've learned the hard way that trusting the wrong people ends in bloodshed."

"Yeah, we've learned that lesson too," Grant says. "Let's untie him, huh, Dax?"

The British Hulk nods.

Grant removes the duct tape, then offers me his hand to shake. "I'm Grant Larson. And that big scary dude is Dax."

"No last name? How chic. He's like a rock singer or an athlete."

"We don't know you well enough to share Dax's last name," Grant says. "It's up to him whether he feels like telling you."

What's that guy hiding? I gave my full name. But the hulk won't reciprocate.

Movement catches my attention, and I move only my eyes to glance at the sexy voyeur. I can see one of her eyes, but their blue color is so pale that it almost seems like silver. I've never seen eyes like that.

"Here's the deal," I say to Dax and Grant. "I'll tell Lady Godiva everything you want to know."

"Lady Godiva?" Grant says. "Oh, you mean Sarah. Why her?"

"We met on the beach. Anything else you want to know about me, you'll have to get from her after I tell the nudist."

Dax and Grant retreat into the far corner of the tent to have a hushed discussion. Then they return to me.

"We have to ask Sarah first," Grant says. "If she agrees—"

"I agree," a feminine voice announces. The pretty voyeur ducks through the rear tent flap. "You guys can go."

"We'll be right outside," Dax tells her.

"Uh-uh-uh," I say. "You'll be out of earshot. That's the deal. Take it or leave it."

Dax pulls a switchblade out of his pocket and tosses it to Sarah.

She catches it. "Thanks."

He nods. Then both men walk out.

The pretty voyeur sits on the cot on the other side of the tent, about ten feet away from me. "Here I am. Now tell me everything Dax and Grant want to know."

"First, I want to know something." I lean forward in my chair, resting my elbows on my knees. "Why do you sunbathe in the nude? Echo creatures might find you and decide you look like a good snack. Or worse, a fun sex toy."

"None of your business. I'm supposed to gather all the intel about you."

"Intel? That's cute. I bet you were a librarian before the Echo."

She bows her head.

"Hey, it's nothing to be ashamed of. Librarians are hot."

"I'm not embarrassed." She lifts her head. "You still haven't given me any information about you."

Well, I did say I'd tell her everything. "The day the apocalypse hit, I got sucked into the Echo."

Sarah stares at me. "Seriously?"

"Yeah, seriously. It's not the kind of thing anybody would joke about." I can't get comfortable all of a sudden, and sitting back in my chair doesn't help. So I get up and start pacing. "I experienced the apocalypse from the Earth side of things for about two hours, and I spent most of that time running away so I wouldn't get ripped apart by the creatures. Then I got thrown into the Echo. Pretty much everything I know about the apocalypse came from my time in that world."

"Did the Echo get destroyed like Earth did on the day the apocalypse started? We've wondered about that."

"Yeah. That happened in both worlds."

She wants to ask more questions, I can tell, and I promised I would spill all the beans—but only to her. Now I'm wondering if that's the wisest choice. I can't claim I made that deal for any good reasons. No, I just wanted to be alone with Sarah. I've seen her naked. She's beautiful and sexy, and I haven't been with a woman in so long that I can't even remember when the last time was. That's the only reason I feel such a strong urge to spend more time with her.

If I stop talking, she'll go get the British Hulk, and he will probably pummel me.

Worse things than him have tried to crush me. They always lose the battle.

Sarah holds the switchblade in one hand, loosely, like she's uncomfortable with the weapon. Every so often, she glances down at it. "Would you tell me who you were before the Echo? Before the worlds collided?"

"Does it matter? Nobody is who they used to be anymore."

"We want to trust you, Gabriel. But evasive answers don't help."

Of course I'm being evasive. I just met these people. For all I know, they're Echo creatures who found a way to disguise their true nature, and any minute they'll hoist me onto a spit and roast me for dinner. Or maybe they're a doomsday cult who believe the Echo is their ticket to the afterlife, and they plan to sacrifice me to get inside the other world.

Yeah, I've spent too much time in the Echo.

Nothing in that hell world is as beautiful as the woman sitting ten feet away from me.

"Would you tell me about your time in the Echo?" Sarah asks.

"You don't want to know what it was like, trust me."

My pulse beats faster, and I start to feel slightly nauseous. Why? Anything I might tell her about the Echo is nothing I haven't experienced firsthand. It never made me uneasy before. But with Sarah's eerily pale eyes fixed on me, I develop a phantom itch that refuses to go away.

"I won't tell anyone else," she says. "Not unless you give me permission to do that."

"But you told your buddies that you'd get the information they want." I shake my head. "Guess you're a liar. Way to build trust, Lady Godiva."

"Please stop calling me that. My name is Sarah."

"What's your last name?"

She bows her head again. "I don't know."

For a moment, I stare at the top of her head. Then I finally manage to ask the obvious question. "Do you mean you have amnesia?"

"Yes."

"Oh. Well, that's, uh…" I have no idea what to say to an amnesiac to make her feel better. Why I care about making her feel better, I have no clue. "Maybe your memory will come back soon. Is it total amnesia?"

She nods. "I have no idea who I am, or how I wound up lying on the beach, facedown, wearing tattered clothes. It's terrifying not to know anything about yourself."

This woman who just met me has shared a secret with me. I don't understand why. But it's pretty clear from her body language that she's telling the truth. She has no idea who she is or how she got here. At least I know my own name. She doesn't know where her family lives, whether they're still alive, or what she might've done to earn a living before the apocalypse. Something about her story makes me feel like I need to share more about myself with her.

"I had friends in the Echo," I tell her. "They were not human. I guess they were Echoes of people who died during the apocalypse. Anyway, they turned out to be good people who wanted to fight with me and find a way out of the new world Sefton Stainthorpe had created."

"You know about Sefton? Did you meet him?"

"Only from a distance. I saw him having a sort of conference with his minions. Then he vanished, and the creatures took off on a rampage."

"I've never seen what the creatures can do. At least, I don't remember seeing it."

"Be glad for that. They're monsters in the truest sense of the word." I sit back in my chair and sigh, letting my shoulders wilt. "Despite the horrors of the Echo, I found allies. We became friends, and eventually, a family."

"Maybe you can find them again and bring them into this world."

"No, I can't." I shut my eyes as the memory barrels through my mind. Screams. Blood. Agony. "They're all dead, and it's my fault."

Soft, warm hands clasp mine.

I open my eyes—and discover Sarah has moved up to my chair, kneeling in front of me. "What are you doing?"

"You seemed like you needed a little comforting. Whatever happened to your friends must have been horrific."

Why does she care about comforting me? I'd behaved like a complete asshole when we first met. Now, she's holding my hand while giving me the sweetest look of compassion and understanding. I should push her away, but

I can't make myself do it. No one has ever looked at me the way she does right now. But it's pity, nothing more.

"I can tell you don't like talking about it," Sarah says. "But would you tell me what happened to your friends? How did they die?"

Weariness drops over me like a lead blanket, and I no longer have the energy to resist whatever she wants. "I'd cobbled together a kind of army, a small one. Then I got the great idea that we should storm the castle and seize control of it. Didn't work out that way. All my friends died."

Did my voice hitch the slightest bit? No, it couldn't have.

"What castle?" Sarah asks, sounding totally confused.

"The one Sefton Stainthorpe built for himself. He's not there anymore, and neither is his Echo, the dweeb who calls himself Will."

"I haven't heard about the castle or someone called Will. But then, I think our leaders have kept a few secrets—to protect us, I'm sure."

"Leaders?" I study her face, trying to gauge how much she might actually know. Is the pretty voyeur as clueless as she seems? I have trouble believing it's all an act. "I'm guessing this camp is run by your friends Dax and Grant."

"Allison and Erin too. But this isn't a dictatorship."

"Then you guys have one up on the Echo creatures. Most of them did whatever their master told them to do." I try to make myself pull my hands away from hers, but I still can't do it. "Not all the creatures are evil. My friends were loyal and brave, but I talked them into breaching the castle and…they all died. Because of me. I didn't realize the bad creatures had found a secret entrance that let them walk right into the castle. My friends and I had to climb up a sheer cliff. We were exhausted by the time we reached the top. I should've known…"

"What? That there was a hidden entrance?" She clasps my hands more firmly while gazing straight into my eyes. "It's not your fault your friends died. I'm sorry that happened. But you shouldn't blame yourself."

"Don't you understand? I taught them to fight. I convinced them they could beat the other creatures, and that together we had a chance at seizing the castle." I yank my hands away from hers and cover my eyes with my palms, then drop them. "There was nothing in the castle. Just empty rooms, and one stone chair. Sefton's throne, apparently. I got my friends killed for nothing."

Why have I told her so much? Maybe because it doesn't matter. Everyone I ever cared about died today. Being alone is nothing new to me, but getting close to other people… I'd never done that before. Never. Then I found a home with creatures created by magic, who live in another world.

But I'm back on earth, and I have no fucking idea how to deal with other human beings.

"Were you in the Capital City?" Sarah asks. "Or did you land somewhere else in the Echo?"

"I didn't reach the Capital City until a few weeks ago. I traveled through the entire Echo world and picked up friends along the way."

"You've seen the whole Echo? Is it a flat plane, or an actual world? Like Earth, I mean. Grant and Erin thought it might be a planet in an alternate universe."

I study her for a moment, trying to decide if she really doesn't know the answer to that question. "Yeah, it's a planet."

Sarah leaps to her feet. "I need to tell Dax and Grant about this. Please stay here, I'll be right back."

The shape of the Echo never seemed that exciting to me, but Sarah clearly thinks it's big news. I guess her friends haven't explored much of the other world Sefton Stainthorpe had created.

Bells jingle. The tent flap flutters.

I look in that direction and see a pale face gazing at me through the partly open flap. The girl can't be more than fifteen or sixteen, I'd guess.

She glances over her shoulder furtively, then tiptoes into the tent. "You must be the guy who invaded our camp. Where did you come from? Are you going to stay? I've never seen anyone who looks like you, but that's probably because your clothes are falling off and your hair is dirty."

"Are you related to Sarah? She's too inquisitive for her own good too. Kids like you should stay away from beasts like me."

Her eyes widen. "Are you an Echo creature? Don't look like the ones I've met."

She tiptoes closer to me.

"Beat it, kid." I bare my teeth and clack them together, growling softly. "Or I'll gnaw on your flesh."

The girl stares at me blankly for a moment, then starts laughing. "You're so weird."

"What's your name, kid?" Not that I care. I'm bored, which is the only reason I'm talking to an annoying child.

"I'm Willow. Who are you?"

"Gabriel."

Sarah waltzes into the tent with Dax, Grant, and a raven-haired woman following her. When Dax notices Willow, her grabs the girl's arm to haul her away from me. "Go to Allison's tent and stay there."

"But—"

"Do it," Dax snarls. "Now."

Once the girl has left, Sarah approaches me. "Please tell my friends what you told me, Gabriel."

"Which part?"

"About what the Echo is."

She must have already told her friends that, but she wants me to explain it all over again. I guess the news really is a big deal to them.

"The Echo is a planet," I say. "Like Earth, only smaller. I think it's smaller, anyway. Since I'm not an expert on things like that, I can't say for sure. But it's definitely a globe. It has a horizon that curves down around the rest of the planet."

"Fascinating," Grant says. "How much of the Echo was devastated by the alchemy of worlds?"

"The what?"

"Oh, sorry. I forgot you don't know about that." Grant sits down cross-legged on the dirt floor in front of me. Then he glances up at Dax. "Should we tell him about it?"

The British Hulk shrugs. "Since you already mentioned it, there's no point in denying you said it. Might as well explain. This bloke did confirm the Echo is a planet."

"Okay." Grant sets his hands on his knees. "The alchemy of worlds is what Sefton Stainthorpe called the method he used to merge the two worlds. He combined alchemy, quantum physics, and dark magics to create the Echo, then he let the alchemical reaction transform the worlds. He intended for the Echo and the Earth to merge into one hell dimension."

CHAPTER FOUR

Sarah

"THAT DIDN'T HAPPEN," GABRIEL SAYS. "I DON'T KNOW WHERE YOU GUYS get your information, but it must be from a brain-dead con artist. Both worlds got destroyed, mostly. Well, the Echo did. I don't know how Earth fared after that. But I know the worlds didn't magically merge into one planet."

"You are correct. The worlds did not merge," Dax concurs. "But only because we stopped the alchemical reaction before it could complete the transmutation."

Gabriel seems vaguely confused, though he tries to hide that. Whatever happened to him after he was thrown into the Echo, it clearly changed him in ways that he doesn't want to consider. I didn't know him before the apocalypse. Yet I feel I can trust him, and I feel that he has suffered more than he lets on, more than he wants to admit even to himself.

He shifts uncomfortably in his chair. "That does explain a few things I'd wondered about for a long time after I got thrown into the Echo. Like why I never saw any other humans in that world. And why the creatures were able to come and go as they pleased. I couldn't. That alchemical reaction thing must have been intended to kill all humans. But it was stopped before it finished."

"Indeed."

"So, did you people know Sefton Stainthorpe?"

Dax narrows his gaze on me. "Did you? Can't see why you would bother trying to breach the castle if you had never met Sefton. How would you even know the castle existed?"

"Because it's on top of a big cliff. Everyone in the Capital City can see it. Told you already, I never met Sefton." Gabriel seems incapable of stopping himself from getting annoyed with my friends. He grits his teeth, then loosens his jaw, and his words come out rough and almost snarly. "Are you people stupid? I thought you knew all about the Echo. You sure act like you do. But apparently, I know more than all of you combined."

"Do you?" Dax leans in, squinting at Gabriel, clearly trying to intimidate him. "You had no idea what the alchemy of worlds was. That means we know more."

"All right, boys," Erin says. "Time to dial back the testosterone so you can think like grown-ups again."

I love Erin. She never lets anybody push her around, and she always knows exactly what to do when an argument gets too heated. I don't have that talent. She also knows how to take down any type of Echo creature, another skill I lack.

Erin walks up to Gabriel and plants her hands on her hips. "It would be in your best interest to tell us everything you know."

"Why? If you're in league with the Echo creatures, or some other bad guys, you'll use that knowledge against me. I've been on this ride for long enough to know how things work."

"You're awfully cynical. Is that because you lost your Echo pals? Or because you're hiding something?"

He grunts. "Take your pick."

"What happened to your actual family?" Erin asks. "Parents, aunts, uncles, brothers, sisters…"

"None of your business. Kill me, or let me go."

"If Aldith really did send you here, maybe you should do what she wanted. Work with us, instead of against us."

Gabriel shakes his head slightly. "Aldith wasn't that specific."

I step up beside Erin. "Why don't we try this my way? Bullying him doesn't work."

"What is your way, sweetie?" Erin asks. "No offense, but you don't have the skills to handle a jerk like him."

"You guys aren't having any luck. But Gabriel will talk to me. Alone." I glance at his tattered shirt and pants. "But let's get him some new clothes first. As a show of good faith."

Grant shrugs. "She's right. We need to trust Sarah's instincts on this. And we'll get him new duds."

Our guest huffs. "Let me guess. You'll give me girlie clothes."

I lean in until my face is inches from his. "Say thank you, Gabriel."

His lips kink into the faintest smirk. "Thank you, Lady Godiva."

"No, thank my friends. They're donating the clothes for you."

Gabriel glances at the others. "They haven't given me anything yet, so I don't need to be grateful to them."

He is the stubbornest man I've ever met. Of course, I only remember the past two months.

The others leave to find clothes for Gabriel and to do whatever else they need to do. I'm alone again with the man who grabbed me on the beach, but I don't feel anxious about that. I think underneath all the bluster and snarling, he's just as scared as anyone else.

"How long have you lived here?" Gabriel asks.

"Two months. I washed up on the beach with amnesia."

"It's awfully convenient," he says, "that you have no memory of anything before two months ago. You can't tell me anything useful."

"You're here to share information with us, not the other way around." I sit down on the cot. "But no, it isn't convenient. Maybe I have parents or a husband somewhere. They might be looking for me, but I couldn't find them even if I wanted to."

"Okay, maybe it's not so convenient."

"Thank you."

"For what?"

I give him a tight smile. "For acknowledging the truth."

He shrugs. "Whatever."

Getting through to Gabriel seems like an insurmountable task, but I feel that I need to do it. Can't explain why. On the beach, he'd behaved like a cretin. He'd threatened to fuck me on the beach, or at least I'd interpreted it as a threat. But then he let me go. And he'd mentioned he hadn't been with a woman in a long time. Living among Echo creatures for months couldn't have been easy.

I shouldn't cut him any slack. But I feel like I can trust him. Maybe amnesia has made me insane.

"Why did you let me go?" I ask.

He scrunches up his eyebrows. "What?"

"On the beach. Why did you let me go? If you really wanted to assault me, you should have held on to me. You were in control then."

"Maybe." He eyes me up and down, though it doesn't seem like sexual interest. "Why aren't you afraid of me?"

"Don't know. I guess you just aren't that scary." I tap my fingers on my knees while I consider how to get him to tell me what I want to know—which is everything about him. "Do you trust me?"

"Yeah."

"Good. Then please answer my questions." I look straight into his eyes. "Do you have a family? Friends? Anybody who might've missed you over the past eight months?"

He freezes. His eyes flick left, right, up, down as if he's contemplating an escape route. But I know he won't try to run. My intuition tells me so.

Gabriel seems more tense now, maybe because my question brought up bad memories. But he said before that he was sucked into the Echo before the really bad stuff started happening on Earth. He can't suffer from memories of the horrible things Echo creatures did to his loved ones.

"How long has this camp existed?" Gabriel asks.

"Answer my question first."

The stubborn man flattens his lips and glares at me, but I ignore his behavior. Frightened men get angry much more easily than women do. Finally, he blows out a breath. "I didn't have any family or friends before the apocalypse. That means nobody is looking for me."

"I'm sorry. Being alone is scary." I bite my lip for a moment before I can talk myself into sharing the information he wants to hear. "Sanctuary has existed for eight months. People tend to stumble onto it without knowing how they found us. Getting dumped here isn't the usual way of entering Sanctuary."

"So, I got special treatment. How nice."

The man seems incapable of speaking without being sarcastic.

He abruptly turns more serious, his gaze boring into me. "What was it like on this side of the apocalypse? I mean, when the Echo first hit? I know how things looked from the other side, but not here."

"I don't know what it was like. Amnesia, remember?"

"Oh. Right." He fidgets in his chair, his face pinching up a little. "It's been so long since I was in this world that I just…wanted to know what I missed, I guess."

"The cities are destroyed, mostly. That's what I heard."

Grant marches into the tent and tosses a pile of clothes to Gabriel. "Get changed. Then meet us outside."

He leaves the tent.

And Gabriel smirks at me. "Sticking around to watch me get naked?"

"Oh, no, I—" Jumping up, I glance around because I suddenly can't remember what I was going to do. Then I remember and clear my throat. "I'll wait outside."

I rush out of the tent and stop just past the doorway. Why did I get flustered just because he smirked at me? It's ridiculous.

After a minute or two, Gabriel saunters out wearing jeans, a T-shirt, and tennis shoes. "Where to now, Lady Godiva?"

"Will you please stop calling me that?"

"No." He shoves his hands into his jeans pockets. "Where are we meeting the Three Stooges?"

"The what?"

He raises his brows. "Well, I guess you wouldn't remember those movies since you have amnesia. The Three Stooges were a bunch of morons."

"My friends are not morons."

Grant, Erin, and Dax approach us. But Grant takes the lead in the conversation. "Okay, it's time to have an upfront discussion. We're trusting you, Gabriel, so don't abuse that faith."

"Wouldn't dream of it."

He says that in a sarcastic tone, but something in his eyes makes me think that's baloney. He told me he had no one before the apocalypse. That must've been a lonely existence, and his life after the Echo had to be much worse.

"Gabriel means 'thank you'," I say, "and he'll do his best to become a contributing member of Sanctuary."

"You're his translator now?" Grant says. "Here I thought he spoke English. Must've been hallucinating that."

"Ugh. Just talk to him. All right?"

"Yeah, sorry." Grant nods to Gabriel. "Okay, here's the deal. We've been trying to understand Sefton Stainthorpe's notes and how he created the alchemy of worlds. If we could get a clear understanding of that, maybe we could find a way to counteract what happened."

"Counteract it?" Gabriel says. "Is that even possible? Not sure what that means, anyway."

"It would be like an inoculation for the whole world. We would be immune to the shit going on inside the Echo, and possibly to the assaults of the creatures living here."

"Do you have reason to believe you can actually do that? Or are you tilting at windmills?"

"Kind of both. We're only telling you this because Aldith sent you to us—and Sarah trusts you."

My opinion sealed the deal? I don't understand why. A girl with amnesia doesn't seem like the most trustworthy person. I can't give them any information about my past or who I was before I washed up on the beach. Yet they trust me. Of course, Aldith's opinion must count more than anything I could say.

A light flashes to my right, visible in my peripheral vision, and I turn my head to glance in that direction. Another flash slices across the sky, though I see no clouds. I point toward the area where the flashes had originated. "Is that a thunderstorm?"

Everyone glances toward that area just as several more flashes erupt. Brows wrinkle. Eyes widen.

"What is it?" I ask. "Have you seen something like that before?"

Dax goes stoic, which is never a good sign. "Not exactly like that. But I have seen strange lightning as part of the alchemy of worlds. In that case, it was extraordinarily powerful and could shatter streets and buildings, causing earthquakes."

Still no clouds have formed, but the lightning mutates into silver tongues of electrical energy that sizzle and snap, not quite hitting the ground. We all stand here immobilized by the sight before us, and I can tell my friends recognize what's going on. Allison and Willow race out of the tent she shares with Dax and huddle beside him. He slips an arm around each of them.

Dax glances down at his wife's swollen belly. "You should find a place to hide. Perhaps I should teleport you to…somewhere else."

"Like where? For all we know, this is happening everywhere. I want to stay with you, Dax. The three of us are in this together, forever. Remember?"

"Yeah, that's right," Willow says.

Dax hugs them both more firmly.

If Dax and Allison are worried… Oh, we're in big trouble.

A bolt of silver lightning slams down at the far end of the camp, just shy of the nearest tents. The concussion rattles my eardrums and makes the ground shudder.

"We need to find cover," Grant hollers. "Everybody, head for the woods! The lightning should strike the trees instead of us."

But it's supernatural lightning. Who knows how or where it might strike? Still, the woods feel like our best option.

Slender ribbons of electricity snake across the sky above us, spanning from horizon to horizon. The crackling and snapping grows louder, to the point where we can't hear each other even when we shout. Dax, Grant, and Erin wave their arms to indicate that everyone should flee into the dense woods and seek whatever shelter they can find.

Everyone flees.

The lightning has become so blinding and deafening that I can't see anyone. I can't move either. Something about the cloudless storm raging in the sky transfixes me, and try as I might, I can't convince my muscles to work.

A bolt slams down a few yards away from me.

The concussion makes me stumble sideways and scream. I trip over something—a rock, I think—and struggle to get back on my feet. Slithering tongues of silver continue to snake across the heavens, and I swear they're searching for me.

A figure races toward me, but my vision has become blurred and the brilliance of the lightning has created black spots that further hinder my ability to see. I stumble forward.

The blurry figure draws closer, shouting something I can't understand, not with my ears ringing.

As if in slow motion, a bolt slams down like a ladder of electricity, one rung at a time, seeming to adjust its trajectory as I stagger toward the woods. A crack and a sizzle resound so close that my heart stutters.

Then the bolt strikes.

A figure pushes me out of the way, and the lightning pounds into that person instead of me. My savior falls backward, knocking us both to the ground and pinning me beneath their weight.

The lightning abruptly stops.

A silence deeper than anything I've experienced before descends on Sanctuary. Smoke emerges from inside several tents, and flames ignite on others. But I don't see any people. Except for the man lying on top of me. I push him off and roll him over so I can see his face.

Gabriel's eyes are open, but he's not breathing.
The lightning has killed him.

CHAPTER FIVE

Gabriel

A RINGING NOISE DEAFENS ME. MY ENTIRE BODY FEELS LIKE I'VE jumped into a swimming pool while holding a raw electric wire in my teeth. Though my eyes are open, and I can see what's going on around me, I can't move or breathe or speak. Did I leap in front of a lightning bolt? That's insane. I would never do anything like that. But I do sort of recall seeing a bolt heading straight for Sarah, almost in slow motion, and I remember thinking that she would die if that thing hit her.

So, I jumped in front of her.

The bolt must have struck a few feet away. Right? That scorched smell must be the grass that got incinerated.

"He's not breathing!" Sarah shrieks, while she kneels beside me. Her eyes are wide, and her lips are trembling. "Help! Someone, please!"

Footfalls pound. Voices say things I can't quite make out.

"What happened?" That's the voice of Dax, the British Hulk. "Lightning hit him?"

"Yes," Sarah says. "He jumped in front of me and took the bolt for me. We have to save Gabriel."

Another figure approaches, though I see the person as only a shadow. "I had some basic medical training in the army. Let me take a look."

Is that Grant? I had no idea he was ex-military, but that doesn't matter right now. I feel oddly disconnected from everything around me. The only thing that comes through clearly is Sarah's voice.

"Please try," she says. "He might've been an ass at first, but he saved me."

If I could chuckle, I would. She described me perfectly. I am an ass.

Someone starts pushing on my chest, probably doing CPR, and I feel my heart trying to pump. Little by little, my body comes back to life, first with my heartbeat, then with my breathing. I blink slowly and groan.

"Take it easy," Grant says. "We nearly lost you, so you'll need a few minutes to recover."

I try to speak, but it comes out as incoherent mumbling. So this is what almost dying feels like. I have to admit, I expected something more dramatic, like a white tunnel with an angel reaching out to me. Not that I believe in that kind of thing. But if heaven does exist, I won't be going there.

Pain ricochets through my body, but it isn't as intense as I'd expected, considering I got fried by lightning. I push up onto my elbows, groaning again, then try to sit up. Grant helps me.

I scrub my hands over my face, then shove them into my hair. "I don't recommend tangling with Echo lightning."

"Yeah, it's a lot more powerful than the regular kind," Grant says. "Can't believe you survived that. Most people would be crispy critters after a strike half as strong as the one you took."

"Guess I got lucky."

Sarah is kneeling beside me, her eyes wide, staring at me like I've started to glow. Have I? No, I'm pretty sure that hasn't happened. But she keeps gaping at me. It makes my skin crawl.

"What's wrong with you?" I snap.

"You died, then you came back." She reaches out to grasp my hand. "And you saved my life."

"No, I just—It wasn't like that."

"Don't be embarrassed. You jumped in front of a bolt of Echo lightning to protect me."

"I didn't think about what I was doing. Don't take it personally."

She shakes her head slowly. "I don't understand you, Gabriel. I'm thanking you for saving my life, and you act like I've insulted you."

Maybe I've kind of forgotten how to accept a compliment, or how to admit I might not be a total bastard. I've spent too long fighting for my life and the lives of my friends, only to lose everything. Sarah would be better off if she slugged me and told her friends to toss me into the ocean.

Sarah wraps her arms around my neck and kisses my cheek. "Thank you, Gabriel. If you hadn't been here, I would've died."

If she says that one more time... I'll probably growl at her and act like a jerk again.

"We're all grateful," Grant says, "that you were there to help Sarah. That took guts."

I push Sarah's arms away and scramble to my feet. "I didn't do it on purpose. That was instinct, plain and simple."

Though I want to get away from these people, I have nowhere to go. So I stand here glancing around, fisting my hands and loosening them again, over and over.

Men and women pour out of the woods, where they'd been hiding. Several approach Grant and his friends, wanting to know what happened and why. Dax gets me another T-shirt, since the one I'd been wearing got scorched. There's a hole in the fabric smack in the middle of my chest, but my skin suffered no damage. Supernatural lightning has different rules.

But in the Echo, lightning like that would kill whoever got in its way.

After things calm down, I follow Grant, Dax, and Erin into the tent where they'd kept me until they decided I'm not a psycho. Sarah walks right beside me. I pull my hand away when she tries to hold it. I get that she feels grateful, and she's probably latched on to me because I helped her. But I wish she wouldn't do that.

Inside the tent, we all sit down to discuss the event that has everyone panicked and confused. Sarah sits on the chair I'd been tied to earlier, while Erin and Grant take the cot. Dax and I sit on the floor.

The British Hulk squints at me. "How did you survive that strike? Echo lightning can destroy a city, and it incinerates the human body."

"I know. Don't ask me how it happened, because I have no idea."

Dax keeps staring at me with his squinty, flinty gaze, like he thinks that will make me confess that I'm secretly an Echo beast who wants to eat everyone in this camp. "No one survives the lightning."

"Clearly, that's not true. How do you know that nobody else has survived it? You can't be everywhere at once, all the time."

"Perhaps not. But over the past eight months, I and my mates have visited many cities and rural towns to scavenge supplies and help anyone who might need our assistance." Dax rests one arm on his bent knee, leaning toward me. "No one has ever seen a human being survive Echo lightning."

"At least I could be the first. Maybe I'll get an entry in the Guinness Book of World Records."

"I doubt that exists anymore."

"Well, I know I'm the record-holder. That's something."

Grant shakes his head at me. "Is everything a joke to you? We're talking about the end of the world, and you're cracking wise."

"The alternative doesn't appeal to me."

Because going full-on doom and gloom would mean surrendering to the Echo. No, I'll never do that. I fought my way through that hell world once, and I can do it again if necessary.

Sarah stands up. "I should go. Everyone here has a role to play in the apocalypse, but not me."

"Of course you play a role," Grant says. "Something or someone sent you to us. That means you belong in this discussion. Besides, that lightning was meant for you."

"But all of you can fight. I can't."

"There are other ways to contribute, Sarah."

She sits back down, hands clasped on her lap.

And she keeps her gaze trained on me.

For some reason, her unwavering focus on me makes me feel the need to share information. "Aldith mentioned that the Echo has a heart and lifeblood, and a brain too."

"We know about the Heart and the Lifeblood," Grant says. "But this is the first we've heard of a brain."

"I only know what Aldith told me. She said the Echo has been without a brain ever since Sefton and his doppelgänger died." I stare at the dirt floor to avoid Sarah's gaze, because her undivided attention still makes me uneasy. "The Echo is a living thing composed of magics, that's what Aldith told me. It's not sentient, and without its master, it needs another being to keep the Brain working."

"Interesting," Grant says. "Aldith never mentioned that to us. But I guess she's been waiting for whoever will become the Brain."

Sarah's eyes go wide. I try not to see that, but my eyes insist on looking at her. She opens her mouth but seems unable to speak for a moment. Then she points a finger at me. "It's you, Gabriel. You are the Brain."

"What? Come on, that's crazy. I got good grades in school, but I'm no brainiac."

"I doubt a high IQ is required," Grant says. "The Heart and the Lifeblood were chosen based on their strength and dedication to protecting others. The Brain was probably selected for similar reasons."

Though I intend to refute his claim, something he just said stops me. I study Grant for a moment, while I decide whether I should alert them to the fact I've figured out one of their secrets. Maybe I'm wrong, anyway. But I have a gut feeling that I'm right.

I nail my gaze to Grant's. "Two of you guys are the Heart and the Lifeblood, aren't you? I'd bet it's you and Erin. Just a hunch, but I think I'm right."

Grant stares at me.

I take that as confirmation I was right. "You don't need to confirm it for me. And I won't spill the beans to anybody else. Who would want to talk to me, anyway? I'm the jerk who scared everyone when I stormed into your little camp."

Dax and Grant exchange a look that I think means they're deciding how much they should tell me. Then Grant looks at Erin, and she nods.

"We should ask Allison first," Dax tells his friends. "She should be involved in the decision of whether to bring someone new into the inner circle."

This is starting to sound like a cult. But I don't think they meant it that way.

Dax strides out of the tent. Minutes tick by while the rest of us wait in silence. Sarah keeps glancing at me, smiling. Every time she does that, I avert my gaze.

The British Hulk returns—with a pregnant woman. He holds her hand, guiding her toward the cot. Erin takes a seat on the floor to let the woman, who I assume is Allison, settle onto the cot. Dax squats on the floor beside her.

"We should tell Gabriel everything," Allison says. "The Echo needs him."

"But it tried to kill me," I say. "Even if it meant to hit Sarah, it still fried me. I just happened to jump in front of the bolt that was meant for her."

"Exactly. You instinctively protected Sarah, even though you just met her and know nothing about her. She doesn't know herself either."

"Yeah, I know that."

Allison glances at her husband, who nods. "What we're about to tell you is top secret. We've kept most of this from the rest of our community because it's explosive. People might panic."

"Do I seem like the panicking type? I can handle whatever it is. Didn't Dax tell you about me?"

"Yes, he did. That's why we agreed you should know the truth." Allison nods to her husband. "You should go first, honey."

The British Hulk faces me. "Sefton Stainthorpe was my twin brother. He used me and Allison as tools in his mad scheme to create the Echo and start an apocalypse. He transformed my body into what you see now and threw me into the Echo."

"He used me too," Allison says. "But not as violently as he used Dax. Sefton made me the Catalyst for his plans. Dax was the Anchor."

"Allison tapped into magics she hadn't known she possessed to stop the alchemy of worlds. As revenge, Sefton murdered Allison." Dax glances at each of his friends in turn, as if seeking their approval. When they nod, he continues. "What I'm about to tell you cannot leave this tent. We want to trust the members of our community completely, but this revelation might hurt a child if everyone knew. You've met Willow, the youngest member of Sanctuary. She's fifteen years old."

"How we met her is a long story we'll tell you later," Allison says. "But it turned out that Willow has the Echo power inside her, just like I do, and so does Dax. Grant and Erin also hold that power inside them. We believe you have it too. But I'm getting away from the main point. Willow used her Echo power to resurrect me from death."

"I've never heard of Echo power," I say. "And I traveled through the entire world that is the Echo."

"Apparently, not many people in either world know about that power. We've found a few people in Sanctuary who have a watered-down version of it that gives them limited teleportation skills."

"This is all fascinating. But I don't see how it relates to me."

"You gathered a small army of Echo creatures who shared your desire to protect the innocents trapped in that world," Allison says. "Then, after you found Sanctuary, you shielded Sarah from the Echo lightning. You are a protector, Gabriel. Dax and I believe you might be the Brain, the key component of the Echo that has been missing ever since Sefton and Will, his doppelgänger, died."

"What does being a protector have to do with being the Brain of the Echo? I'm not a genius like Sefton Stainthorpe. He was a scientist, right? I've learned that much from exploring the Echo world."

Dax lifts one brow at me. "You assume 'the Brain' refers to intelligence. But even a human brain contains more than knowledge. It's the seat of knowledge, yes, but also the seat of everything that turns a living thing into a human being—the heart, soul, and lifeblood."

"But Grant and Erin are the Heart and the Lifeblood."

"Yes, but they haven't been able to affect much change in the Echo. We've believed for a while now that the Echo lacks the balancing power that will bring it under control, and that's why Grant and Erin can't erase the remnants of the alchemy of worlds."

I stand up and start pacing, which is difficult in a small tent with people sitting on the floor around me. But I try it anyway. Movement might help with the tension that's been building inside me ever since Allison walked into the tent and started explaining crazy things to me. "I am not the Brain of anything. I'm just a guy who got thrown into the Echo and had to learn to survive. And I got my friends killed. That's not heroic, and certainly nothing that would qualify me to become the balancing whatever in the Echo."

My pacing speeds up, and I almost trip over Grant, mumbling a half-assed apology.

"Stop, Gabriel," Sarah says.

And I stop. Why? Because her voice always does something to me. It's like a shot of Valium injected directly into my veins. Well, no, it's more like a double shot of Valium and Viagra. Yes, I'm attracted to Sarah, but it's weird and nothing I'm ever going to admit to or surrender to, no matter what. Sarah and I gaze at each other without speaking, without showing our reactions to each other. But I have the strangest feeling she's experiencing the same things I am.

Thunder explodes overhead, making the ground beneath us shudder so violently that I stumble into Sarah. Without realizing what I'm doing, I pull her into my arms.

"We need to get into the woods," Grant says. "Everybody was safe there when the Echo lightning started."

Dax grabs Allison. "We need to find Willow. Gabriel, make sure Sarah gets to safety. Let's all meet at the hot spring. She knows where that is."

The tent begins to sway as another round of thunder detonates. As we hurry out of the tent, Dax and Allison veer to the left, while Grant and Erin announce they're going to make sure everyone makes it into the woods. I've been tasked with protecting Sarah, and I focus on that. I keep hold of her hand as we sprint toward the trees, which tower so high above our heads that I don't see how lightning could reach us down here. Other people rush into the woods too, and we make sure they know everyone should meet at the hot spring.

Whatever is about to happen, it can't be good.

CHAPTER SIX

Sarah

WHAT ON EARTH IS HAPPENING TODAY? THE ECHO HAD BEEN STABLE for months, with only the occasional hiccup. Now, it seems intent on destroying me. I might think I'm being paranoid if I hadn't witnessed the lightning coming after me, strike after strike. Why me? I'm just an amnesiac who has no special skills or magical powers.

Unless I do have skills and powers. Maybe I just can't remember having them.

Gabriel's hand in mine relieves the worst of my fear, though I can't figure out why. I met him today. We've barely spoken to each other. Yet he nearly died for me, and I trust him to be there if I need him again. I trust him not to lie too. Even when he attacked me on the beach, I felt no fear of him.

The thunder fades away, and lightning sizzles across the sky. I can just see it through the treetops, but I know it will grow closer and more powerful. Am I inadvertently leading the Echo lightning to the others? I don't want my friends to die because of me. If the Echo wants me dead, maybe I should just let it have me.

I stumble to a halt beside a wide tree.

Gabriel tugs my hand, but I still don't move. "Come on, Sarah. We need to keep moving."

I shake my head. "Everyone's in danger because of me. I should go back and face the lightning. Let it take me."

"Don't be stupid. Your friends are waiting for you."

"Go on. I'm staying here."

I'd seen everyone from Sanctuary rush past us, heading toward the hot spring. Allison and Dax, Grant and Erin, Willow too. They're out of the path of the lightning, provided that I don't follow them. The strongest thing I can do is to let the Echo take me.

So I yank my hand free of Gabriel's and run back toward Sanctuary.

I can hear footfalls behind me, and I know it's Gabriel. I run as fast as I can, praying he won't catch up and stop me. I need to do this. Maybe it's my destiny. If this has even a snowball's chance of saving my friends, I'll do it.

"Sarah, stop!" Gabriel shouts. "What do you think you're doing?"

I ignore him and keep running. My legs have started to hurt, and I feel like I can't catch my breath. Doesn't matter. I need to get out of the woods so the lightning can take me. *Please let this end the madness, please let it save everyone, please, please, please.* I've just broken out of the woods, and I can see the camp up ahead, not more than thirty feet away.

Arms lash around me, halting me so swiftly that I stumble, and the man trying to restrain me loses his footing. We both crash to the ground, with Gabriel on top of me. He quickly rises and flips me over, kneeling there as he glares at me and struggles to breathe.

"You fucking idiot," he snarls. "What kind of stunt are you trying to pull?"

"I need to get away from the others."

"Why?"

"Because I don't belong here. They do. You do. I have no useful purpose except to stop the lightning from destroying everything and everyone in its path." Tears burn in my eyes and stream down my cheeks. "Let me go. I need to sacrifice myself to the Echo."

"Are you totally brainless? Or just suicidal?" He grabs my arms and pulls me up into a sitting position, holding me inches away from him. Face to face, we stare at each other. "Killing yourself won't solve anything."

"But the lightning wants me. I need to give it what it wants."

"That's bullshit." He's so angry that his eyes have narrowed and he's gritting his teeth. "What makes you think you're so damn important that the Echo wants to murder you? You're just some girl from who knows where, probably a socialite who never worked a day in her life. I bet you spent your days getting manicures and agonizing over which pair of shoes go best with your hair."

Is he trying to tick me off? To dissuade me from what I've resolved to do? If so, it's working. I want to deck him. But I can't move any part of my body. All my muscles have turned to jelly, thanks to my panicked flight through the woods, and I can't tear my focus away from Gabriel's eyes.

"Don't you think your friends need you?" he asks. "Or do you only care about your own fears? What about that girl, Willow? I guess you'll just leave her to grieve for you, like everyone else. How thoughtful of you."

"Stop trying to piss me off, Gabriel."

"Why? You pissed me off, running away like that. I'm supposed to protect you, remember?"

Something in his eyes convinces me that he's genuinely worried about me. We're essentially strangers, yet he won't leave me alone to sacrifice myself for a stupid belief that only my death can stop the Echo lightning.

"Okay, I won't run out there," I say. "I won't let the Echo kill me."

All the anger in his expression melts away. He's breathing hard, but he no longer seems upset. No, I sense something else from him, something I've never experienced before. He wants me. I can't explain how I know it, but I guess my amnesia is letting me know what it means. He wants to have sex with me. I crave that too. Even while the lightning slams down on the camp, I grow wet and tingly between my thighs, and I instinctively understand what that means.

Lust. Hard, hot lust.

Gabriel pulls me into his body and crushes his mouth to mine. His rough lips scrape across mine, and my stiff nipples rub against his chest. Then he thrusts his tongue into my mouth and devours me so completely that my heart pounds and my ears ring because I've stopped breathing. God, this feels incredible, and I want more, need more, can't take another breath again until he consumes my body in every way imaginable. He slides a hand down to my ass, grasping it firmly, and pushes one finger between my cheeks.

I moan and fling my arms around his neck, pushing my tongue between his lips. My sex throbs while slickness dribbles down my inner thighs. I can smell a musky scent that I instinctively know is the proof of how much I hunger for him.

He drops to the ground with me beneath him. Above us, Echo lightning ravages the sky, crashing down to penetrate the earth too. The ground vibrates beneath our bodies as he yanks my jeans and panties down to my ankles and unzips his pants, then plunges inside me so suddenly that I cry out and arch my back. He slaps his hands down on the ground at either side of my head. I bend my knees to cradle his body with them, and though I have no memory of sex, I realize that what's about to happen will change everything in ways I can't comprehend.

Gabriel begins thrusting, hard and fast, the pace brutal, while I grip his biceps and hoist my hips up into his thrusts. I need him to fuck me like the world is ending, and maybe it is. The Echo started the apocalypse, but our blistering lust for each other might eradicate both worlds.

And I don't care.

He growls and snarls and fucks me even harder, making my body bounce while lightning pulsates above us. He fills me so completely that it almost hurts. I don't care about that either. The ground shudders as monstrous bolts penetrate the earth one after another, zigzagging across the sky.

The thickest, most explosive bolt yet punches into the earth—and I come.

My body curls in on itself while mind-blowing spasms seize my inner muscles, and I scream again and again. Gabriel punches into me twice more, roaring to the heavens as I feel him releasing everything inside me. The sensation makes me come harder.

The entire world falls into a deep, tranquil silence.

Gabriel still has his cock inside me. He gazes down at me with a look of wonder and shock on his face. Then he pulls out of my body, sitting up, and glances down at himself.

His eyes go wide. He jerks his head up to gape at me.

"What's wrong?" I ask, pushing up on my straight arms.

"You, ah…" He rubs his jaw and won't look at me. "This is… I'm sorry."

"For what?" I look down at my hips, which seem to have transfixed him with horror. And I see why. I have blood smeared on my inner thighs. When I glance at his dick, I see blood there too. "Um, I don't understand."

"Did it hurt the first time I, ah, thrust into you?"

"A little. But only for a second."

"Fuck." He tucks his dick back into his pants and zips them up. Then he gets to his feet. "You were a virgin."

"I'm…what? No, that can't be. Everyone thinks I must be twenty-eight years old."

"Maybe you were a—" He winces and averts his gaze again.

"What did you almost say? Maybe I'm what?"

He shoves his hands into his hair. "Maybe you were a nun."

"I don't feel like a nun." Sitting up, I struggle to pull up my jeans and panties. "What we just did, it felt familiar. Like I've done that before."

"That can't be. You were obviously a virgin."

He sounds irritated again. Is it my fault I was a virgin and didn't know that? *Hello, amnesia girl here.* Besides, I do feel like I must've had sex before. But that makes no sense. I recognized what an orgasm should feel like, and I sensed that before I reached my climax. I just knew what was coming and how good it would feel.

Nothing about me makes any sense.

Gabriel grasps my hands to pull me up off the ground. "The lightning stopped."

"I know. It completely stopped right when we came."

"That's insane. Sex has nothing to do with it."

"How do you know? You're not an expert on Echo lightning."

Gabriel snares my hand, half dragging me out into the clearing where the camp lies. A few tents have fallen down. Nothing else seems to have been damaged. Would the lightning have kept going if Gabriel and I hadn't screwed each other? I wonder if the lightning somehow fed us erotic energy. I've been attracted to Gabriel since the moment we met, even when he was acting like a jackass. But I didn't experience intense lust until we ran through the woods together amid an Echo lightning storm.

What does that mean? I don't know, and I'm not sure I want to find out.

Gradually, the residents of Sanctuary wander back into the camp. Though everyone wants to talk about what's going on and what it might mean, I can't focus on the conversation. My mind keeps rewinding to those moments at the edge of the forest when Gabriel had taken me like a maniac and I'd loved it.

Can anyone tell we did that? Does it show on our faces? I can't look at him without my entire body growing warm, and every time Gabriel glances at me, he immediately swerves his gaze away. I wonder if the lightning somehow made us insanely hot for each other. It was paranormal lightning, after all. As much as I'd love to blame the Echo for what I did, what we did, I know I can't do that. I wanted him, and I did something incredibly stupid because of that lust.

Never again.

I sneak away to my tent so I can try to erase that incident from my memory. I got amnesia once without wanting it to happen. Why can't I pull off self-induced memory loss that only wipes away those moments with Gabriel in the woods?

Someone rings the bell on my tent flap. "May I come in, sweetie?"

That's Erin. Every tent has a small clump of jingle bells attached to the outer flap that acts as a doorbell. We all understand the value of privacy.

"Sure, come on in," I say.

Erin walks in and sits on the canvas chair across from the cot, where I sit. "Are you okay? You haven't seemed quite like yourself ever since the lightning came again."

I know she didn't mean that in a dirty way, but hearing the words "came again" makes me flash back to Gabriel in the woods, inside me, thrusting wildly.

"Sarah? What's wrong?"

"Nothing, I'm fine." I shake off the memory and try for a smile. I don't think I pulled it off. "The lightning keeps coming for me, doesn't it?"

Erin says nothing for several seconds, then she moves onto the cot beside me. "Yeah, we think it is after you or Gabriel—or both. You guys were together both times the lightning struck, right?"

I nod.

She lays a hand on my thigh. "Don't worry. We'll figure this out, all of us, together."

Maybe I should tell her what Gabriel and I did, but I just can't make myself speak the words. It's humiliating. But also hot and incredible. How could I still have been a virgin? How could I have let Gabriel seduce me? If I used to be a nun, then I'm going to hell for sure.

"Is there something else?" Erin asks. "Seems like you want to tell me more."

"No, it's nothing."

"Okay." She doesn't sound or look like she believes me. "Do you feel up to hashing out ideas about the lightning and other stuff? Or would you rather take a break? The rest of us can talk about things without you, and you can join us when you're ready."

"No, I don't need to rest. I'd rather be a part of the discussion."

"Okay. Then let's head for Dax and Allison's tent. That's where the confab is happening."

As we head through the camp, I notice people gathering around the spot where we often have bonfires. It looks like they might be getting ready to do that this evening. The sun will set soon, and I wouldn't be surprised if nobody wants to sleep tonight. Memories of the lightning will keep us awake.

Erin and I reach Dax and Allison's tent just as Gabriel walks up to it. I manage not to blush or act like a flustered teenager. Gabriel barely glances at me. He holds the flap open as Erin and I walk into the tent.

I can't figure him out at all.

Someone brought in several more chairs to accommodate our group. Allison sits on a cot, and she encourages me to sit beside her. The others take the chairs.

"That lightning was after something or someone," Dax announces. "On both occasions, it sought out either Sarah or Gabriel. Perhaps the lightning wants a different person, but it can't find them. Either option seems plausible."

I wish I remembered what my life had been like pre-apocalypse. What was the world like before the Echo? I want to know, but I suppose I might never remember.

My gaze flicks to Gabriel.

He glances at me sideways and winces faintly.

I stare down at my hands, where I'm wringing them on my lap. "What are we going to do? If the lightning came back once, it might come back again. I don't want anyone to get hurt because of me."

Allison clasps my hand. "No one has been hurt, except for Gabriel. And he survived. This is not your fault, Sarah."

"I should leave. Go somewhere far away."

"And if the lightning follows you there? Then what?"

"Don't know."

A prickly sensation spreads over my skin, raising goosebumps. It swiftly transforms into a warmth that penetrates my skin and sinks deep inside me, settling between my thighs.

When I lift my head, Gabriel is watching me.

I'm getting turned on in front of all my friends. What is wrong with me?

"No one is asking the obvious question," Gabriel says. "What if the lightning is caused by the Brain? What if it's searching for the right person to take over that role?"

He keeps watching me while he speaks.

"I used to be a computer programmer," Gabriel says. "The Brain might be like a living computer, capable of being programmed. The lightning could be its way of dealing with the missing circuits—the missing neurons and brain cells that Sefton Stainthorpe gave it."

"What do you suggest we do?" Grant asks.

"Tell me everything you know about Sefton's plans for the Echo and Earth."

CHAPTER SEVEN

Gabriel

I CAN'T STOP THINKING ABOUT SARAH, LYING HALF-NAKED BENEATH ME while I fucked her in the woods. I don't know what came over me in that moment, but I couldn't fight the lust. It seized control of me and wouldn't let go until I came deep inside her body. She was a virgin. I took her innocence on the ground, in the dirt, with lightning exploding everywhere. Every time the lightning punched into the ground, I thrust into Sarah harder and faster.

Does that mean the lightning made us want each other? I can't say that's insane and impossible. The rules of the universe changed on the day the Echo breached the Earth and the two worlds merged. But Sefton didn't complete the transformation. Now the Echo is suffering from the loss of the only being in either world who could control the Brain.

And the people seated inside this tent think I'm the new Brain. Finding Sefton's castle hardly qualifies me to become the human controller of the Echo's mind.

Can my computer skills help? Well, we don't have electricity, so I can't do any actual programming. But maybe I can employ the mental skills I learned as a computer geek. I'm no longer the man I'd been before the apocalypse. The time I spent inside the Echo changed me in ways I still don't fully understand.

That's one more reason why I shouldn't have screwed Sarah, and why I will never do that again.

I rest my elbows on my knees and rub a hand over my cheek. "The lightning didn't kill me. Maybe that means the Echo wants me to…do something. To figure that out, I need you to tell me everything about Sefton's plans."

"He wanted Allison to rule both worlds with him," Dax tells me. "She was the catalyst for the alchemical reaction, but he never intended for her to die. He killed Allison out of sheer rage when she ruined his plans. Willow brought her back to life."

"Right," Erin says. "Your brother didn't want Allison dead. He only wanted everyone else on Earth to die."

Dax shakes his head. "That's not quite right. He meant to force every human on earth to merge with their Echoes, which would imprison every human inside the bodies of the twisted copies of themselves. My brother called that the alchemy of souls. But he wasn't able to complete that part of his plan."

"Because you killed him," I say. "What else did Sefton want to do?"

"Turn himself into a godlike figure who would have total dominion over both worlds."

"What about his castle?"

Dax shrugs. "He never mentioned that. I had no idea he created such a place until Grant and Erin learned the truth during their mission into the Echo."

I gaze down at the dirt floor for a moment while I try to digest everything they've told me. How do I fit into this? Am I supposed to be the new Brain of the Echo? Or is my fate to protect Sarah? Now I'm seriously considering the idea that fate plays a role in my future. The world really has turned upside down and inside out.

My eyes force me to glance at Sarah out of the corner of my eye. I try not to wince, but every time I see her, I flash back to earlier in the woods. She had felt so fucking good, and I came harder inside her body than I'd ever come before. The woman annoys me. I don't want to want her. Maybe I shouldn't be surprised that we wound up losing control and screwing each other like crazy, since she loves to sunbathe in the nude. She's got a naughty streak, for sure.

But I have no excuse for what I did. I never even asked if she wanted it.

"Maybe I should give you Sefton's journal," Grant says. "You might see something in it that the rest of us missed. He was a scientist, after all. So are you, Gabriel, in a way."

"Computers are my thing, not quantum physics."

"Give it a try," Sarah says. "I can help you."

I raise my brows. "You're a physicist?"

"No. But I'd like to help. Maybe I was a scientist of some sort. I don't know."

Because she has amnesia. I still think it's bizarre that she just appeared on the beach one day, according to her friends. She looked like she'd been assaulted, though not sexually. I know that for sure because I took her virginity earlier today. And I hate myself for that. But we've got bigger problems than my guilt.

"I will take a look at the journal," I say. "And any other information you guys have. But I need to start where Sarah's story begins."

Her brows knit together. "I don't have a story. I'm amnesia girl."

"But you came from somewhere," I growl. Why? No frigging idea. Guilt, I guess. "We should start on the beach, just you and me."

Dax squints at me. "Why only you and Sarah? The rest of us know more about how the Echo has affected this world than you do."

"Yeah, but I have years of experience with the other side of the apocalypse."

Sarah stares at me, her eyes wide. "What do you mean years?"

"Are you deaf? Or just stupid? When I say years, I mean years."

"I think I understand," Dax says. "The same thing happened to me when Sefton initiated the alchemy of worlds."

"What are you talking about?"

"Time can behave differently inside the Echo. My brother threw me into that world, and I was trapped there for five years. How long was it for you, Gabriel?"

For a moment, I can't respond. My brain is struggling to reconcile what the British Hulk just said with what I'd always taken for an absolute truth of the universe. Time moves forward. Sure, I'd watched documentaries about how time travel might be technically possible. But I treated it as theory, not fact. The Echo changed everything, turning myths into truths and theories into reality.

"Three years," I say. "I lived in the Echo for three years."

Sarah rushes over to me and kneels beside my chair. Her soft, warm hand encloses mine. "I'm so sorry, Gabriel. That must have been awful. But it does explain how you managed to explore the entire Echo world."

"I had nothing else to do. No way out. No way home, if that even existed anymore. Might as well explore, that's what I decided."

She gives my hand a gentle squeeze. "I will go with you to the beach. I trust your instincts, and if you believe retracing my steps will help, I'm in."

"That's a good place to start," Grant says. "But I'm wondering if Gabriel's knowledge of the Echo could provide clues none of us ever found. You've seen all of the other world. That has to be useful."

"I want to go to the beach first," I say. "Just me and Sarah."

"You shouldn't go with him alone," Dax declares, and he almost growls like I did. "He is a stranger."

"Dax and I could go with you two," Grant says. "For safety. Yours and ours."

"Sarah and I need to go alone." Why? I have no clue. But I sense that we need to do this without her friends watching.

"Like hell," Dax snarls.

"I could always kidnap Sarah while you're all sleeping."

The British Hulk looks like he's about to rip my head off.

But Sarah steps in. "Relax, he's joking."

"Let them do this," Allison says. "We're all adults here and capable of making our own decisions."

The gang exchanges glances, as if they're seeking each other's permission. Then Grant says, "Okay. You and Sarah, alone. But you should take some kind of weapons. Erin and I can advise you on what to take."

I smirk at Dax, just to annoy him, though I speak to Grant. "That's a good idea."

This time, I will not have sex with Sarah. It's an informational mission only. I don't care if lightning erupts and makes us both so horny that we can't stand it. I will not repeat my mistake.

What if Sarah is pregnant?

I can't worry about that right now. We have bigger problems.

"Let's go," I say, as I push up out of my chair. "I don't want to waste any time. Who knows when the lightning might come back."

Sarah's cheeks dimple, and her eyes sparkle. "I knew you weren't as much of a jerk as you acted like you were when we first met."

"I'm no hero. But everybody does what they have to do to survive in this new world."

The rest of the gang follows us as we march through the camp. We stop along the way at the tent where they keep the weapons and grab a few things. Then we head for the woods. At the edge of the forest, the others halt and just watch us disappear into the gloom. Our trek over the mountain takes longer than I remember, but then, I've only hiked this trail twice before. The second time, we hadn't gone all the way to the beach. Sarah and I hadn't even made it to the hot spring.

Now, we hike up the mountain until we reach the summit. There, we pause to take a break and drink some water. We both have backpacks filled with supplies, which was something Grant and Erin had suggested. Since they've both trekked into the Echo, they know what we might need if we should "get sucked into hell through the sewer drain," as Erin phrased it. Now, we have weapons, food, and water stashed in our packs.

After our brief rest, we head down the other side of the mountain to the beach.

"What now?" Sarah asks.

"Let's put our stuff down and walk over to the shoreline. Do you know if it was high tide or low tide when you washed ashore?"

"Sorry, no idea. I was unconscious at the time."

"Yeah, I know." I drop my pack on the sand and survey the area. "But when you woke up, what did you see? Anything you can remember might be helpful."

She bites her lip, then gnaws on it as if she's thinking hard. "Erin and Grant found me, and they mentioned something about the tide. I know for sure they said I was lying facedown on the beach with the water washing up around me. And now that I think about it...I'm pretty sure they said it was low tide."

"When is low tide?"

"Around noon, I think. Grant keeps track of it."

I bite back a curse. "We're too late for it today. Better hold off until morning. I want to see where you washed ashore, but at low tide."

Because I'm suddenly an expert on that stuff. But nobody else seems to have a clue, so I might as well pretend I know what the fuck I'm doing. It's been two months since Sarah turned up here on the Northern California coast. Don't know what I think I'll learn by visiting that spot at low tide. Maybe it doesn't matter either way. Or maybe I'm delaying because the thought of what I might find out makes me uneasy.

No, it can't be that.

"Okay," Sarah says. "We'll wait. In the meantime, what should we do? Walk back to Sanctuary?"

"No, let's just settle in for the night here."

She glances around, hunching her shoulders. "Shouldn't we stay in the woods? I mean, if the lightning comes back…"

"You'd feel safer in the woods."

She hugs herself. "Yeah, I would. I know I'm being a wimp—"

"No, you're not. Let's go find a good spot for the night."

We hike back up the slope, but we turn down a path worn down by wildlife and choose a spot there to spend the night. We don't have any sleeping bags, but I made sure we brought blankets just in case. I try to give both blankets to Sarah, so she can lie on one and cover herself with the other. But she won't agree to that. I need to have a blanket too, she says. Sarah might think she's a wimp, but she knows how to be tough when she wants to get her way.

Though she declares that she can't really sleep and will only doze, after a while I look over at her and see she has fallen asleep. Good. At least one of us will get some rest.

I lie on my back and gaze up at the sky, what little of it I can see through the trees. Before the apocalypse, I'd rarely gone out into the suburbs, much less the wilderness. My idea of experiencing nature involved driving through a national park. Now, I'm sleeping under the stars. Would it be weird to thank the Echo for taking away my ability to stare at my cell phone for hours? I might never have studied the stars otherwise.

And I would never have met Sarah.

But I can't get too attached to her. I just lost the only family I'd ever known, and I don't want to watch Sarah or her friends suffer the same fate. I need to keep my distance.

Sarah moans softly, stirring a little. Her eyes remain closed, though her lips have curved up just enough to make her look so pretty that I want to cradle her in my arms. Christ, I met her today. I shouldn't have feelings like that. I don't want to feel that way.

Eventually, I doze off and wake up at dawn.

Can't believe I slept at all. But now, we both need to get up and try to find answers. I yawn and stretch, then grasp Sarah's shoulder to give her a little shake. "Wake up. No time for snoozing."

She opens her bleary eyes and frowns at me. "You're even grumpy when you wake up in the morning."

"Just get up." I scramble to stand, though I keep slipping on the grass, where morning dew has made things slick. "Come on. You're still just lying there."

"I need a few minutes to wake up."

Grumbling, I hunt around in my pack until I find the snack bars I'd stashed in there. Apparently, Sarah's friends like to scavenge food from destroyed cities. Grant told me they also hunt, so they can have meat sometimes. All I've got for me and Sarah is snack bars and jerky. Not my favorite foods. But nobody can be picky these days. Hell, I'd even eat pea soup if I found some, and I hate that garbage.

Sarah finally gets up. "What's the plan?"

I toss her a couple of snack bars. "We go down to the beach. Weren't you listening yesterday? I told you already."

She rolls her eyes at me.

Whatever that's supposed to mean, I don't care. I grab my pack and wave for her to follow me. "Hurry up, Lady Godiva."

"How many times do I have to say it before you listen? I don't like being called Lady Godiva."

"Then don't sunbathe in the nude where even Echo creatures could see you."

She scowls at me as she stalks past me down the hill.

I chuckle and follow her. She's hot when she gets mad.

We reach the shore, but it's too early to see low tide yet. So I decide to search the vicinity for anything out of the ordinary, though I have no idea what that might look like. What's ordinary these days? I suppose I'm searching for evidence of how Sarah got here, but that happened months ago. What are the odds I'll find anything?

Sarah refused to come with me on my perimeter search, but I keep an eye on her peripherally. She chose to stay on the beach where I can see her. Maybe she did that because I ordered her to do it, and I might've also snarled at her. But at least she complied. During my three years inside the Echo, I learned that you can't be sweet and nice, not if you want to survive. The Echo beings I'd befriended didn't follow my orders at first. I had to give them reason to do it, which meant getting tough with them. Becoming the general of our ragtag army saved lives—until the day it didn't anymore.

I need to convince Sarah to follow my orders, even if that means I have to get nasty with her. Noncompliance could get her killed. But I got my friends killed despite my orders. She might be safer back at Sanctuary.

After completing my perimeter search, I trek back down the hillside to the beach, heading for Sarah.

She's lying on the sand, fully clothed. The fact that she's dressed doesn't make her any less beautiful and sexy. She has one knee bent and her arms clasped above her head. The sun beams down on her face. Her lips curl into a sweet little smile. I get a strange pang in my chest as I watch her. That doesn't mean I like the girl.

I will never care about her or anyone ever again.

CHAPTER EIGHT

Sarah

THE SUN FEELS SO GOOD THAT I COULD FALL ASLEEP, JUST LYING HERE ON the beach, and I could almost forget about the apocalypse. I think I understand why Gabriel keeps acting like a jerk, but losing his friends is no excuse for his behavior. I haven't done anything to warrant this kind of treatment. I convinced my friends to let me interrogate him, rather than Dax. That man knows how to scare people without even touching them, sometimes without even speaking.

I doubt Dax's red-hot glare would impress Gabriel.

Though I do not like him, I have to admit Gabriel is attractive and sexy, and sometimes he even does selfless things like taking a bolt of Echo lightning for me. But that incident confused me. Now, he wants to help me understand how and why I washed ashore here. Yeah, I'm totally confused now.

A shadow falls over me.

I crack one eye open. "Find anything, General Jackass?"

"No. Get up. This isn't a vacation."

"Really? I thought you were the hotel concierge coming to tell me my massage appointment is at ten o'clock."

"Just get up. The tide is receding. Might be low enough now that I can figure out where you washed ashore."

"Grant and Erin told you that already."

"I want to see it for myself."

What evidence does he think he'll find two months later? Sheesh, he's stubborn. But I might as well indulge his obsession with the tide. Just as I start to sit up, he offers me his hands. To help me? I stare at his hands for a moment, while that idea sinks in, then I let him help me up.

"Thank you," I say. "But I could've gotten up on my own."

"And you think I'm rude. You could've stopped at 'thank you.' But no, you had to tack on some girl-power BS."

"You just have to be obnoxious, don't you? At least I was speaking in a pleasant tone, instead of growling like you do."

He stalks away from me, heading for the shoreline.

I follow him only because I want to do that, not because he silently ordered me to do it by walking away. Just to make sure he understands that, I walk beside him. That means I need to move fast to keep up with his longer strides, and I start to get short of breath.

"Slow down," I say. "What's the rush, anyway?"

He stops abruptly. "Show me the general vicinity where you think you washed ashore."

"I was unconscious at that point. Duh. I woke up when Grant and Erin found me."

"Yes, but you weren't blind. You must've noticed your surroundings, at least a little bit." He grasps my shoulders, gazing intently into my eyes. "This is important. Please think hard about what happened when you woke up. Close your eyes, try to relax, and let the memories flow naturally."

He's actually trying to help. I appreciate that, so I need to try to do what he suggested. I shut my eyes and listen to the gentle ebb and flow of the surf while the scent of the sea and the pine trees waft over me. The warmth and firmness of Gabriel's hands on my arms lulls me too, though I won't try to examine why, not right now. I've got the Zen mood going, and I need to release my worries, floating on a warm wave of relaxation.

At first, nothing happens. But I let my mind drift, as random thoughts tease the edges of my consciousness.

"Just let go," Gabriel murmurs, his tone smooth and almost sensual. "And when you're ready, tell me what you see."

Sounds tickle my memory, faintly at first, growing louder little by little but remaining an indistinguishable mess.

"That's it," Gabriel murmurs. "Relax into the memories as they flow into you."

His voice has grown so deep and sensual that a tingle starts up between my thighs, and my nipples tighten. But I shouldn't focus on that. I sink back into the Zen moment I've woven around myself—and Gabriel. Somehow, I know what I'm feeling has infiltrated him too. The mishmash of vague noises I've been hearing gradually coalesces into recognizable sounds. Pounding feet. Sirens. The roars of angry beasts. The screams of human beings.

"The Echo," I say. "I was in a city somewhere when the alchemy of worlds began, and the Echo invaded Earth."

"Good. Keep going, but remember to stay disconnected from the memories. You're safe, Sarah."

I feel that way with him, right here, right now. I know nothing will hurt me as long as Gabriel is with me. So I sink into the memories once again, anchored by the steady hands of Gabriel as I float on an ocean of tranquility. Even the screams of terrified people can't raise my pulse, and at last, I begin to experience events of the past as more than blurry images. I don't feel connected to what I see and hear, though, and I don't think that's solely due to my semi-trance state. Angry voices roar while lightning bolts punch into the earth and fireballs rip through buildings.

"Don't let her get away!"

"Wait, she's over there!"

"Stop running, you stupid—"

My lids spring open. My gaze connects with Gabriel's. I can't catch my breath, and my heart is pounding so hard and fast that I feel like I might pass out. Cold sweat dribbles down my temples while my teeth begin to chatter.

Gabriel pulls me into his arms, rubbing my back and murmuring soothing sounds that aren't quite words. My pulse begins to slow down. I let my body sag against him and close my eyes again, with my cheek to his chest, listening to the rhythmic thump-thumping of his heartbeat.

Once I feel able to hold myself upright, I wriggle free of his embrace. "Thank you for...doing that. I started to drown in the memories, though I don't understand any of it."

"What did you remember?"

"Fragments, that's all. Fireballs, lightning, people screaming. That must have been the start of the apocalypse, right?"

He nods. "What else?"

"Angry male voices. They shouted not to let 'her' get away and that 'she' was over there. One guy shouted for 'you' to stop running. I think they were talking about me."

"But you couldn't see who those men were, or in what city that happened."

"No. I'm sorry, I tried."

He lays a hand on my cheek. "You did great."

"Yeah, sure. Vague shouts are super helpful."

"It's a start. And it suggests your memories aren't gone, they're just hidden deep inside your psyche." He makes a pained face. "But I'm hardly an expert on psychology."

"You've helped me more than anyone else has since the day I washed up on this beach."

He scratches his neck and clears his throat, as if he's embarrassed by what I said. "Let's head back to the camp and report what you remembered. Maybe your friends will have some other ideas about how to resurrect your memories."

"They're your friends too, you know."

"Yeah, sure. We're good buddies."

Despite his sarcastic tone, I think he honestly wants to become a part of our family. After three years in the Echo, he's probably forgotten what it feels like to live among a camp like Sanctuary. I'm sure his Echo friends were loyal and good people, but they didn't have the skills that Grant, Erin, Dax, and others in our group can bring to the table. And Gabriel needs a new family. Here, in Sanctuary. Now, how can I convince him that he belongs with us?

A tiny thrill shivers through me. I want Gabriel to join our group. I want him to stick around, even after we discover the truth about me.

I try to hold Gabriel's hand as we start walking toward the mountain slope, but he shakes my hand off.

"They *are* your friends," I tell him. "You're not alone anymore. You have a home here in Sanctuary."

He grunts and refuses to look at me.

A bolt of lightning slams down on the beach just yards ahead of us. The blast throws us backward, and we both go tumbling across the sand into the surf. My ears ring, drowning out all other sounds. I scramble to my knees, hindered by my backpack, and crawl over to Gabriel, who lies flat on his back with his eyes open, seeming dazed. I shake him. He blinks slowly, twice, then grimaces.

A flash overhead makes me tip my head back to stare at the heavens, just as another flash coruscates across the blue sky. I would call it cloud-to-ground lightning, except there are no clouds.

"Get up!" I shout to Gabriel, who still seems a little dazed. "We need to find shelter."

I grab his hand, tugging hard as I rise to a half-crouch. With my help, he gets to his feet.

A bolt slams into the ground, striking so close to us that the sand erupts and showers onto our bodies.

Gabriel seizes my hand, and we take off toward the trees.

Yet another bolt slams down in front of us. But this time, it doesn't retreat into the sky. No, it just hovers there, shimmering and sizzling, the energy rippling inside it. The bolt blocks our path to the trail that leads up the mountain.

We veer to the left, toward the other side of the little cove.

Another bolt punches into the sand and hovers there, like the other one is still doing.

Running for the narrow swathe of beach that skirts the rock outcroppings doesn't work either. The lightning has boxed us in, and we have no escape route.

Gabriel grips my hand so tightly that it almost hurts, but I don't care. Echo lightning has trapped us here, which makes me wonder what will happen next. Will creatures appear to abduct us? In the two months that I've lived in Sanctuary, we've only seen the occasional creature. If a horde of them lived nearby, surely they would've made their presence known.

The sky splits open. The rift spirals outward, forming a black disk high above us that enlarges with every passing second. A ratcheting noise accompanies the ever-expanding disk. Is that… No, it can't be. There has never been an entrance to the Echo in this area. Those are only in cities or some of the small towns. Not here, in the wilderness. Not in Sanctuary.

Something flies out of the opening.

I swallow hard, but my throat has constricted.

A winged Echo creature swoops down to seize us, whisking us up toward the whirling black disk. Before I realize what's happened, we've been pulled through the entrance and into the Echo.

The flying beast drops us and soars away.

We land sprawled on the ground, with me on top of Gabriel.

He smirks. "Well, I'm liking this position."

"Sarcastic come-ons are not appropriate right now." I scramble to my feet. "We're in the Echo, aren't we? How did that happen?"

He sits up and glances around. "Home sweet home."

Yeah, he was being sarcastic again.

I plant my hands on my hips. "But how—"

"What makes you think I have a clue? No idea why a flying monster dragged us into the Echo and dumped us in the middle of nowhere."

I hadn't realized the Echo consisted of more than cities, but we currently stand in a scorched wasteland that seems to have once been countryside, maybe even farmland. I think I see the remnants of corn stalks. Echo creatures farmed? Wow, I have a lot to learn about this world. But my main concern right now is how to figure out why a creature dumped us here.

"Do you think that Aldith woman brought us here?" I ask. "Maybe she wants to talk to us."

"I doubt that. She was in the castle, though she might also have the ability to go into the stronghold. I got the impression she can't roam free, though."

"You mean she's a prisoner?"

He shrugs. "Could be. She didn't give me much info before she tossed me out of the Echo."

"She told you the Brain can't work properly on its own, right? She might be expecting you to take over that role now."

"Then why banish me to Earth? And why bring you here? None of this makes any sense."

Well, I can't argue with that. Lightning has tried to fry me several times. I have nothing to offer in terms of healing the Echo's Brain. Maybe Aldith didn't do this after all. At least we have our backpacks. That gives us some water and snacks, weapons too.

"What should we do now?" I ask. "You've traveled this whole world, so I'll defer to your knowledge of the Echo."

"Do you think I memorized the geography of this entire planet? I don't have a photographic memory."

He's getting grumpy again. Perfect.

A metallic grinding noise erupts behind us, but when we turn around to look, we can't see anything. The ground trembles with every *whump* of what sounds like gigantic feet. Then a white flash behind us makes me spin around and shout, "Gabriel! The lightning is back."

In the distance, bolts pound into the ground one after another after another, sweeping closer every moment.

"Run," Gabriel says, almost whispering the word.

We take off, having no clue where we're going or how to escape from the dual forces coming after us. More metallic grinding. More thunderous lightning. And we keep running, running, running. The ground shudders so violently that we stumble and hit the ground.

A lightning bolt strikes too close.

Gabriel hoists me onto my feet, but just as we turn to run, another bolt erupts from the sky.

A massive metal hand reaches out from behind us, raising its open palm, and the lightning bounces off it. The being that hand belongs to remains shrouded in darkness as the thing deflects bolt after bolt, using both palms as shields. Then the being scoops up both me and Gabriel. Cradled in the monstrosity's palm, we both stare up at the creature.

"Jarek," Gabriel says. "Thanks, buddy. We needed a hand."

The gigantic being seems to be made of metal and flesh, like a cyborg in a sci-fi movie. Gabriel knows this creature, and he doesn't seem angry or afraid of the thing. He called it Jarek.

"Did Aldith send you to bring us into the Echo?" Gabriel asks. When the cyborg shakes its head, Gabriel says, "No, of course you didn't. You would've scooped us up straight off Earth, and whoever brought us here needed an Echo creature to abduct us."

With one hand, Jarek continues deflecting the lightning bolts, but I swear he winces a little every time.

I whisper to Gabriel, "Your friend is getting tired."

"Yeah, he is." Gabriel shouts to Jarek, "Big buddy, can you take us to the castle?"

Jarek shakes his head.

"What about the stronghold?"

The cyborg nods.

"Good. Take us there, please."

Jarek cups his other palm over us, forming a protective shell. Then he lopes away, presumably ferrying us to the stronghold, whatever that is. I can't see Gabriel, but I feel his hand holding mine.

"What is this creature?" I ask. "Everyone says Echo beasts are the size of normal humans, but this guy is like Godzilla."

"He's nicer than that monster. Jarek is good, and he helped me scale the sheer cliff that has Sefton's castle at the top of it."

"But what is Jarek?"

"He's a golem. That's a creature created by magic to serve its master's bidding. But Erin and Grant managed to free him, and he does what he wants now."

I'm glad to hear that, because it means Jarek chooses to help us. The ride in the golem's palm isn't the smoothest, but it seems like Jarek is trying to make it as easy on us as he can. After a while, he slows to a walking pace and pulls one palm away to let us see the landscape. It's vacant land, scorched beyond recognition. I swear I can smell the smoke, though the bulk of the apocalypse has been over for months now. It could've been longer here in the Echo. If time behaves differently in this world, I wonder how long our friends will have to wait for us to return. Will they assume we're dead?

No. They will never give up on us.

CHAPTER NINE

Gabriel

JAREK'S LONG STRIDES CREATE A SLIGHT ROCKING SENSATION AS WE travel toward the stronghold, wherever that might be hidden. The rocking motion seems to be making Sarah kind of dizzy, given the way she keeps biting her lip and gripping her knees. So I sling an arm around her shoulders. "Don't worry. The stronghold is a bastion of good magics, not bad ones. That's what I've heard, anyway. I tried to find it, but I think the stronghold is cloaked to prevent just anybody from getting inside."

"Grant and Erin have been inside the stronghold. They met Aldith there."

"Well, I hope she's still there. I want to know what the hell she expects us to do."

Yeah, that woman did not explain herself very well. Maybe she kept things vague on purpose. I get the feeling she's more than just an Echo creature, but some kind of higher being within this domain. She might even straddle both worlds. I don't know, and that's why I need to interrogate her.

Right, because that worked out so well last time.

As we pass through a blackened and lifeless zone, I notice a familiar shape off to my left, far away but close enough that I can recognize it. That's the castle, poised high up on a narrow and hard to reach cliff. All my friends died there. Only I survived, and I still don't know why.

"Do me a favor," Sarah says. "When we reach the stronghold and see Aldith, don't get grumpy with her."

"Why not? She hasn't been the most helpful person."

"Did you ever think that maybe she's scared too? And she might not be able to tell you more than she already has? You seem to assume she's all-knowing."

I sigh. "Yeah, okay, you've got a point. I'll try to restrain myself." I smirk at her. "But I can't swear I won't get sarcastic."

She smiles a touch and shakes her head. "I figured that would be too much to ask of you."

I know I'm a sarcastic jackass. I never used to be, but the apocalypse changed everything. It changed me, for sure. I don't feel qualified to determine whether I've changed for the better or the worse. Only other people can judge that.

How would Sarah judge me?

I don't care. Her opinion doesn't matter. I asked myself that question because…I'm bored, stuck inside a golem's hand. What else have I got to think about?

Sarah kisses my cheek.

I jerk and whip my head around to stare at her. "What are you doing?"

"Thanking you."

"For what? I didn't do anything, good or bad."

"Of course you did." She rests her head on my shoulder. "You're being much less grumpy. And you helped me recover a sliver of my memories back on the beach."

"You did that. I just stood there."

"Stop trying to downplay how helpful you've been."

I don't bother responding to that. I have no response. If Sarah has developed a hero complex about me, she'll be disappointed, eventually.

But right here, right now, she snuggles up to me.

I resist the urge to grimace and try not to fidget. Nobody has wanted to snuggle with me since way before the alchemy of worlds began. I guess I've forgotten how to accept affection. Three years in the Echo hardened me, and I don't know if I can ever again become the kind of man any woman would want to get involved with for more than sex.

Jarek halts, then raises his hand high above his head, lifting us toward… nothing.

What is he doing? Are we supposed to jump into the clouds?

Suddenly, our surroundings shift. We no longer sit on Jarek's palm. Instead, we stand inside a building, in a long hallway that has flickering oil lamps positioned at intervals along the walls. This place feels like a castle, but I've been inside Sefton Stainthorpe's fortress, and it was nothing like this. His castle seemed vacant and sterile, not at all welcoming. The stronghold we now stand in has warm, flickering light and wooden doors. What lies inside those rooms? Not bare stone, I'm sure. Call it a hunch.

A doorway to our left swings open, and Aldith steps onto the threshold. "Welcome to the stronghold. Please step inside this room, where we can discuss matters in a more comfortable environment."

Sarah slips her hand into mine as we follow Aldith into a spacious bedroom. I consider shaking her hand off, but I can't make myself do that this time. Something about the stronghold makes me uneasy. I guess I need a little comforting too. This room is beautifully decorated, not that I'm an expert on that sort of thing. But even I can appreciate the warm tones and the splashes of brighter colors that make the space feel welcoming.

"It's nice to see you again, Aldith," I say. "But why did you send me away only to bring me back here again?"

She cants her head, seeming curious. "I did not bring you here. I sent you to Sanctuary, that is all."

"But Jarek gave us a ride to get here."

"Jarek is an autonomous being, no longer a slave to anyone since Erin and Grant freed him."

I feel myself about to get grumpy and remember what Sarah told me. I shouldn't get angry at Aldith. She might be as much a pawn in this game as we are. So I take a breath and exhale it slowly to calm myself. "Do you know anything about the lightning on the Earth side of things? It seemed to be going after Sarah. Then it penned us on the beach so a flying creature could grab us and drag us back into the Echo."

"I was aware of the lightning," Aldith says, "but only on this side. The Echo has been enduring strange weather similar to what happened during the alchemy of worlds."

"That wasn't going on when I left here."

"No. It began shortly after your departure." She cants her head again, this time aiming her curiosity at Sarah. "The lightning wished to hurt you?"

Sarah hunches her shoulders. "It kept trying to hit me, that's all I know. Gabriel jumped in front of a bolt to save me. But you just asked if the lightning 'wished' to hurt me. That implies you think it's sentient."

"I regret if I implied that. What I should have asked is whether the lightning might've been directed toward you."

"Of course it was," I say, almost snarling, but not quite. I need to do more work on not getting grumpy. I manage to calm down and unfist my hands. "Sorry. I didn't mean to snap at you. But this is all damn confusing and unnerving."

"Yes, I imagine it is." Aldith clasps her hands in front of her body. "Perhaps we can solve the mystery together."

"Any help you can provide would be appreciated."

When I glance at Sarah, she's smiling at me. It's a small but sweet smile. I'd rather she didn't look at me that way.

"About the lightning," I say, focusing on the pretty Echo creature so I don't have to see Sarah's expression. "Do you have any information about that? Any guesses? I'd like to know why those bolts were after Sarah."

"If I knew, I would tell you. But I cannot see what the Echo is doing on Earth, only what happens here."

"Have you ever known the lightning in the Echo to chase a person? Or corral someone?"

"No. And the fact that an Echo creature abducted you is rather disturbing."

Yeah, no shit. The whole situation is disturbing. Especially since I just realized something. "Jarek was working with the Echo creature that brought us here."

Aldith's eyes widen for the briefest moment. Then she rolls her shoulders back and clears her throat. "I don't believe he would have aided anyone in harming you. There must be an explanation."

"Let's ask him."

Aldith marches past us, through the open doorway and across the hall to another door. She glances back. "Are you coming? This was your idea, after all."

I lead Sarah across the hall as Aldith opens the door. We all tromp into another bedroom. This one features big picture windows that overlook…the clouds. We're in the sky? Well, Jarek had lifted us very high, but I'd assumed he pushed us through some kind of portal to the stronghold.

But no, we're actually floating in the clouds.

Aldith waves a hand. One of the picture windows vanishes. She leans out and tips her head down. "Jarek! We need to speak to you, please."

What on earth is that woman doing? Even Jarek can't reach this place. It's high above his head. I think. We just kind of poofed into the stronghold, so I can't say for sure. Can't believe I thought the word poof. At least I didn't say it out loud.

A large metal-and-flesh hand clamps onto the windowsill, and Jarek's head rises into view.

Did he jump up here? Guess it doesn't really matter how he got here as long as he can answer our questions. Since it's yes or no answers only with the golem, this could take a while.

Aldith pats Jarek's head. "Thank you for coming. We need your assistance, if you're able and willing to help."

The golem nods.

"Go on, Gabriel," Aldith says. "You and Sarah may ask Jarek whatever questions you like."

"Okay." I approach the window and gaze at Jarek's enormous face. "A flying creature brought us into the Echo. Were you working with that beast?"

Jarek shakes his head.

I'm surprisingly glad to hear that. I've only met Jarek a few times, but the golem always seemed like a good, uh, guy. Not sure what else to call a creature like him. So I'll stick with "guy." It sounds weird, though.

"Do you know who sent that creature?" I ask.

Jarek shrugs.

What does that mean? I need to rephrase my question. "Are you saying you aren't sure whether you know who did it?"

The golem nods.

Great. Ambivalence is really helpful. "Do you have any idea why the lightning keeps coming for Sarah?"

Jarek shakes his head.

"Well, thank you for answering my questions." I look at Sarah. "Did you want to ask him anything?"

"I can't think of anything." She bites her lip, her brows furrowed, then leans out the window. "Jarek, why did you bring us to the stronghold?"

"That's not a yes or no question," I point out. "He can't speak. You need to keep it simple so he can respond."

Jarek lifts one finger and points it toward Aldith.

Interesting. I nudge Sarah out of the way and lean out the window. "Are you saying Aldith knows why you brought us here?"

He nods. His arms have begun to tremble slightly, which seems like a sign he can't hold on to the window for much longer.

"Okay," I say. "You can go now, Jarek. Thanks for the help."

The golem lets go of the sill and drops down through the clouds, out of sight.

"Well, that was a waste of time," I mumble.

"No, it wasn't," Sarah says. "At least now we know Jarek didn't conspire with an Echo creature to abduct us."

"And he will help if you need him," Aldith says. "Jarek always wants to help those who deserve to be helped."

Sarah deserves it. Still not sure I do.

"Why does Jarek think you know why he brought us to the stronghold?" I ask. "You claimed you didn't summon us here."

"I did not. But Jarek must believe I will come to understand why he brought you here. I need to think about that. Despite what you may think, I don't have special powers of perception."

A yawn overtakes me, and I rub my hands over my face.

"How much did you sleep last night?" Sarah asks.

I lift one shoulder. "A couple hours, maybe. I've gone with less sleep for much longer."

"You need to rest. We both need to be in top form if we're going to figure out what's happening." Sarah looks at Aldith. "Would you mind if we rest here in the stronghold for a while? It would give you time to think about what Jarek said too."

"Take any room you like. All the doors are unlocked." She walks toward the doorway, then pauses to glance back. "The bedrooms in the stronghold sometimes have an unusual effect on couples, particularly those who make love while in residence here."

Is she suggesting we should have sex? No, I can't get up for that. Even after I get some rest, I doubt I would ever feel comfortable doing that in this strange place.

Right, because fucking in the dirt while crazy Echo lightning bombed the woods wasn't strange at all.

I let Sarah lead me down the hall so we can peek into every bedroom. She chooses one she likes, then asks if I like it too. I shrug. What the room looks like hardly matters. I want to sleep, not admire the sheets or whatever it is she thinks I should care about. A bed is a bed. I haven't slept in comfort for so long that I barely remember what a nice, soft mattress feels like, anyway.

We lie down on top of the covers, and I fall asleep almost instantly. It happens so fast that I think I didn't sleep at all, until Sarah points at a clock situated on a dresser.

"It's been seven hours," she says. "I noticed the time when we lay down. You passed out the second you closed your eyes."

"Did you get any sleep?"

"Yes. But I wasn't as exhausted as you were. I did have a dream, though. It was about what I saw in my vision, the one where men were yelling for me to stop running."

Maybe I shouldn't care, but I have to ask. "What did you see this time?"

"They seemed to want to protect me rather than trying to hurt me."

I suddenly realize we've been spooning. I can honestly say I've never done that before. Pretty sure I fell asleep lying on my back. But at some point, I rolled over to cradle her body with mine, and I have one arm draped over her hip. The warmth and suppleness of her body feels…right.

Which is bullshit.

I sit up and swing my legs off the bed. "Better find Aldith. Maybe she finally realized what Jarek meant."

"There's no need to be embarrassed."

"Why would I be? I got some rest, that's all."

She crawls up behind me and wraps her arms around my torso. "We shared an intimate experience. You get touchy about that kind of thing."

Did we have sex while I was asleep? No, I would've woken up if that happened.

She nuzzles my neck. "We took a nap together, Gabriel. When was the last time you went to sleep with a woman holding you?"

For reasons I can't understand, I tell her the truth. "Never. The women I dated weren't into, uh, cuddling."

"Really? I thought all women loved that. But then, I have amnesia, so maybe I just don't remember disliking cuddling." She kisses my throat. "I loved sleeping with you."

"Uh, yeah, it was…fine."

Her hands, her lips, and her voice are doing things to me that won't be helpful right now. So I peel her arms away and stand up, trying not to let her see the growing bulge in my pants. I'm a guy. I can't help that feeling a woman's body wrapped around me, and hearing a woman's sensual voice, makes my dick wake up.

A woman? No, it's only Sarah who does this to me.

I slither off the bed. "Let's find Aldith."

Sarah tries to hold my hand, but I manage to dodge that attempt. I've let her get too close to me, and that's a recipe for disaster.

Distance, that's what I need.

CHAPTER TEN

Sarah

GABRIEL DOESN'T WANT ME TO TOUCH HIM ANYMORE. HE HAS pulled away from me before, but not as abruptly as he's doing now. Our sleepover must have disturbed him. We've had sex, for heaven's sake. How can he feel weird about taking a nap with me? Maybe I just don't understand men. Since I have amnesia, I can't be sure I understand anything that other people do.

Aldith appears in front of us.

We'd been walking down the hall, and now we're forced to halt. I try once again to grasp his hand, but he folds his arms over his chest to thwart me. Why is he so determined to avoid even the tiniest amount of intimacy? It must be related to what he went through before he dropped out of the sky and landed on the beach at my feet. Losing his friends must have scarred him more than I'd realized. I wish I had my own experiences to guide me, but I'm flying blind when it comes to helping Gabriel recover from his losses.

Maybe all I need to do is be here for him, whether he likes it or not.

"Did you sleep well?" Aldith asks.

"Yeah, sure," Gabriel says. He seems to be trying to get away from me, shuffling sideways when I rest my cheek on his upper arm. "Aldith, did you figure out why Jarek thinks you know what's going on?"

"I believe so. But I don't have a direct interface with the Heart or Lifeblood of the Echo, and the Brain is still in limbo."

"You said the Brain requires a human being to function."

Aldith's features crimp the slightest bit.

"The Heart and the Lifeblood are humans," I tell Gabriel. "Grant and Erin took over those roles to stabilize the Echo and Earth when the worlds were having conniptions. They don't have any particular duties related to becoming the Heart and the Lifeblood, and they've only come back to the stronghold a few times to check on things."

Gabriel stares at me for a moment, his mood impossible to gauge. "You must be the Brain. That's why the lightning keeps coming for you."

"No, it must be you. I mean, you saved me from the lightning. That has to mean something."

Aldith clears her throat. "You are both ignoring an obvious aspect of the Brain."

"Like what?" Gabriel says, and he's starting to sound grumpy again.

"Every human brain has two hemispheres, which control opposite sides of the body."

"So what?"

Aldith lifts her brows. "The answer is obvious. The Brain of the Echo would seem to require two humans to function properly."

Gabriel narrows his gaze on Aldith. "But you said Sefton Stainthorpe was the Brain. That means one man, not two humans, controlled the Echo."

"And you forget one vital fact." She walks straight up to Gabriel and aims her glowing eyes at him. "Sefton Stainthorpe had an Echo, the being known as Will, his alter ego who was created when Sefton activated the Catalyst and the Anchor to begin the alchemy of worlds. Sefton did not foresee that his plan would result in an Echo of himself being created, but that is what occurred. He also did not appreciate sharing the Brain with Will."

"Allison and Dax are the Catalyst and the Anchor."

"I trust you to keep the information confidential," I tell Gabriel, "because it affects the lives of three people."

Gabriel swerves his attention to me. "I know how to keep a secret, Sarah."

I wrap my arms around myself, rubbing my hands up and down, suddenly feeling a chill. "Allison was the Catalyst, the human who initiated the chain reaction without knowing she'd done that. Sefton used her without her permission. Dax was the Anchor, the human who kept the alchemical reaction from spinning out of control. He was also used by Sefton without his permission. We don't know what might happen if this information got into the wrong hands. For all we know, the Catalyst and the Anchor might reignite the alchemy of worlds or start the alchemy of souls."

"You said the secret affects the lives of three people."

"The third life is Dax and Allison's unborn child. We've been afraid that if Echo creatures found out the Catalyst and the Anchor had conceived a baby, those beasts might try to steal the child. Their baby might become the golden fleece of the apocalypse."

"Because their kid might have the Echo power."

"Or it might have magics that no one can even imagine yet."

Gabriel shoves his hands into his pants pockets and sighs. "Okay, I get why that needs to be kept a secret. But I am not one hemisphere of the Echo's Brain."

"Do not fight your destiny," Aldith says. "When you breached the castle, I knew you must be the one who would join with the other half of the Brain and take control of the Echo."

"But who is the other half?"

"Sarah, of course."

Gabriel glances at me, but he quickly swerves his attention away. "Why would the Echo want two strangers to be the Brain? Neither of us even knows what that means, what we're supposed to do. You must be wrong. Sarah, sure, I can see that. But not me."

Does he honestly believe that I know what the heck is going on here? I don't want to be the Brain either. But Erin and Grant accepted the roles the Echo assigned to them, and they've managed to sort out what they needed to do. They'd known each other for a month or so before they entered the Echo, so they could try to fix the conniptions. Gabriel and I met yesterday. We don't get along, and he clearly wants nothing to do with becoming one hemisphere of the Echo's Brain.

I don't want to do that either. But we have no choice. What the Echo wants, it gets—or else the worlds will be destroyed. How can I convince Gabriel of that?

"Where is this Brain thing, anyway?" Gabriel asks. "Or are we supposed to find it on our own?"

"The Brain is housed inside the castle, but I'm not privy to its exact location. It does not have a physical form, as it is composed entirely of magics."

"Uh-huh. So what the fuck are we supposed to do? Can't become the Brain if we have no way to find it."

I smack his arm. "Don't be rude."

He doesn't look at me even when he hisses, "I wasn't being rude. I asked a valid question."

"You said the F-word."

Gabriel rolls his eyes. "Now you're suddenly a goody two shoes. Didn't act that way back in the woods yesterday."

"Let's not talk about that in front of *her*."

Aldith gazes at us with a neutral expression. Did she hear what we whispered to each other? If so, she doesn't seem to realize what Gabriel was talking about, and I see no reason why she would. Unless she has psychic powers. God, I hope that's not the case.

"You need to digest what I've told you," Aldith says. "Please, take as long as you like. I have frozen time within the stronghold."

I stare at her. "You froze time? I had no idea you could do that. What about time in the Echo and on Earth?"

"Regrettably, I have no control over that."

"So, time will keep moving at the normal pace for our friends."

"Perhaps, or perhaps not. The Echo does what it wants to do."

Wonderful. I love all these vague explanations.

Aldith vanishes.

Gabriel and I both seem unable to look at each other, instead exchanging furtive sidelong glances. But we don't speak or move.

Finally, I can't take the silence anymore. "Should we, um, talk about this?"

"About what? That chick strongly implied we should have sex because the rooms here have a strange effect on couples. We aren't a couple, though."

"She's trying to help. And Aldith does know more about this stuff than we do."

He grunts. "So, what, she's a sex therapist too? Getting laid won't help anything."

"Won't it? Something changed when we had sex in the woods. I know you felt it too."

He grunts again.

We go back to awkwardly standing here in the hall while we awkwardly glance at each other. Though we had sex once, it happened so fast that I have trouble remembering exactly what we did. No, that's a lie. I remember every second of it. But even while I can't stop thinking about that, I also feel like that experience was a blur too. It makes no sense, but I don't care. And I have a weird feeling that Aldith knows what might happen if Gabriel and I get naked again. Will sex make us stronger somehow? More in tune with the Echo?

"Aldith said we should take our time," Gabriel says. "So let's do that."

"Do what?"

"Take our time."

I tip my head back and glare at the ceiling. "You're being just as vague as Aldith."

"Sorry." He scratches the back of his head. "Let's find a place to sit down and then talk about…stuff."

"Fine."

I let Gabriel lead the way, and we wind up peeking inside every room on this floor. We didn't realize the stronghold had more than one floor until we reached the end of the hall and a wooden door magically appeared. It slid open to reveal the elevator car. Gabriel walked right inside, so I did the same. If the elevator wants to kill us, I don't have the mental capacity to think about that. I don't feel physically tired. My brain needs a rest, though.

Crazy revelations will do that to a girl.

On the lower floor, we explore the rooms we find there. Gabriel finally chooses one, and we drop our backpacks on the floor beside the bed. Luckily, this room has four chairs and a comfy sofa, so we don't need to lie on the bed together. I'd be fine with that, though I doubt Gabriel would. He flipped out after accidentally spooning with me.

He sits in a chair.

I drop onto the sofa at the end nearest to him. "What should we talk about?"

"Whether we want to become the Brain."

"Aldith made it sound like that's not optional. I assume the Echo will start to have problems again if we don't do that."

"She told us to think about it. Why bother considering the issue if we have no choice?"

I tuck my feet under me cross-legged and tap my fingers on my knees. "It was my understanding that Aldith meant we need to come to terms with our destiny."

"Our what?" He makes a rude noise and shakes his head. "You're jumping to conclusions."

"No, I'm extrapolating from what Aldith told us."

"We have no choice. Fine." He gets up and starts unzipping his pants. "Let's fuck right now and get it over with."

"Are you insane? I can't get turned on when you're acting like a jackass."

"Of course you can." He stalks up to the sofa, pulls my legs out from under me, and flips me onto my back. Then he kneels on all fours above me. "I bet you're already wet. Back in the woods, I didn't need to do any prep work to get you ready. I've never been with a woman who gets as wet as you do and does it so fast. You're easy, Sarah."

"What? No, I am not." But I get dismayingly turned on when I'm around him, even when we're having a discussion with Grant, Erin, and the others. Nobody could've noticed that. Right?

He lunges his head down to take my nipple into his mouth, through my shirt and bra. The strong sucking motion makes my clit pulsate. I bite back a gasp, because I do not want him to know he's right.

Gabriel ducks his head to shove his nose between my thighs and pull in a big breath through his nostrils. "Damn, I can smell how hot you are for me. Your clothes can't mask it because you want me so badly."

The rough tone of his voice makes my sex throb. I'm trying so hard not to start panting, though my racing heart doesn't help me resist him. How can I want a jerk like him? I wish I could forget that one time we screwed, but I dreamed about it last night in the woods. I woke up with my panties drenched, but I won't admit that to him. He'd just love knowing I'm desperately hot for him.

But I think he kind of figured that out already. *Damn.*

I should order him to stop. Better yet, I should kick him in the head. But I can't convince myself to do either of those things.

He rises to his knees, finishes unzipping his pants, and pulls out his cock. While he stares at my chest, he begins stroking his length with one hand. "Do you want it right here, on the sofa? Or on the bed? Your choice, but it'll be a filthy fuck either way, and I guarantee you'll beg me to do it again once we're done."

No sex, period. That's what I should say. It's not what my mouth decides to tell him, though. "On the bed. Please, hurry."

The desperation in my voice makes me hate myself for being as easy as he claims I am. But I don't care anymore. The way he made me feel when he had sex in the woods… I want more of that. Not for a few minutes. No, this time I want him inside me for hours and hours. We have all the time we want, thanks to Aldith freezing the clock for us. And I need to experience filthy sex just once more before I die.

And yeah, I assume we will both die soon. Neither of us knows how to become the Brain, after all.

Gabriel picks me up and drops me onto the bed without even bothering to remove the covers.

Watching him undress mesmerizes me, and I couldn't move if I tried. I follow his every movement as he unbuttons his shirt and shrugs out of it, revealing all those rippling muscles that I'd seen when he fell from the sky yesterday. But now not even tatters of clothing conceal his physique. I long to lick a path along every one of those muscles.

But then he pushes his pants and underwear down to his ankles and kicks them off along with his socks. He'd already kicked his boots off before he got started stripping. My attention stalls on his cock, that thick, smooth, beautiful dick that I can't wait to feel inside me again.

"Strip," he commands.

And I do it. As quickly as I can, I ditch all my clothes and lie down on the bed again. "Gabriel, I—"

"Don't move."

I watch while he finds his backpack and pulls out a length of rope. "What's that for?"

"Always keep some rope with me just in case." He climbs onto the foot of the bed and crawls up my body on his hands and knees until his face hovers above mine. "And I need it right now."

"Why?"

"You know why, because you want it too. Don't you?"

I can't tell him to go to hell because the power of my arousal has stolen my breath. I feel the slickness of my cream all over my inner thighs, and I can smell it too. Whatever he wants to do, I want him to do it to me.

"Yes, Gabriel, I want it. I want you."

Chapter Eleven

Gabriel

WHAT AM I DOING? I'VE NEVER GONE ALPHA-MALE ASSHOLE ON A woman before. I never wanted to behave that way. But three years in the Echo changed me in ways I haven't fully explored yet and that I don't fully understand. Now that I have Sarah all to myself, in a place where no one will find us or interrupt us, I've developed a powerful urge to dominate her.

And she seems okay with that.

Fuck, I need to do this.

Sarah's tits rise and fall with her every breath, and her chest has become dappled with rosy pink. Her stiff nipples jut up, begging me to devour them.

But not yet.

I carefully bind her wrists to her ankles with the rope, leaving just a bit of leeway to make sure she doesn't get chafed. "Don't speak unless I tell you to, and don't come unless I give you permission."

"But how—"

"I said don't speak."

She bites her lip, her eyes glossy with desire. Sarah has never looked more beautiful than she does right now.

I push her legs apart, keeping her knees bent, exposing every inch of her glistening pink flesh while I drink in the evidence of how much she wants me. Then I lie down with my head between her thighs and suck in a deep draft of her scent, groaning at the musky, addictive aroma. Now that I have her at my mercy, I need to tease her until she can't stand it anymore. So I drag my tongue up and down the edge of her cleft, flicking my tongue out occasionally to tease her inner folds.

Sarah moans and rocks her hips.

The sound, so erotic and hungry, pushes me to do more, to make her so aroused that she won't be able to think, much less speak. I hoist her hips and seal my mouth around her opening, thrusting my tongue deep again and again until she whimpers and thrashes, her breaths growing shorter and more erratic. When I feel like she's on the edge, I stop.

"Do you like what I'm doing?" I ask. "You can speak this one time, because I'm allowing you to do it."

"Yes," she breathes, "I love this. Don't stop."

I flick my tongue around the rim of her opening, and she writhes, as much as she can when I have her bound. While I keep teasing her entrance, I stretch an arm up to close my hand around her breast and rub my thumbnail over the rigid tip.

Her mouth falls open as she seems to struggle against the need to cry out.

As much as I thought I needed her to stay silent unless I gave her permission to speak, now I realize I want to hear whatever she needs to scream or whisper to me. I need it so much that just thinking about it makes my cock throb. I'm so hard that I don't know if I can last much longer.

"You can speak," I growl. "But I'm still in control."

"Oh, yes, I want you to tell me what to do. It's the hottest thing ever."

She loves having me in control of her. Would I want to give up control to Sarah? I can't think about that right now, because I need to drive her toward a climax that will shatter her. But not yet. I rise to my knees and hoist her hips, then rub the tip of my erection around the rim of her entrance in slow, steady circles. The motion drives me crazy too, but it's the look on Sarah's face that might break me. I'm struggling to catch my breath while she loosely bites her bottom lip and her eyes flutter half-closed. Her mouth curls into the sweetest, naughtiest little smile I've ever seen.

Just as I feel myself on the verge of coming, I pull away and shove my hand into the curly hairs on her mound, teasing them with my fingers. Her slickness dampens those hairs and my fingertips.

Sarah watches me, her breasts heaving.

I hold my fingers to my mouth and lick away the drops of her cream one by one.

"Oh, God, Gabriel," she moans. "Make me come, please."

"Not yet." I trail my fingertips up her belly and back down again, then take hold of the rope and tug it, making her gasp. "You want me to fuck you right now."

"Yes, please."

"I won't do that, not yet."

Rising to my knees, I stroke myself while I gaze down at her nude body. I love watching her writhe as if she can't wait for me to fuck her, but I don't want to do that yet. All right, I *want* to do it. But we have literally all the time in the world, and I won't rush.

"Do that again," she says, her tone sultry and her eyes darkened by lust. "Take me to the edge and leave me hanging. I love what you're doing to me."

I've discovered something about myself since I met Sarah—several things, actually—and I will tell her about it later. Right now, I need to drive her wild again and again until we both can't stand it anymore.

"How flexible are you?" I ask. "Don't want to push you too far and hurt you."

She smiles playfully, then pulls her bound legs and hands up over her head, hooking her ankles in the headboard rails. "Does that answer your question?"

"Hell yeah." I run my hands up and down her legs. "You must do yoga to be that flexible."

"I practice with Grant and Erin. Grant's teaching me how to be Zen too."

My gaze has become glued to her body, where her new position has exposed all that glistening, slick, pink flesh that I need to devour—eventually. I slant forward to grasp the headboard rails, and I start rubbing my dick up and down her cleft. Every time the head of my cock grazes her flesh, I suck in a sharp breath, and she gasps too. I struggle to keep control of my breathing while I rock my hips to rasp her sensitized flesh, and my pulse accelerates, pounding in my chest and thundering in my ears.

I sit back on my heels and wipe sweat from my brow.

Sarah moans and manages to wriggle her ass even while bound to the headboard. She's very flexible. Unbelievably flexible. The fact that she does yoga and meditates turns me on even more.

On my knees, I waddle even closer until my dick hangs right over her face. "Suck me, baby."

She doesn't hesitate. Sarah lunges her head up to catch my cock in her mouth, and she lets out sharp little grunts while she sucks me. I groan and hiss in a breath, clutching the headboard while I let her do whatever she wants. Her tongue coils around me like a sexy snake, and she takes as much of me into her mouth as she possibly can, then she withdraws. With a sly smile, she rakes her tongue over my crown.

"Fuck, Sarah," I growl.

I know I'll come any second, and I don't want that to happen yet. So I back away to kneel near her exposed cleft, then cup both her breasts in my palms. I flick my thumbs over her nipples in a slow rhythm, and her breaths shorten, becoming erratic while I torment her stiff peaks. Just when she's gotten used to the rhythm, I stop. Then I bend over to gently lick her nipples. That makes her jerk and gasp. I blow air over those wet peaks.

"Gabriel, please," she pleads. "Don't ever stop."

I chuckle. "You're a dirty girl, aren't you? Guess that shouldn't surprise me since you sunbathe in the nude."

She must be in agony—the best kind, brought on by intense pleasure with no release—but she wants even more. I feel the same agony, but I'm not ready for this to end yet either.

And she begged me not to stop.

I plant my hands at either side of her body and ease my cock inside her, relishing the silky smoothness of her sheath as it molds to me, hot and wet, the scent of her desire inundating my senses. Once I'm buried as deep inside her as I can go, I hold that position. Yeah, I need to come so badly that I'm clenching my teeth and I can hardly breathe, but I need this to last a little longer. So I pull out completely and just hover here, my dick inches from her opening, and gaze into her eyes. She gazes right back at me, her cheeks pink and her lips a deeper shade of rose.

Can't stop myself. I lunge down to claim her lips, pushing my tongue between them, ravaging her mouth and relishing the taste of her. She thrusts her tongue between my lips. Our teeth clash, our breaths gust over each other's faces, and her heart must be pounding as ferociously as mine, but neither of us can stop. We keep kissing like the world will explode any second, and maybe it will.

The world did explode once, when the Echo punched through into Earth.

If this might be the last day of my life, I need to make it incredible. I thrust my cock into her while we keep kissing, and I punch into her over and over, so hard and so fast that the bed bounces and thumps and our cries fill the room. Almost there... Any second...

With a snarled shout, I pull out of her body and give up her mouth. My ears are ringing. I take some slow breaths and encourage Sarah to do the same. Once we've both calmed down just enough that we won't pass out, it's time to finish. I slide my cock into her sheath inch by inch, letting myself experience every sensation, and I keep my gaze locked on hers. My God, she's beautiful and sensual, the perfect woman, the only one in the universe who could make me feel human again. The heat of her body surrounds me. Nothing else has ever felt this good, but I know what I'm about to do will become the most incredible feeling I will ever know.

I pump into her, slowly at first, then faster and faster until I'm pounding into her and the wet sucking sound of our bodies colliding reverberates in the room.

"Come for me, Sarah," I say, my voice a hoarse growl. "Come right now."

I adjust the angle of my thrusts until my balls rub against her flesh. Her body tightens around me, a sure sign that she's about to go off. The pressure to come builds inside me like an industrial boiler ramping up to an explosion, and I can't do more than gasp and keep pumping faster and harder.

Sarah freezes. She doesn't even blink. Doesn't breathe either, I think. Then her entire body curls in on itself while the spasms of her climax grip my cock, and she screams. The pressure inside me has become too intense to fight, and

I let go. My release erupts out of me while I pound into her twice more, shouting as the last spasms of my cock subside. I'm breathing hard, sweat sheaths my body, and I don't have the wherewithal to pull out of her. All I can do is stare at Sarah.

Did we just do that? Or did I hallucinate the whole thing? When I gaze down at her, I know it was real.

Her lips curl into a smile of intense satisfaction. "That was amazing, Gabriel."

"Yeah, it was." I finally realize she's still bound. "Shit, let me untie you."

I release her bindings and drop onto the bed beside her.

Sarah snuggles up to me, her head on my chest and her arm draped across my torso. She traces little circles on my skin with her fingertips. "I've never felt this good before."

"Me either. Damn, that was…" I can't figure out how to end that sentence. No words feel right.

"What we did in the woods was incredible," she says. "But this was even better."

"Yeah, it was." I slip an arm around her. "Can I tell you something?"

"Of course. You can tell me anything, and I won't repeat it to anyone else."

"I know that." While I caress her hair, I feel more relaxed than I have in years, maybe ever. "The way I've been with you, it's nothing like the way I was before the Echo. And you are the only woman I've been with since then."

She lifts her head to look at me, though she keeps her chin on my chest. "Really? I haven't been with anyone either. Just you. Not sure if I liked this kind of sex before the apocalypse since I have amnesia."

"I can tell you unequivocally that I've never been like this with any other woman." I hesitate because I might be kind of worried about what she'll think of me if I confess. But she needs to know the truth. "I've been celibate since the apocalypse. But even before that, I was never great with the ladies. I had girlfriends, but nothing serious. When I fucked a woman, it was pretty basic, boring sex."

"You could never be boring."

Can't help chuckling. "Thanks, but you didn't know me then. My years in the Echo changed me. Pre-apocalypse, I was a computer programmer—a geek."

"I know that already."

"But I don't feel like the geek I was back then, not anymore. I've changed since the Echo."

"Everyone has. Besides, geeks can be hot."

"How would you know? You don't remember what geeks are like."

She folds her arms on my chest and gazes into my eyes. "I don't care what you were like before. I would've liked you then too, and you can't convince me otherwise."

"Okay, fine, have your way. I was a hot geek."

"That's more like it." She kisses my chest. "Should we get dressed and…do something? You know, something useful."

I close my hand over her ass cheek. "I happen to think sex with you is very useful."

"But we need to understand how the Brain—"

"Yeah, yeah, I know." I sigh with no small measure of sarcasm. "You just can't let me enjoy the afterglow, can you?"

"Sorry." She rests her head on my chest again. "Let's enjoy the afterglow for a while. Time is frozen right now, anyway, so we can do whatever we want."

I wrap my arms around her. "Let's just lie here, then."

Though I know we can't lounge in bed forever, we can take a few minutes to revel in the afterglow. Her body feels warm and soft, and the scent of sex wafts around us. I love the way her breasts are mounded against me, her hair tickles my cheek, and her fingers tease my skin. I've never experienced relaxation like this, and I doubt I ever will again—unless I have Sarah with me. I barely know her, yet I feel like I belong with her.

Nobody can deny anymore that fate exists. The Echo taught us all that the unbelievable can be true.

Are Sarah and I destined to become the two halves of the Brain? I don't even know what that means. We need to find out before we commit to something that monumental. Grant and Erin have become the Heart and Lifeblood, but I don't understand what that means either. When I mention that to Sarah, she props her chin on her folded hands to look at me.

"It means they help keep the Echo in balance," she says. "This world was having seizures, of a sort, before Erin and Grant came to the stronghold."

"Yeah, but what did they actually do?"

"If you're expecting a nuts-and-bolts explanation, no one can give you that. We're talking about magics here."

"Right. But I need to understand what the Brain is before I can sign on for becoming one hemisphere of it."

She sits up and shakes her head. "Honestly, you lived in the Echo for three years. How can you still be skeptical about magics? They exist. We can't explain how or why they work, but we do what feels right to fix any problems."

"You mean problems in the Echo."

"Or on Earth. The two worlds are intertwined, Gabriel."

This conversation is not clearing up the issue for me, not at all. "Living in the Echo didn't give me any insight into how this world works. And it definitely didn't give me knowledge of how magic works."

"You're still trying to squeeze the supernatural into a box designed for the mundane."

"I have no idea what that means."

"Until you can accept that magic exists and you will never understand it, I don't see how we can save the worlds."

Chapter Twelve

Sarah

How can I convince a stubborn man to accept that he will never understand the supernatural? I get that before the apocalypse Gabriel led a life built on logic. But he lived in the Echo for three years. He must have seen all sorts of things he couldn't explain or understand. Yet he refuses to accept that we are the two halves of the Echo's Brain, the only people who might have a chance to change the fate of both worlds.

I don't know how that will work. But I'm willing to accept the unknown. That's the difference between me and Gabriel. We forged a bond when we had sex, both times. But he still won't accept that it meant more than really hot orgasms.

Gabriel slides off the bed and starts hunting for his clothes.

I watch him, only in part so I can admire his body.

Once he's pulled on his pants, he pauses to glower at me. "Why are you staring? Get dressed."

Wonderful. We're back to grumpy Gabriel.

Sex with me must've knocked him off kilter. It threw me for a loop too. Our quickie in the woods had stunned me, but our little bondage experience in this bed had shown me things about myself I never knew. Like that I enjoy being tied up. And I love it when he gets bossy in bed.

Bossy the rest of time? No, I'm not crazy about that.

Time to make him talk. "Did you have a family before the apocalypse? Friends? Anything like that?"

He just pulled on his shirt, and now he flashes me a scowl. "What difference does that make?"

"I'd like to know. Please."

Gabriel grabs his socks and boots and drops onto the bed. "I was alone. Happy now?"

"No, of course that doesn't make me happy. What happened to your parents?"

He shrugs while pulling on his socks. "Never met them. I was an orphan, tossed around to various foster homes."

"Oh, Gabriel—"

"Don't do that. Don't pity me."

I waddle across the bed and wrap my arms around him. "I would never pity you. But I feel for you, Gabriel, for the boy who never had a family. It's no wonder you have trouble connecting with other people."

"What makes you think that?"

"You said yourself that you never got serious about anyone you dated. Did you have friends?"

"Only the people I knew at work. We weren't particularly close."

I lay my cheek on his shoulder. "You aren't alone anymore. You have everyone at Sanctuary—and you have me."

"Because you think I'm the other half of the Brain."

"No." I climb onto his lap while keeping my arms around him. "I'm with you because I like you, Gabriel. You're more than just a guy I had sex with twice."

He grunts.

I think that means he's embarrassed. "It's true. No amount of grumpy behavior will make me change my mind about you."

"What if I growl at you?"

"Nope. That won't work either." I wriggle my bottom on his lap, which makes him wince faintly. "I let you tie me up and order me not to come. How can you think I don't like and trust you?"

He falls back onto the bed and shuts his eyes, leaving me still crouched on his lap. "You're impossible."

"Thank you. I take that as a compliment."

Gabriel peeks at me through one half-closed lid. "You're weird."

I grin. "And I take that as a compliment too. I never realized how spunky and naughty I could be until I met you. But I love it."

He opens both eyes and smirks. "You are a very naughty girl, and I'd love to explore that some more. But I think you'd better get dressed. We need to…figure things out."

"You mean the Brain thing."

"Can we stop calling it that? Makes me feel like I'm Frankenstein's monster."

I pat his chest. "And I'm the monster's bride."

"Uh-huh." He sits up, throws his arms around me, and stands up. Then he sets me on my feet. "You really need to get dressed. Don't know how much longer I can look at your naked body without fucking you again."

Yeah, that would be a shame. I know I shouldn't want to do that again, since we have problems to deal with, but I wish we could have sex one more time. What we've done makes me wonder if I loved sex this much before the apocalypse, or if living under the constant threat of death and destruction has changed me. Does it really matter what I was like before? I want to stay the person I am now. If I regain my memories, maybe I won't like what I learn about myself.

Gabriel likes me this way, that's for sure.

Once I'm dressed, we head back out into the hall. Gabriel suggests we should look for a way out of this place, in case Aldith doesn't come back. I can't imagine she would just abandon us here, but we haven't seen or heard from her since she told us to spend time together. If Gabriel wants to search for an exit, I'll go along with it.

We've just reached the end of the hall, but the elevator door is gone.

Oh, great. We're trapped. I should feel scared by that fact, shouldn't I? But I don't. That's kind of weird. I feel safe, not cornered, and I don't really mind if we stay here for days or weeks, even months. I don't understand my reaction. I almost feel like...

"Someone is using magic on us," Gabriel says. "Can't you sense it? Suddenly, I want to take you into the nearest bedroom and make you scream again."

"Yeah, I do feel it. Not sure what's going on."

Gabriel opens his mouth, but the words we hear are not his.

"The Brain wants you to cement your bond in a deeper way. You won't be permitted to leave until you've done that."

We both spin around to face Aldith. She stands there with her hands clasped in front of her, seeming quite relaxed.

"You can't be suggesting we should have sex again," Gabriel says. "Come on, orgasms aren't the engine running the apocalypse."

"How do you know?" Aldith asks. "Sexual intercourse has powered several important changes in the Echo."

"Like what?"

She bows her head, and I swear she's blushing a little. "You must ask your friends. It's not my place to reveal such information."

"But you know about it. Are you a voyeur? Did you watch me and Sarah getting it on?"

"I do not watch. But it was fairly obvious afterward what transpired in the stronghold."

Gabriel starts to speak, but I can tell he's about to get grumpy again.

So I speak first. "Aldith, what do you mean that we won't be able to leave until we cement our bond? We, um, already did that."

I couldn't help the dopey little laugh that came out of me when I said that. Yeah, I feel very awkward about discussing sex with a woman I barely know who also happens to be an Echo creature.

Aldith shrugs. "I relay the information, nothing more. That's all I can tell you."

She vanishes.

My body wants me to do exactly what Aldith suggested and have bone-melting, earth-shattering sex with Gabriel again. And again. And again. For as long as it takes to finish cementing our bond. But the idea that the Echo's Brain wants us to do that… Yeah, it's beyond disturbing.

"What should we do?" I ask.

Gabriel scratches the back of his neck. "Keep looking for a way out. Screw the damn Brain. I choose when I do things, not some supernatural computer system."

"You think the Brain is a computer?"

"No idea. But it can't be an actual brain, with two hemispheres and blood vessels and neurons and whatever else. It must be more like a computer."

He grabs my hand, leading me back down the hall.

Not sure if a computer brain is less creepy than a real brain. Either way, we're supposed to merge with it or something. Aldith hasn't really explained that part. From what Erin and Grant have said, Aldith simply doesn't have access to all the information that's needed to do the things she informs us we need to do.

Why can't the universe just send me a postcard with all the details printed on it?

Gabriel approaches a door, not the one that leads into the room where we got naked, and throws it open. I see a bed and a couple of chairs. No window.

He shuts the door and moves on to the next one.

We had already searched this floor. But who knows, maybe the Echo decided to change the rooms and one of them includes an exit.

Nope, we don't find anything like that.

Gabriel insists on searching all the rooms three times. Why? Because he's a stubborn, grumpy man who refuses to accept the inevitable. We are trapped in here, until we do whatever the Brain wants us to do. I get that he doesn't like being ordered to do the bidding of a supernatural computer, but I don't see that we have a choice. Gabriel finally gives up and sits down on the floor with his back to the wall.

I pace back and forth in front of him.

What if "cementing" our bond doesn't mean only having sex? There might be another component. Not sure what that would be. Sealing a bond sounds intimate, like something that would involve emotions and trust. I trust Gabriel, but maybe I haven't completely surrendered to the bond between us. Could it be that the Echo's Brain requires us to come to terms with our feelings for each other and accept them?

I met him yesterday. But I already feel closer to him than to anyone in Sanctuary. If I didn't have amnesia, maybe I would find that idea disturbing and slightly insane. But having a giant blank spot in my mind gives me a different perspective. I think. It makes sense, at least to me, that not knowing how I used to feel about anything could make me more open to the idea of bonding with a virtual stranger.

But I know some things about Gabriel. He told me he has no family because he was an orphan, and that he didn't have any real friends.

To bond means to share ourselves with each other. How can I share parts of me with him when I don't even know who I am? Instead of talking to myself about this in my head, I should discuss it with Gabriel.

He'll probably tell me I'm a moron.

But I do it anyway. I sit down beside him and say, "We need to talk about this bond thing."

"It's bullshit. There's nothing else to say."

"Stop that. We need to have a real conversation."

He sighs and leans his head against the wall. "Fine. But it was your idea, so you start the conversation."

"Okay." I resist the impulse to squirm and avoid looking at him. Instead, I turn partway toward him. "We sealed our sexual bond, but there's more to it than that. You saved me from the lightning before you even knew anything about me. You confided in me too. That means something."

"Like what?"

"That maybe we share a bond deeper than lust. You felt protective of me quickly, which makes no logical sense."

He glances at me sideways. "What are you suggesting?"

"That we need to accept our feelings for each other, even though they don't make sense. I think that's what the Brain wants. A real, emotional bond."

"I threatened to assault you on the beach."

"You didn't mean it. I know that. You were scared and doing what I've learned you always do when you're upset. You got grumpy and lashed out."

He grunts.

"And I've also learned that you grunt when you're embarrassed."

Gabriel shakes his head, though it's still leaning against the wall. "You are even more stubborn than I realized."

"And you are even sweeter than I realized."

"Sweet?" His lip curls. "You're insane."

"It's the truth. You are sweet, though you try to hide that fact."

He grunts again.

Well, Allison did tell me that most men don't like to be called "sweet." I'll move on to another topic. "We need to do this bond-sealing thing so we can take control of the Brain. Hopefully, that will give us the power to end the apocalypse. The worst of the devastation might be over, but the Echo keeps throwing things at us. We need to do something before both worlds go nuts."

"You assume they will."

"The Echo already did go nuts, for a while. Erin and Grant stopped it. But now the Brain apparently needs our help. I wonder if it was the Brain that sent the lightning and the Echo creature that kidnapped us."

He swivels his head to look at me. "You never mentioned that possibility before."

"Just occurred to me."

Gabriel studies me for a moment. "That would make sense, I guess."

That's probably the best admission I'll get. He's telling me I'm right without actually saying it.

Of course, I don't know if I am right. Not yet.

He clears his throat. "So, uh, how do we seal our emotional bond?"

"I don't know."

"Of course not." He stands up and offers me his hands. "Come on. We can't do it sitting down."

"How do you know that?"

"Because I just decided it's true." He flaps his hand at me. "Get up, Sarah."

I accept his hand in getting up. "Now what?"

He stares at me. "How should I know? This was your idea."

Of course he expects me to come up with a plan. Well, I think I've got one. I doubt he'll like it, but that's what he gets for making me take charge.

I grasp his hand, then guide him into the bedroom where we'd had sex earlier. "Lie down."

"You said this wouldn't be about sex."

"That's right. But do what I say." I point at the bed. "Lie down, Gabriel. Right now."

I'm really starting to like being bossy, especially when I get to boss him around.

Gabriel lies down on the bed.

And I lie down beside him, rolling onto my side so I'm tucked against him. I lay my head on his chest and slip my hand into his, threading our fingers. "Do you like me?"

"Sure. You're okay."

"Gee, thanks. I got a warm glow all over when you said that."

"I'm a guy. We don't get mushy about this stuff."

"That's the best you can do? Telling me I'm okay?"

He fidgets and screws up his mouth. "I never had a family or friends. You know that."

"Are you saying you don't know how to give affection because you never received it?"

"Uh, yeah, I guess."

I snuggle up to him even more. "I like you, Gabriel, a lot. And I've given up on worrying about the fact that we met yesterday. You make me feel safe and strong and fulfilled. Being with you has changed my life. I'm not just the amnesia girl who needed strangers to give her a name. I'm part of something more, something vital and scary and undeniable."

"What is that something?"

"Us. The two halves of the Brain. But it's more than that too. If you can stop fighting it, I think we could become one with each other and the Brain."

He smirks. "Are you suggesting we should merge bodies, like in some goofy movie?"

"No, I'm suggesting we could merge spiritually and emotionally. Dax and Allison have a supernatural bond. So do Erin and Grant. It's not unprecedented."

"Yeah, you keep telling me about your friends. But I don't know if I can submit to something like that."

He is an alpha-male type. I shouldn't expect him to accept my idea immediately. Submission is probably the last thing he wants to do, especially if it means submitting to me. But I let him take control of my body, willingly. He just needs a little more time to get used to the idea.

"Please, Gabriel," I say. "Do this for me."

Chapter Thirteen

Gabriel

SARAH WANTS ME TO BECOME SUBMISSIVE, AT LEAST WHEN IT CON-cerns what the Echo's Brain wants. After living in this world for years, I've forgotten how to be anything except hard and tough and the master of my own destiny. I don't even like that the Echo threw me into this world, since I had no choice in that. As a normal guy who was a computer programmer, I didn't have much autonomy. My bosses told me what to do.

But the Echo gave me a kind of freedom I'd never imagined I could have. That might sound weird, since the apocalypse destroyed two worlds, but it's true. Could Sarah ever understand that?

She taps my lips with her fingertip. "I can see that you're mulling over what I've said. You can tell me anything. I won't get mad or make fun of you."

I know that. But I can't help feeling uncomfortable with what she wants me to do. Sarah makes me feel things that I don't understand. Mostly good things. The strength of those feelings disturbs me. But I agreed to try this bonding thing, so I need to tell her all of that. *Damn.* I'd rather sit down in a fire ant mound. But I will do it, for her.

So I blow out a breath and tell her. "I have these, ah, feelings for you. Not sure what it means. When we had sex, I felt it more strongly, but I've been experiencing these feelings more and more often since the moment we met."

"I have the same kind of feelings."

"But you don't fight them, do you? That's the difference between us."

She pushes up on one elbow to gaze down at me. "Our differences can become our strength. Allison—"

"Can we please stop talking about your friends? I get that they all have supernatural bonds, but I'm not ready for that yet."

"The Echo needs us to be ready. Right now."

"Why? Everything seems relatively stable. I'd say there's no rush."

She lifts her brows. "So, you want to stay trapped inside the stronghold forever?"

If we never leave this place, I can fuck her over and over without anything interfering. But I know that's not plausible. I'd make her sore, for sure.

"Time is frozen inside the stronghold," she says. "But the rest of the Echo and the Earth might not be faring so well. We should check that out."

"Great idea. Let's order Aldith to let us out of here."

Sarah drops her head and moans. "Honestly, Gabriel, that's not helpful. We can't leave until the Echo lets us, and it wants us to seal our emotional bond. You're the one holding things up with your stubbornness."

"I admitted I like you and have strong feelings for you. What more do you want?"

The most beautiful woman I've ever seen sits up, growls, and smacks my chest—hard. "Do I need to tie you up to make you comply?"

She wants to dominate me? Not sure how I feel about that. I trust her, so maybe it wouldn't be a horrible thing. But she was probably joking. I should make sure, though.

"Are you seriously suggesting that you want to dominate me?" I ask. "Because, no offense, but you aren't strong enough to do that. I would kick your ass in three seconds flat."

"Kick my ass?" She wags a finger at me. "That's not the way to cement a bond, Gabriel. But yes, I think you need to experience being submissive, so you can give yourself over to our deep, supernatural connection."

A strange tingle of excitement raises the hairs on my arms and at my nape. Maybe her suggestion does arouse me, but I know I can't do what she wants. Not yet. And I need to explain to her why that is.

"I'm sorry, Sarah," I tell her. "I just can't do that, not yet. It isn't because I don't want to. But you have no idea what my life was like inside the Echo for all those years. Showing weakness will get you killed. I got used to always acting like an asshole because anything less would be a cue for the Echo creatures—the bad ones—to attack."

She leans over and kisses me, though it's only the barest brush of her lips on mine. "I understand that. And maybe you don't need to fully give in to the Echo's Brain. It might be enough right now for you to accept that we have a powerful connection. Do you think you can do that?"

"I can try." Though I'd love to say I would do anything for her, I won't lie. When it comes to protecting her at any cost, I'll do that without hesitation. But the touchy-feely stuff is a lot harder for me to embrace.

"Trying is a good start."

"How do I do that?"

She lies down beside me again and drapes half her body over me. "Accepting intimacy is phase one."

"How many phases are there?"

"As many as you need."

I touch my finger to the tip of her nose. "Who came up with these phases?"

She smiles brightly. "Me."

"Uh-huh. I figured as much." I lay my arms on the mattress and take a deep breath, exhaling it slowly to relax my body. "I'm ready. Tell me what to do."

"Touch me, Gabriel."

"I thought this wasn't about sex."

She rolls her eyes. "Do you think 'touching' automatically means the sexual kind? I'm talking about intimacy."

"You'll need to help me out here. We seem to have different ideas about what 'touching' and 'intimacy' mean."

"Right. You're a rough-and-tough guy, and I'm giving you girlie explanations."

She genuinely wants to help me understand and experience intimacy. Nobody has ever cared so much about my emotional well-being. I could fall for this girl, I know it. Maybe I've already started that process. After all, I'm letting her boss me around. That must be a sign of…something.

The fact that I can't even think the words probably isn't a good sign.

"You're tensing up again," Sarah says. "Let me help you with that."

"How?"

She smiles with her lips sealed as she shimmies on top of me, getting herself situated on my lap. I'm still lying down, but she sits on my thighs with her hands resting on my lower belly. When I open my mouth, she wags a finger at me and shakes her head. I guess this must be the submission part of our bizarre ritual. She unbuttons my shirt, and her tongue pokes out between her lips as she focuses on the task. It's the cutest, sexiest thing I've ever seen. Then she spreads her palms on my chest and begins skating them around my torso in slow circles, pressing a little harder with every revolution until she's massaging my muscles. I can't help relaxing into her ministrations. I also can't stop myself from watching her fingers as they work my muscles. My dick starts to thicken, but she doesn't seem to care.

Sarah moves her hands up to my shoulders, pushing my shirt out of the way, and digs her fingers into my flesh to loosen up my tight muscles.

Damn, this feels good.

My eyes drift half-closed, but I don't want them to close all the way. I need to see everything she does and the look on her face while she does it.

The sexy angel unhooks the button on my pants and drags the zipper down.

"Uh, that's not going to relax me," I say. "It'll have the opposite effect. You're getting me turned on."

She rubs the hollows of my hips with her thumbs.

A deep groan resonates in my chest, and I swear all the blood in my body is flooding into my dick.

"You want to fuck me, don't you?" she says. "Tell me why you want that."

"Because you're getting me hot. I thought this little massage thing was supposed to relax me and help me accept intimacy. You told me it wasn't about sex."

"That's right, it's not. I haven't touched your dick or your balls."

A laugh snorts out of me. "Your criteria for not-erotic massage is that you haven't touched my dick or my balls? You are one weird chick."

"Ha-ha." She slides her hands up my belly. "Tell me why you want to fuck me, Gabriel."

"I already told you, and it's obvious, anyway."

Have I started to growl again? I didn't mean to do that. But the more she touches me, the more I need to flip us over so I can tie her to the bed rails and take her again, while she's at my mercy and can't hurt me.

"Come on, Gabriel. Be honest with me. You want to take control again because…"

She wants me to say it, but I won't. I can't. No matter how many times I've tried to convince myself the past doesn't matter, it still does and it always will. Sarah refuses to see that. I push her off me and slide down to the foot of the bed. My feet touch the floor, but I can't move any farther.

She crawls toward me on her knees, halting right beside me, though she doesn't touch me. When she speaks, her voice is hushed and filled with empathy. "Please let me in, Gabriel. I want to help you."

"It's too late."

Memories flash through my mind, vivid and sharp and inescapable. Screams. The crunching of bones. Anguished pleas for mercy. Children running. Monsters pouring out of the newly formed entrance to the Echo, tearing people apart, feasting on their flesh and blood.

I suddenly can't breathe. My chest feels like ten cement blocks have fallen onto it, and I'm starting to hyperventilate. I can't let Sarah see this. I need to get out of here before—

Her arms come around me. She murmurs things that aren't words, just soothing sounds.

And the panic subsides. I shut my eyes, take in slow, deep breaths, and wait it out. That simple act of putting her arms around me has erased the memories. Well, not erased. I will never forget what I saw that day. But her arms around me and the soothing sounds she makes have pulled me out of the past and back into the present.

"What was that?" she whispers. "A flashback?"

"Yeah. How did you know?"

"Because I've seen it before, with people who found Sanctuary. Do you have nightmares too?"

"Not as often as I used to."

She brushes the backs of her fingers over my cheek. "I can't imagine what you went through, and I wish I could erase all of that for you. If you want to tell me about it, I can handle whatever it is."

I believe she can. Sarah might've seemed like an amnesiac with no backbone, but I know now that she's a fighter. Should I tell her everything? If I do, maybe she will finally realize I'm not the kind of man she needs.

"On the day the alchemy of worlds began," I say, "I was walking to work. It was a beautiful summer's day in Oklahoma City, sunny and warm. I'd just passed a park where kids were playing catch, when that eerie music started up and everyone froze. The music was beautiful and terrifying, mesmerizing too, and a force beyond our control compelled us to walk to a specific spot in the city."

"Quite a few people in Sanctuary experienced the music too. Not everyone heard it on that day, though."

"I heard it, and that music always echoes in my dreams."

Sarah hugs me a little tighter, but she doesn't speak.

"When the creatures poured out of the Echo," I say, "I tried to save whoever I could. Those monsters went after the kids first. I tried to help, but I couldn't save even one of them. Then I got sucked into the Echo, and I couldn't save anyone anymore."

"You tried. That's what counts."

"No, it's not," I snarl. "Trying isn't enough. The parents of those kids don't care that I tried. It's bullshit. But the parents are probably dead too."

I set my elbows on my thighs and drop my head into my hands. My eyes sting. I'm not about to cry, no way. I never do that, not even when I watched those children being torn apart and couldn't do a thing to stop it. But when I suck in a sharp breath, it's ragged, which implies that I'm getting choked up. That's bullshit.

Sarah combs her fingers through my hair, her touch gentle and more soothing than seems possible. How she always knows what to do and say, I have no idea. She just knows.

"I apologize for interrupting, but I thought you both would want to know immediately."

The sound of Aldith's voice makes me snap upright. The pretty Echo creature stands there with her hands clasped in front of her, the way she always does, and her slightly pinched expression suggests she thinks she's interrupted an intimate moment.

Well, I guess she has. I just shared the worst experiences of my life with Sarah and almost started to cry. At least Aldith couldn't see that. I hope.

Sarah claims my hand, lacing our fingers. "What is it, Aldith?"

"The Brain has released you and Gabriel. Your connection has been solidified."

"But we didn't do anything," I say. "How did we solidify our connection?"

Aldith shrugs. "That is not for me to say. The Brain has received the information it requires, but you still need to join with the Brain to stop the Echo from falling apart."

"Who cares if it falls apart?"

"The Earth will be destroyed too if that happens. Both worlds will die."

"I thought the whole point of this was to take control of the Brain so we can destroy the Echo."

Sarah leans in to whisper in my ear, "She is an Echo creature. You're suggesting we want her to die."

Oh, shit. I hadn't considered how Aldith might take what I said. Thinking before I speak has never been one of my virtues. Not sure I have any virtues at all.

"I'm sorry, Aldith," I say. "Neither of us wants good people like you to die. Maybe we can take you and any other good Echo beings to Earth with us."

Aldith smiles just a little. "I was not offended, Gabriel. I was created for the sole purpose of protecting the stronghold, and I never expected to leave this place."

"Have you ever left it? Even for a few minutes?"

She lowers her head. "No. I have never seen the world of the Echo or the Earth."

I study her for a moment, trying to decide whether I trust her. After thirty seconds at most, I realize the truth. I do trust Aldith, and I've learned to listen to my intuition about Echo creatures.

Rising, I tug on Sarah's hand to encourage her to stand up too. "Aldith, when we leave the Echo for good, you are coming with us."

Her lips tick up a little more at the corners, and her eyes brighten. "You would do that for me?"

"Yeah, sure. You help people, you don't hurt them. Our friends Grant and Erin vouched for you, and we've gotten to know enough about you that Sarah and I feel the same way."

Maybe I should've asked Sarah if she agrees with me about that, but I somehow know she does.

"That's right," Sarah says. "We would never leave you here alone when the end comes."

I glance at Sarah. "What do we do now? If we already made the Brain happy, I assume our next move is to find a way to destroy the Echo."

"Not necessarily. We need more information."

"How do we get that?"

She nudges me with her elbow. "We have Sefton's journal, remember?"

"Oh, yeah. I forgot." My gaze lands on our backpacks on the floor by the doorway. "Should we study it here? Or go back to Sanctuary?"

"How could we get back there? Neither of us has Echo power."

"Jarek helped me get back to Earth."

"He cannot do that again," Aldith says. "The issues with the Brain have caused problems with the doorways to the Echo as well. Jarek may escort you to and from the stronghold, but he can no longer open the doorway for you."

CHAPTER FOURTEEN

Sarah

"WELL, DAMN," GABRIEL SAYS. "I REALLY WANTED TO GET OUT OF HERE. No offense, Aldith, but the Echo isn't the most relaxing place for a vacation. It doesn't even have a good beach or a hot club."

Gabriel is reverting to sarcasm. I've come to realize that's his coping mechanism when things get bad or weird. Reliving his memories of the day the alchemy of worlds began must have made him antsy about staying here. The Echo has previously had "conniptions," as Grant and Erin call them. What if that happens again? We would be trapped here and vulnerable to every kind of horror the Echo can produce.

"Can anyone get into or out of the Echo right now?" Gabriel asks Aldith. "Or are we all stuck here?"

"Only the Brain has the power to reopen the doorways."

Someone had us brought here, and I have a feeling they knew we wouldn't be able to leave. Was it the Echo flier? He abducted us, but then flew away.

"You are wrong, by the way," Aldith says. "You both possess the Echo power. The Brain would not need you otherwise."

We have Echo power, and the Brain needs us. Wow, that's crazy to even think about.

Gabriel rests his hands on his hips and stares down at the carpeting. "A smarter man would know exactly what to do. But I'm no genius, mad or otherwise. You've got the wrong guy."

Aldith tips her head to the side. "You do not believe me, but you will soon."

"We need to find the creature that brought us here," I say. "If we have Echo power, maybe we can do that. Bring him to us."

"You're suggesting we should summon a dangerous creature into the stronghold."

"That's right. But we would contain it. Maybe in one of the rooms that has no windows."

He watches me for a moment, as if he's trying to gauge how serious I am about this plan. I think he knows me well enough by now to realize I'm completely serious about it. Finally, he exhales a big breath. "Fine, let's try that."

Aldith leads us across the hall to a small room that has no windows. Gabriel and I discuss how to make the room safer for us, and that results in removing all the furniture except the bed, which is too big to move. I doubt it would fit through the door.

"Would you like me to assist you?" Aldith asks. "I helped Grant and Erin achieve the necessary state of oneness to access their shared Echo power."

"Sure, help us," I say. "We'd be grateful for your advice."

"Join your hands, one atop the other."

We do that, and Aldith hovers her hand over ours. The air seems to thicken, while invisible energy crackles in the air around us. I can't see it, but I feel that energy on my skin. Glittering light begins to emanate from our hands, and even when Aldith pulls her palm away, the energy continues to build and spread out. My hair stands up, like static electricity has affected it.

Gabriel's eyes have a faint green glow.

Do my eyes look that way too? I don't have time to think about that, because the energy has begun to pulse inside my body. It's not unpleasant. The sensation reminds me of a heartbeat, though it's not my heart causing it. Soon, the rhythm of the magics aligns with the thumping of my heart, and I begin to feel another heartbeat joining mine, merging until I no longer feel it as a separate beat, but simply another layer melding with me.

Gabriel and I are tuned in to each other. I know that, but I could never explain how or why it happened.

An Echo creature appears beside us. Its wings were retracted behind its back when it arrived, but now the beast flutters his wings in a slightly threatening gesture.

"Why have you brought me here?" he asks. Yeah, it's obvious this is a male creature. He's not wearing any clothes, which means I can see his equipment.

"You kidnapped us from Earth," Gabriel says. "I want to know why."

The creature chuckles. "Because the Brain wanted you, of course."

My intuition has kicked into high gear, and I'm getting an idea about what might be going on. "Did you voluntarily do what the Brain said? Or did you have no choice?"

The Echo flier scowls at me. "I choose my own path."

"Okay, then why did you kidnap us? You said it was because the Brain wanted us, but that doesn't explain why you did it. What did you get out of the deal?"

"There was no deal. The Brain commanded, and I—" He scowls again. "No more talking to you."

He spreads his wings wide, forcing us to back away. Then he tries to kick the door open, but he can't do it. After multiple kicks and punches, he's still trapped in this room with us.

The Echo flier throws his head back and roars.

"Not the master of your own destiny, after all," I say. "So answer our question. Why did you kidnap us?"

Our winged friend stands there fuming for a minute or two, then folds his wings and slumps his shoulders. "I had no choice. The Brain commanded, and I had to obey. I know nothing else. Not why it wanted you, or what it planned to do with you."

Gabriel and I exchange glances, and I know we agree about what to do next.

We send the Echo flier back to where he'd come from, though we have no conscious knowledge of where that might be. We just know we sent him there.

The Echo creature didn't instigate our abduction. That leaves me with another question.

I face Aldith. "How can the Brain command an Echo creature? It's not a sentient being, is it?"

"No, but we are talking about supernatural forces."

Right. I shouldn't expect magic to make logical sense. I don't recall what the world was like before the apocalypse, but I'm pretty sure magic didn't rule the Earth. I miss those days, even though I can't remember them.

Boom.

The entire stronghold shudders, and I stumble into Gabriel. He slings his arms around me.

Boom. Another explosion detonates, shaking the stronghold.

We all race into the other bedroom to peer out the picture windows. Our gazes veer downward, to the ground far below us. Buildings look like toys, but the bolts of lightning slamming into the earth seem all too real. Is the Brain trying to capture us again? I don't see how lightning beneath us will do anything except destroy the ground. We're too far away for it to harm us.

But the Brain doesn't want to hurt us. It must not, right? Why else would it try so hard to capture us and stop pounding the worlds once we came to the stronghold? What is it after now? We're here, where it wanted us.

Did the Brain actually stop pounding Earth once we left?

"I don't understand," I say. "Why is the Brain causing mayhem down there? We did what it wanted. We came to the stronghold and sealed our bond."

Gabriel hugs me to his side. "The Brain doesn't have its hemispheres, right? It's basically an empty vessel struggling to fulfill its purpose."

"I guess so. But how can we stop it from destroying both worlds before we have the chance to figure out what we're supposed to do?"

"The Brain can't think on its own. That's the way I see it." He hugs me a little tighter as more lightning bolts strike the ground, sending plumes of dust and debris high into the atmosphere. "It needs to be told what to do. That means we need to give it instructions."

"How? I don't think we're ready to join with the Brain, or whatever we're supposed to do."

"I agree. But we can sort of give it a gift to make it happy for a while."

Though I open my mouth to complain about what he said, I stop short of actually speaking. Maybe he's right. We used our Echo power to summon that flying beast. Why can't we magically send the Brain a gift? A power boost to keep it going while we sort out the details. We need to know a lot more before we take the plunge and take command of the Brain.

Another boom detonates out there, but it sounds much closer.

We peer out the windows again—and my heart thuds.

Two fireballs are streaking down from the highest levels of the atmosphere to rain their fire and destruction down on the land below. One fireball has already struck, setting a large building ablaze and destroying most of the structure. The two fireballs streaking toward the ground seem much bigger.

No time to talk about it. I know Gabriel will agree with my idea, and I feel the energy of our Echo power already surging between us. I grab his hand while focusing on the lightning and fireballs below us, and the magics we share grow warmer and stronger, tingling through me more powerfully than before. Gabriel grips my hand even more tightly. The magics expand and strengthen, invisible yet palpable, a living energy that heeds our bidding.

The two remaining fireballs are snuffed out.

Smoke billows up from the destroyed structures on the ground, but at least we stopped most of the fireballs. The lightning seems to have disappeared too.

I look at Gabriel, and he looks at me. His grim smile probably mirrors mine. Yes, we're glad we circumvented the devastation. But that was only a stopgap measure. Unless we can take control of the Echo's Brain, things could get much, much worse in both worlds.

"We should check on our friends in Sanctuary," I say. "And see what's going on elsewhere on Earth too."

"How? We can't get out of the Echo."

"I think we can. We just stopped fireballs and lightning, after all."

Gabriel gazes out the windows, his grim smile now just a grim expression with no hint of anything resembling satisfaction, despite the fact we saved potentially innocent beings from suffering a terrible death. But I think I understand now why he doesn't seem happy that we might have the power to escape the Echo. I know we'll probably need to come back to fix the Brain, but then we can go home, I assume. Gabriel spent years in this world. He doesn't know how to fit in with normal people on Earth anymore. And he feels like he failed, because he couldn't save his Echo friends.

I grip his hand with both of mine. "You deserve to go home, Gabriel. You don't belong in the Echo anymore."

He tries to pull his hand away, but I hold on. "You're being stupidly stubborn. I am not a hero, or even a good man. I did whatever it took to survive here, and I can barely remember what my life was like before the apocalypse."

"And I don't remember it at all. Don't see me moping and acting grumpy."

"You're different."

I raise my brows. "Because I'm a girl?"

"No. Because you're an angel."

Laughter splutters out of me, though I tried to squelch it. "Angel? I had hot-and-sweaty dirty sex with you—twice."

"I corrupted you."

"Get over yourself, Gabriel. You don't intimidate me, which means I do what I want because I want it. Only I control my desires."

He stares out the window, and his voice becomes flat. "But we're both planning to hand over our free will to something we don't understand and have never seen."

"We'll take control of the Brain, not the other way around."

"You don't know what will happen. Neither do I. Even Aldith doesn't know."

I glance around the room. "Where is Aldith, anyway? She was here a few minutes ago."

"That chick loves to mysteriously disappear."

"Yeah, she has the mystery thing down pat." I lean closer to the windows and lay my palms on the cool glass. "There must be a way to get out of the Echo. Let's ask Jarek to take us to the nearest gateway. Then we can test our powers and see if we can open that door."

"Okay."

For several seconds, I can't move or speak. Did he just agree to my plan? With no growling? No grunting? Yeah, he did just do that.

I open the biggest window and lean over even more. "Jarek! We need you, Jarek!"

Nothing happens. We just stand here waiting and listening.

"Maybe he didn't hear you," Gabriel says. "Let me try."

He thrusts half his body out the window and hollers, "Jarek! Get your ass up here, buddy."

He does shout much louder than I do. Men have bigger lungs, right? So that explains it.

I notice a dark shape rising through the clouds, barreling closer and closer and closer.

Gabriel pulls away from the window, then slings an arm around my waist to drag me away too. "Better not get too close. He might not see you until it's too late."

A large metal-and flesh hand clamps onto the windowsill, then another identical hand clamps onto the other end of the sill. A grinding noise ensues, as Jarek hauls himself up to the level of the window.

I grin and wave at him. "It's nice to see you again, Jarek. Thank you for coming so quickly."

He nods, and his lips curve into the barest approximation of a smile.

"Can you give us a lift?" I ask. "We need to get to the gateway of the Echo."

He shakes his head.

"Are you saying you won't take us there?" I ask. "Or that you know the gateway is closed and won't open again?"

Jarek doesn't respond.

"He can only answer yes or no questions," Gabriel says. "You made it too complicated."

"Oh, right. I forgot."

"Let me try." Gabriel moves closer to the window. "We know the gateway is sealed. But will you take us there anyway?"

Jarek nods.

"Thanks, buddy. We appreciate it."

The golem stretches out one hand toward us, holding it palm up. His other arm, the one still clamped onto the windowsill, has begun to tremble faintly. Must be really hard to maintain a position like that. Gabriel climbs onto Jarek's open hand first, then helps me up.

Aldith reappears to wave goodbye as Jarek releases his hold on the window.

We sail downward, rushing through the clouds, with the ground zooming ever closer. Just when I think we're about to get creamed, Jarek's massive feet whump down with surprising gentleness. Then he starts striding across the barren landscape, heading back toward the Capital City. Since I have nothing else to do, I take stock of the damage caused by the lightning and fireballs. Scorched earth surrounds the crater where the first fireball struck. The other two never made it to the ground. The lightning had slashed into the ground with electric force, creating glass-encased tunnels.

Gradually, I begin to see signs of civilization ahead of us. Well, I'm using the word civilization loosely. The apocalypse decimated the Echo too, and according to Grant and Erin, not many living things have remained in the Capital City. I got only a glimpse of that metropolis when the Echo flier grabbed me and Gabriel, whisking us away.

Jarek lumbers past the edge of the city, which has a sharp line of demarcation, unlike any city in the normal world. No suburbs, no smattering of shops that peters out the further you go from the skyscrapers. Yeah, I can remember what cities on Earth look like. It's my memories of my own life and the apocalypse that vanished. Jarek speeds up his pace as we head down a four-lane street, and I get my first glimpse of the gateway to the Echo. The sight makes my skin crawl and my mouth go dry.

The black disk in the sky swirls round and round, releasing slithering fingers of darkness that dissipate into smoke-like wisps. The gateway generates no sound, but the gravity of it vibrates in my bones.

Now it's time to find out if the Echo will let us leave—or if it will hold us hostage.

CHAPTER FIFTEEN

Gabriel

AS I GAZE UP AT THE GATEWAY, MY MEMORIES REWIND TO THAT DAY when the sky split apart and the world as we knew it ended. The apocalypse began in the cities with eerie, terrifyingly beautiful music taking over the world, serving as the precursor to the devastation that followed. The spinning tendrils of magics that lashed out from the gateway's center heralded the coming of creatures disgorged from the Echo to wreak havoc.

Today, I see only the placidly swirling disk of darkness.

Despite my mind wanting to pull me into the past to relive my personal journey into the apocalypse, I can't let myself sink into that oblivion. We have too much to do, and no idea how to do it.

Sarah gapes at the gateway like she's never seen it before. We had both gone through the gateway earlier, but it happened so fast that I doubt she got a good look at it. Now we both have no choice but to watch as we draw ever nearer to the disk-shaped abyss that swallows a large quadrant of the sky. Even the damage to the city around us can't tear our focus away from the gateway.

Jarek halts below the black disk, which I can now see lies at his head level. The gateway consumes such a large part of the sky that it's hardly surprising the golem can reach it. When he raises his hand to his chin level, Sarah and I find ourselves staring straight into the roiling blackness of the gateway. Jarek extends his hand toward the opening.

And hits an invisible barrier.

The jolt surprises Jarek, who instinctively jerks his hand away. The sudden movement sends me and Sarah tumbling off the golem's palm, sailing down toward the street far below us. She screams and flails as if to grab on to me. I seize her forearm but lose my grip.

And the ground rushes toward us.

Jarek scoops us up just before we would've hit the ground. We both lie sprawled on the golem's palm, somewhat dazed by our narrow escape from becoming human pancakes. My gaze lands on the gateway, but it's not simply spinning anymore. No, it now roils and rumbles, pulsating with a rhythm that I can feel but not hear.

We just ticked off the Echo.

But we aren't done yet.

I sit up, then cautiously rise to my knees. Once I determine I'm not going to fall off Jarek's palm, I grab Sarah's hands to help her stand too. "We need to tap into our Echo power so we can force the gateway to open."

She nods, though she's biting her lip.

I don't blame her for feeling off kilter. The Echo slammed the door in our faces, and now we plan to kick it in. I clasp Sarah's hands as we face each other, our gazes bound, and summon the magics. The power sizzles between us, hot and liquid, slipping into every cell in our bodies. I concentrate on thoughts of the Echo, of kicking that door open so we can jump through it.

A blast of energy fires into the gateway and bounces right back at us. I fly off Jarek's palm to the left, but Sarah flies off to the right. I tumble toward the pavement below us, face up, and can do nothing but watch as Jarek bends his knees and thrusts out both hands to catch us. We wind up crumpled on separate palms, but Jarek tips one hand over to dump me onto his hand beside Sarah.

Breathing hard, I just lie here recovering from my second brush with pancake-hood. "That worked out well."

"I hope that's a joke." Sarah sounds breathless too. "We failed miserably."

"Because the Echo wouldn't let us out. I'm guessing that means nobody else can get in either."

"That would make sense." She rolls onto her side to look at me. "If the Brain wants our cooperation, why won't it let us leave? We need help from our friends."

"Seems like we aren't allowed to get help. We have to do this on our own."

"What now?"

I sit up and stare at the gateway, with its whirling blackness and slithering tongues of energy. What does the Brain want? Not like we can ask it, since the thing isn't a living being. It's a collection of magics, I assume. Even Aldith seemed uncertain of what the Brain is or how Sefton Stainthorpe used it. I doubt the Echo can keep the Brain functioning for much longer. The desperation evidenced by the lightning and fireballs, and our abduction, proves the point.

The Echo needs us. Maybe we can leverage that.

I scramble to my feet. "Jarek, would you mind taking us to the castle?"

He shakes his head, which I assume means he doesn't mind and will take us there. I sit down beside Sarah, who has already pushed up into a cross-legged sitting position, and hold on while Jarek lopes down the street away from the gateway. He turns down another street, and another, and another, moving faster with each turn until I finally spot the sheer cliff that houses the castle at its summit.

Jarek halts at the base and raises his hand to the level of the summit.

Sarah and I step off the golem's palm, onto solid ground.

"Thanks, buddy," I say. "We'll call if we need you. And let us know if you need anything too."

He nods, then turns to walk away.

Sarah and I stand on the cliff's pinnacle, with the castle looming behind us.

"Now that we're here," she says, "what's the plan?"

"Uh, there is no plan. We wing it."

"Perfect. Guess it was too much to hope for a sliver of a strategy, much less a fully formed one."

I grasp her hand. "Let's go inside and see what we can see."

She lets me lead her across the rock-strewn ground, heading for the castle gates. "How long have you known Jarek?"

"A few days."

"In Echo time, which is different from mortal time."

"According to Aldith, it can be different. I'm no expert on that stuff. I didn't even know time behaved differently here until Aldith told me."

Sarah glances at me, seeming puzzled. "I still don't understand the time stuff. I hope stopping the apocalypse won't involve me needing to understand quantum physics. I don't remember geometry, though I probably took that in high school—or so Allison says."

"Everybody has to endure geometry class."

"Think I'm glad I don't remember it."

I chuckle. "Wish I'd lost that memory. I got a C in geometry. And don't even get me started on trig."

At the castle gates, we pause. Well, I make us pause because I'm a little worried that the castle might reject us too, and we'll end up tumbling off the cliff with no Jarek to catch us.

Sarah gives me a brows-raised look, then sighs and knocks on the gate.

The barrier swings open slowly, creaking all the way.

No, that's not disconcerting. I love walking through creepy creaking gates that lead to a creepy, empty castle. As we cross the threshold, a chill sweeps over my skin, like a ghost has passed through my body. Maybe it has. Sefton Stainthorpe might have died in the mortal world, but he left his Echo here, a man called Will, which must mean he left something of himself, or at least his magics, inside this building.

Something is keeping the Brain going. It has to be those leftover magics.

Hand in hand, we shuffle across the vacant courtyard. The place feels unnervingly quiet and empty. What happened to the bodies of the creatures who died here? My friends hadn't perished in the courtyard, but we had taken out several of our enemies in this place. We continue toward the doors to the castle and find them hanging slightly ajar. I gently nudge one out of the way so we can sidle through the opening into the entryway.

No bodies here either.

I suddenly realize I'm gripping Sarah's hand more tightly, though she doesn't seem to mind. She grips my hand firmly too. We move at a faster pace as we go down the hall to the throne room. The doors should be closed, but instead, they stand wide open. Inside, I see nothing but the throne sitting on its raised dais.

All the bodies are gone. The remains of all my friends have vanished, as if they never existed.

"This makes no sense," I say, speaking in a hushed tone because this feels like a mausoleum. "Who got rid of the bodies? I was the only one left in here after the battle."

"Are you positive of that? Could someone have sneaked in without you noticing?"

"I suppose that's possible. But it doesn't explain what happened to the bodies."

Sarah releases my hand, approaching the dais. "Maybe someone dumped the bodies over the cliff."

I hope that's not what happened. To think of my friends being discarded like trash… It's my fault they died, and it will be my fault if it turns out someone destroyed their remains.

Sarah stretches out an arm toward me, holding her palm up. "Come here, Gabriel. You need to see that it's only a chair, and the demons in this room are all in your head."

But they're not. Real demons murdered the only family I'd ever known.

"Take slow, deep breaths," she says, still offering me her hand. "And come over here. You're almost hyperventilating."

Am I? My chest is heaving, and my ears have started to ring. So yeah, I guess I am almost hyperventilating. Gazing into Sarah's eyes, even from a distance, does more to calm me than any breathing exercise. So I walk over to her and slip my hand into hers. The sensation of her soft, warm fingers threaded with mine relaxes me even more. This connection between us used to scare me, though I would never have admitted it. The time we spent in the stronghold changed things between us so profoundly that I can't even describe how it feels. Magic didn't do it. Sarah was the driving force behind everything inside me that has transformed.

But I still don't know if I can do what she believes we need to do—become one with the Echo's brain. Yeah, the idea of merging with a magically created brain that used to belong to a mad man is kind of…disconcerting. But it's the idea of merging with Sarah that terrifies me. I haven't told her that. Don't know if I can tell her. It sounds weak and pathetic, especially after all the years I'd lived and fought in the Echo. How can having a deep connection with one woman make me feel this off balance?

Right now, here with her, holding hands…maybe I don't feel quite so off balance anymore.

"Tell me about your friends," she says. "The ones you fought with here in the castle. What were they like?"

"Our little army didn't have any training. I didn't either. But when I got thrown into the Echo, I had to learn a lot and learn it fast. Every good Echo being I met became an ally first, and a friend later. It takes time to forge a bond with a stranger." I realize what I just said, and it spurs me to look at Sarah. "But not with you. I felt a connection the instant I first saw you, though I fought it hard."

"I felt the same way." She turns toward me and slips her arms loosely around my waist. "But I'd like to know more about your friends, please. They clearly meant a lot to you."

"Just like your friends mean a lot to you." I can't resist the impulse to slide my arms around her too, linking them at the small of her back. "I never had anyone to start with, no friends or family, just coworkers and women I slept with. In the Echo, that changed, slowly. I couldn't protect myself alone, so I had to ally with anyone I could find who wasn't hell-bent on killing any living things they saw. I met Kai first. He was just a kid, eighteen years old and scared to death. But as we got to know each other and fought together, we forged a bond. Then we picked up more allies along the way, when I decided to explore the entire world of the Echo to understand what was happening."

"Do you understand it now?"

"Not as well as I'd like. But I figured out that the castle on the cliff must be important somehow, and my team agreed that we should check it out. We came back to the Capital City to search for clues. It is Sefton's city, after all. We couldn't find much, so I suggested we should try to breach the castle."

"What did you hope to find there?"

I shrug. "Didn't really know. But after the convulsions in the Echo recently, it seemed like we needed to take drastic action."

"Yeah, the convulsions were what made Grant and Erin decide to go into the Echo. Everyone was afraid it might be the start of something much worse. I wasn't living in Sanctuary then, and I don't remember any of that. It's what my friends told me."

I remember too much, and she has no memory. I still think that's strange. Is it a coincidence? Or does the dichotomy mean something? I should talk to Sarah about that, but first, I need to tell her more about the

Echo beings who became my family. "Kai and the others, they were the bravest people I'd ever met. Even when they were scared, they kept going, kept fighting, kept trying. I was proud of them, especially at the end when they refused to give up despite knowing they were about to die."

Sarah wraps her arms around me more firmly, with her cheek on my chest. "I'm so sorry you lost them."

"I didn't lose them. The Echo took them from me. I spent my whole life as a loner, except for the three years in this world. But even with my friends here, I didn't share everything with them. I held things back. Maybe I deserved to be alone again."

"You're not alone, Gabriel."

With her, I don't feel alone anymore. But I can't make myself tell her that. So I ask a question instead. "Have you seen your friends fight? I mean, in a battle."

"No. They don't let me go on supply missions with them because it's too dangerous. But I've seen them sparring for practice. Dax always beats Grant. But when Grant spars with Erin, you never can tell who will win."

"I thought Grant was a Zen hippie, and Erin was a badass."

"You're half right," Sarah says with a laugh. "But Grant is a badass too, and he's taught Erin how to be Zen. That's what couples do. They make each other better."

Do I make Sarah better? No, I seriously doubt that. But she makes me better, for sure. I don't growl nearly as much as I used to, before I met her.

She lifts her head, aiming a sweet smile at me. "Dax and Allison taught each other lessons too. He was a prisoner in the Echo, banished here by his brother. Allison showed him how to be human again, and he taught her self-defense tactics."

"Hmm, I'm starting to see a pattern here. One half of each couple didn't like to fight, but the badass other halves showed them how it's done."

"You're oversimplifying things. Their relationships are way more complex than that, just like ours is."

We have a relationship, that's what she just implied. I suppose we do in the wider sense of the term. But I suspect she means a romantic relationship. We did have sex, twice, but that doesn't automatically mean we have some kind of emotional connection. Maybe I did sort of share stuff about my past and my feelings, but that's not proof of a relationship either.

So what would be proof? I have no fucking idea.

But something changed between us inside the stronghold, and I'm not sure it's a good thing—for her.

CHAPTER SIXTEEN

Sarah

I SWEAR I CAN HEAR THE GEARS TURNING IN GABRIEL'S MIND WHILE HE struggles to accept that we have a relationship—a real, emotional relationship. It doesn't make sense for us to have this kind of connection so soon after we met, but the Echo has taught everyone that every day is precious and we shouldn't take any moments for granted. I might not remember more than the past two months, but I've listened to everything my friends said and took it to heart.

They're amazing people, and I'd be lucky to find half of what they have.

Why do I care so much about Gabriel? Because he saved my life, yes, but that's only a small part of it. I care because he showed me his pain, he opened up to me in a way I doubt he's ever done in his life before now, and he's determined to stop the Echo from destroying itself and Earth along with it. That's what will happen if we can't command the Brain. The worlds are connected, inextricably. If one dies, so will the other.

Along with all life in both worlds.

"Let's explore the castle," I say. "I know it's full of bad memories for you, but we need to make sure there's nothing in here that could help us. Are you okay with that?"

He blusters out a big breath. "Yeah, I'm okay with it. As long you're with me."

Gabriel winces, like he thinks he said something stupid.

I bracket his face with my hands. "Don't be embarrassed. I feel the same way. As long as I'm with you, everything will be okay."

He peels my hands away from his face and clasps them. "I wasn't embarrassed. But I'm not used to saying things like that—or feeling them." He kisses my hand, then releases both of them. "We should probably spread out to explore the castle, though we shouldn't go out of sight of each other. You take the far side of this room. I'll look around on the dais and behind the throne."

"Sounds good."

We lost our backpacks somewhere along the way, probably one of the times Jarek almost dropped us. Not sure it matters. If we can't figure out how to take control of the Brain and find a way out of the Echo, we're screwed anyway.

I start at the doorway to the throne room and work my way across it in a diagonal pattern. That seems like the most efficient way to explore. As I sweep this side of the room, I search the walls and the floors for any sign of a hidden doorway or panel that might open up to reveal…something. Not knowing what we're looking for makes the search more difficult, but I know we can do this. I wish Aldith could have given us more info about the Brain, but I'm sure she has limitations, just like we all do.

My friends would know how to search. They might even have some equipment that could help. But they aren't here, and we can't go to them.

Gabriel and I can do this. I know we can.

Once I've finished my examination of this half of the room, I wander over to where Gabriel is scrutinizing the throne. He'd been executing a similar search pattern while exploring his half of the room, but he clearly didn't find anything. Now, he's on his hands and knees, feeling around for who knows what.

I squat beside him. "What are you doing?"

"Searching, obviously."

"For what? I haven't found anything. Do you think there might be a hidden compartment or something in the throne?"

"Not sure." He sits back on his heels. "This is pointless. I'm pretty sure the throne and everything in this room is composed of one unbroken piece of stone."

"Everything? I don't see how the floor and ceiling could be like that."

He huffs. "The Echo is a world composed of magic, remember? Sefton could easily have created any damn thing he wanted. The guy had enormous power."

"Good point. We should search the rest of the castle."

We head into the corridor that leads deeper into the castle. Gabriel is right, I think. This entire structure does seem to have been crafted from one continuous piece of stone, which seems impossible. Magics have a way of turning the impossible into reality, though. That makes our task even more difficult.

Every room we find is empty, like it was never designed to house people, not even its creator. The only chamber that seems different is the dungeon, but that room was empty too. Grant had been trapped in the dungeon briefly, until Erin rescued him. But why did Sefton need a prison cell? Why did he build this monstrosity if he never intended to live inside it?

When I voice that question to Gabriel, he stops dead in the middle of the cold stone hallway and stares straight ahead at nothing.

"Are you okay?" I ask. "Gabriel?"

He slowly swivels his head toward me. "That's exactly what he intended—never to live here. It's not a castle in the traditional sense. It's a place to house the Brain."

"I suppose it could be. But we haven't found any evidence of that either."

"We have no idea what the Brain looks like. That means we might be standing right in front of it and not know."

That suggestion sends a shiver up my spine. What if the Brain has a physical form that can reach out to grab us? Nothing is impossible in the Echo.

"So, how do we find it?" I ask. "If we can't see what we're looking for."

He aims a smug smile at me, but it doesn't seem like arrogance. He just looks like he's pleased that he thought of something I didn't. "We made the Brain happy when we sealed our bond. We need to stay here and look through Sefton's journal to figure out how to command the Brain. We also need to do some more bond-forging while we're inside the castle, to make our buddy the Brain happy."

"And you think we should have sex to make that happen."

"Yeah, of course. The Echo seems to like it when we fuck, and I love making you scream."

I can't help smiling. Yes, I would love to get naked with him again. But my smile fades quickly when I realize we have another problem. "We lost both of our backpacks, and the journal was in one of them."

"No problem. We'll bring our packs to us with our wicked new powers."

"Your sudden love for our powers is making me uneasy."

He rolls his eyes. "I thought you wanted me to embrace the magics. I finally figured out how to do that, and you're giving me a disapproving look instead of kissing me."

"I'll kiss you when you explain why you've suddenly changed your attitude toward our Echo power."

Gabriel bows his head and sighs. "Maybe I did get a little too excited about that. But we should try to bring out backpacks to us. Don't you think?"

"Yes, of course we should. Let's try it now."

We sit down on the floor cross-legged, facing each other, and hold hands. When we tried to open the gateway to the Echo, it failed because the Brain doesn't want us to leave yet. We shouldn't run into that problem now, since we're only trying to retrieve our packs. If we get zapped, I will be very annoyed with the Brain. I mean, we're trying to stabilize it. The thing should be grateful.

Now I'm expecting a mystical, formless Brain to thank me. Jeez, I need to get out of the Echo.

Gabriel and I gaze into each other's eyes and focus on bringing our packs to us. The magic rises within us as a gentle, tingling energy that emerges in our chests and spreads outward into our arms, then our legs, and finally up into our heads. I can't explain how I know that he feels the same thing I do. Don't need to explain it. The supernatural energies rise through our skin to waft in the air, swirling and shimmering, zinging whenever they touch us.

Our backpacks appear behind Gabriel.

"This isn't working," he says.

"Yes, it is." I point past his shoulder. "Look."

He twists around to see, and his smug smile returns. "I was right. We did it."

"Get out the journal. We should study it."

"Will do." He pulls both our packs out from behind his body, setting them between us. "Could use a snack and some water too."

"Yes, definitely."

He digs the journal out and offers it to me.

I shake my head. "You should read it."

"Why? You're the smart one."

"Honestly, we're both smart."

"Tell you what." He flips the cover open. "I'll read the first twenty pages, then you can read the next twenty, and so on. Sound good?"

"Yes. Very equitable."

He leans over to lay a hand on my thigh, then slide it up toward my hip. "I love it when you say big words. Makes me want to fuck you again right now."

"Later, Gabriel. We have work to do."

"If you insist."

While he begins reading the journal, I get out some snacks and water bottles, enough for both of us. I offer him food, but he waves it away. I watch him as I eat a snack bar, chewing slowly because I'm fascinated by the look of intense concentration on his face. My friends back in Sanctuary had told me a bit about what the journal contains, but I want to know the details. It might prove vital to figuring out how the Echo's Brain works.

Did Sefton imbue the Brain with his own thought patterns? That would be beyond creepy, but it might also provide insight, if it's true.

Finally, Gabriel raises his head and rolls his head side to side as if ironing out kinks. "This book is boring and full of whackjob nonsense."

"Let me have a go at it."

He hands me the open journal. "Be prepared to go cross-eyed."

"I can handle it." I toss him a snack bar. "Recharge your brain."

While he rips open the foil package, I flip to the next page of the journal to start where he left off. After reading three pages of dense text about quantum physics, and not understanding one sentence of it, I give my eyes a brief rest by shutting them. The light inside the room filters through my lids, creating phantoms of writhing darkness and light. I take slow, deep breaths in the hopes I can achieve a Zen state the way Grant can. He's had years of experience. I've had a few meditation sessions with Grant and Erin. So no, I doubt I can achieve true Zen-ness here in a spooky, empty castle while a hot guy sits across from me, watching and munching on a granola bar.

I can hear him chewing. And breathing.

Let the rest of the world recede from your consciousness, Grant always tells me, *and relax into the silence and mindfulness*. I reel my thoughts backward to the last time I had a mindfulness session with Grant, when I was trying to regain my memories. It didn't work. But I learned how to block out all the noise and focus on my body. I start at my head, feeling my scalp and my hair without touching them or moving even one muscle. Mindfulness is about perception, not physical touch. So I feel my way down my face as I experience my eyelids, my facial muscles, my lips, and my chin.

"What are you doing?" Gabriel asks. "You aren't reading the journal."

"Shush. I'm trying mindfulness meditation to get a clearer perception of the journal."

"But—"

"I said shush, Gabriel. That means be quiet."

He goes back to chewing, and I retreat into my mindfulness again. I work my way down my body, perceiving muscles and skin and hair without touching anything, just sinking into the feeling. When I reach my lap, I experience the sensation of the journal lying on my thigh and my hands resting on the smooth pages. I swear I can smell the paper too, and even the ink Sefton Stainthorpe used to write his nonsensical text.

A strange sensation trickles through me, lifting every fine hair on my body and shortening my breaths. I found something. I can't see it, but I feel it. The journal contains important information hidden beneath the surface of the text itself.

I open my eyes.

Gabriel is staring at me. He narrows his gaze. "You look like you just discovered some vital clue, but all you've been doing was falling asleep while sitting up."

"No, that's not all I was doing. Besides, I wasn't asleep. Mindfulness meditation can release tension and allow you to discover things you might have overlooked."

"Like what?"

I spread my hands over the journal pages. "Not sure yet. But I sensed that the journal is more than a written record of Sefton's plan to create an apocalypse."

He huffs. "That means you found nothing. You wasted time on navel gazing instead of studying the journal."

"Don't turn back into a jerk. I know you're anxious. I am too. But this journal is important, and we need to use more than our physical senses to understand it. Magic was at the heart of everything Sefton did, so we can't treat the journal like it's nothing more than a record of his plans."

Gabriel rubs his forehead. "Yeah, you're right. You'd think I'd be used to all this magic shit by now, but I'm not."

"It's okay. You just relax while I study the journal some more."

He lies down on the floor, hands clasped over his belly, and shuts his eyes. Does he want to take a nap? Well, I wouldn't blame him. We've had a rough couple of days.

I close my eyes and return to the mindfulness routine, starting with the journal on my lap. I feel the texture of the ink on the pages, as well as the leather cover and the stitching that holds the spine together. The scent of the leather wafts into my nostrils, and I suck in a deep breath to experience the scent.

A wriggling sensation begins in my fingers and spreads up through my palms, moving toward my wrists. It stops there, but the wriggling doesn't die away. It teases my skin as if it wants me to do something. What? I have no idea. But the book needs me to explore it, to feel every page and understand its meaning viscerally rather than physically. I flip to the next page.

The wriggling mutates into tingling.

My breaths have become heavier, almost as if a weight has settled onto my chest. I inhale slowly and exhale the same way until the weight lessens enough that I can continue my sightless exploration of the journal. Though I've never had vision issues, I can tell this isn't the kind of blind exploration that some-one with reduced sight would experience. What I feel is magics. They want me to dig deeper into the journal and discover something vital.

Why can't the Echo just say what it wants? Trying to interpret magical signals gets pretty damn annoying.

As I turn the next page, I feel another presence intruding into my men-tal space. No, not intruding. I recognize and welcome the invasion, be-cause it's coming from Gabriel. Does he realize what he's doing? Probably not. He hasn't been entirely comfortable with our shared power. But the silky warmth and sensuality of his presence spreads through me, awaken-ing my body and instigating a slick heat between my thighs.

My eyes fly open.

So do Gabriel's. He springs into a sitting position, his chest heaving and the bulge in his pants much larger than it had been a few minutes ago. We gaze into each other's eyes as the weight of lust bears down on us both, and I know what the Echo wants from us right now.

"We need to fuck, Gabriel. Right now."

Chapter Seventeen

Gabriel

LITTLE MISS AMNESIA JUST DECLARED THAT WE NEED TO FUCK AGAIN, right now, here in the creepy castle. Yeah, I've got a raging hard-on. But we're supposed to be studying the journal, not getting hot and bothered. Maybe I had felt something strange a moment ago, while I lay on the floor trying to relax. Maybe it had felt like Sarah crawled inside my pants and started sucking my cock. But that was a daydream or…something. It hadn't been real.

But it felt real. Not literally, but yeah.

I hate magics. The boring, supernatural-free world was so much easier to navigate.

Sarah sets the journal on the floor and starts unbuttoning her shirt.

"Whoa there, cowgirl," I say, as I rise to my knees. "Slow down. What happened to studying the journal?"

"I did that. And it told me that we need to have sex before we can understand."

"Yeah, that sounds completely rational."

"Don't get sarcastic." She glances down at my dick. "The magics affected you too. Since when does a man turn down an offer of sex?"

"Since you declared that the journal wants us to screw each other's brains out."

"Trust me, Gabriel. We need to do this." She unhooks the last button on her shirt and shrugs out of it. "And we both want it too."

I groan and rub my hand over my mouth, because she just released the first clasp on her front-hook bra. "Of course I want you, but this is too bizarre. A book tells us what to do now? And there isn't even a bed in here. Just hard stone floors."

She tosses her bra away, then crawls over to me. The way her breasts dangle beneath her makes my dick throb. "We can go back to the stronghold, if you'd feel more comfortable there. But I'd love for you to take me on the cold, hard floor."

"Why?" Can't believe I'm resisting so much. I'm insanely hot for her, all the time, and now I keep saying no.

Sarah laughs softly. "Why? Stop asking questions and just strip, Gabriel."

We can't go back to the stronghold, not unless we call for Jarek to take us there. I can't hold out for much longer with Sarah tempting me like a siren luring me to my death on a foggy coast, where I will blindly smash into the jagged rocks. I wouldn't mind if she ripped me to shreds and left nothing but a pile of bones behind afterward. Death would be worth it, if I get to be inside her again.

She unzips my pants and curls her soft hand around my hard-on, pulling it out so she can stroke my length. A deep groan resonates in my chest, and my eyes fall half-closed. I can still see her, though, and I watch while she rests her hands on my thighs and lowers her head to take me into her mouth. I can't move, or even tell her to stop. Not that I want her to stop. But this is crazy, and—

The little siren is devouring me, sucking and licking while making ravenous grunting noises. I throw my head back and growl, then I shove my hand into her hair and let the woman have her way with me. She massages my balls with one hand while pumping me with the other, all while she keeps licking and sucking. Fuck, I know I'll come any second. I feel like I'm on a runaway train that just reached a ninety-degree incline, and now it's inching up the tracks so slowly that I can't breathe anymore. Once the train reaches the peak, I'll go barreling down it toward bliss.

She pulls her mouth away. "Mm, you taste so damn good."

I'm breathing too hard to speak.

"Get naked, Gabriel," she says. "Then lie down on the floor."

"Why?" I actually managed to speak one syllable. That feels like a major accomplishment, considering how turned on I am.

"Stop asking questions. It's my turn to dominate you."

The little siren rises and strips off the rest of her clothes. My gaze stalls on the thatch of hairs between her thighs, the ones I know are as soft as silk. I want to eat her up, but she just commanded me to get naked so she can dominate me. Still not sure I can submit to that. But if anyone can seduce me into relinquishing control, it's Lady Godiva.

While I undress, she breaks into my backpack and brings out the rope. She holds it up, smiling with the sexiest look of triumph. "I'm ready whenever you are."

I shed the last item of clothing—my socks—and saunter up to her. "Sure you wouldn't rather I ordered you around? You loved that last time."

She wags a finger at me. "It's my turn. So lie down on the floor. Now."

I can't refuse her command, because I want her like crazy. But my heart rate has accelerated, and I know it's not entirely because I'm turned on. The thought of letting her tie me up has increased my anxiety. But I do what she wants and lie down on the floor, on my back.

Sarah kneels beside me. "Are you okay? You looked kind of anxious a minute ago."

"Yeah, I was. I still am."

"Why does what I want to do to you make you uneasy? It's nothing you haven't done to me."

"I know. But..." I cover my face with my hands and growl, because I hate talking about this shit.

"Please tell me. I don't want you to let me do this if it will make you uncomfortable."

I should tell her the truth. I want to tell her. But something keeps me from saying the words. When I look into her eyes and see the concern there, I know the time has come to share my last secret. "When I was thrown into the Echo, a gang of creatures caught me. They tied me up and tortured me for three days, until I finally managed to get away. It wasn't sexual, just plain old torture."

"Oh God, Gabriel." She lies down beside me and lays half her body over mine. "I'm so sorry. Forget about the ropes. Let's just make love."

I hold her for a moment while I consider what to do now. She let me take control of her body, tying her up and not letting her come until she was desperate for it. She said she loved that, and I loved it too. But it was a one-sided game. What those creatures did to me has no bearing on the time I've spent making love to Sarah. Now that I've told her my last secret, I feel that weight lifting. It's time to give her what she wants, because I want to do it, not because I feel compelled to satisfy her.

"Have your fun," I say. "Don't hold back. Whatever you want, I want it too."

"What about your past trauma?"

"I'll be fine. In fact, I think letting you be in control will be good for both of us."

"Really?"

"Yeah." I palm her ass. "Can't resist a hot woman ordering me around."

Sarah gets to her knees and grabs the rope. "If what I'm doing bothers you at all, speak up. Okay? Don't go all macho and hold it in."

I smirk. "Yes, ma'am. No macho holding-in. Any other orders?"

"Not yet. But I haven't gotten started yet." She snaps the rope taut, and her lips curl into a sexy smile. "Your ass is mine, Gabriel."

Sarah the dominatrix makes my cock throb again. She is the most incredible woman in the universe. Even amnesia can't keep her down.

The woman who wants to dominate me swings one leg over me to straddle my thighs. Then she tells me to sit up, so she can tie the rope behind my back and bind my wrists there, leaving just enough leeway that I won't strain myself if I can't keep from writhing while she's having her way with me. Can't wait to see what the naughty nudist has planned for me.

She slaps a hand on my chest and pushes me back down on the floor.

Next, she grabs another length of rope to tie my ankles, leaving some leeway there too, and she uses the same length of rope to bind my knees. I should probably feel anxious about this, and my pulse does speed up, but I experience only a twinge of anxiety. With my dick so hard I think I could use it as a baseball bat, I can't think about anything except what Sarah wants to do to me.

She crawls forward on her hands and knees, still straddling me. Though I notice her movements, I reserve all my attention for her body. Those tits sway when she bends over me to adjust the rope behind my back, and I want to lunge my head up to seize one nipple and suck until she cries out. The scent of her cream intoxicates me, especially because I can see it dribbling down her inner thighs.

I need to taste her, but she's in charge.

Her face now hovers above mine. She catches her bottom lip between her teeth and bites down hard, then releases it ever-so-slowly. "I love it when you get me so turned on that I beg for you to make me come. Now it's your turn. Feel free to plead with me to push you over the edge, unless that would make you feel unmanly."

"Don't give a shit about that, not when I'm with you."

"Are you sure you're ready for this?"

"Yes, baby, do it. I trust you all the way."

I could probably manage to flip us over, if I really wanted to, but I realize I need to let her do this as much as she does. Though her nipple dangles millimeters from my lips, I don't even try to latch onto it. She's earned the right to boss me around, after our bondage interlude in the stronghold.

Sarah bends her elbows to lower her head and turns it side to side to tease my lips and my cheeks with her silky hair. I pull in a sharp breath. She skims her lips over mine, barely grazing my skin while her hair tickles me again. "I'm just getting started."

"Good. Not ready for it to be over yet."

The little vixen crawls backward, licking and nibbling my flesh as she moves, catching one of my nipples between her teeth only to let it go gradually, then repeating the process with the other one. I gasp and instinctively arch my back. She licks my nipple, then blows a hot breath over it, and finally nips it hard. I hiss in a breath. She keeps inching backward. Her tits graze my chest when she ducks her head to flick her tongue into my navel, then licks a trail down to my groin.

She sits up and drags her nails down my chest from my shoulders all the way to my hips.

"Fuck, you're a wicked girl," I growl. "Not the goody two shoes I thought you were when we met."

"Never trust first impressions. I thought you were an arrogant, rude jackass."

I smirk. "But I am a jackass."

She shakes her head slowly, then leans in to whisper in my ear, "You're hung like a bull, not a donkey."

"Let me taste you, please."

She sits back on my thighs, and now her wet cleft is pressed into my cock. "Maybe I should let you make me come. You won't be coming anytime soon, though."

"This is your show."

With a wicked smile, she rocks back and forth, spreading her cream all over my erection. Then she rises to her knees and waddles up my body until her groin lies inches above my mouth. "Close enough?"

"A little lower, baby."

I groan when she lowers herself until my nose rubs against her mound and the silky hairs there, and her glistening slickness teases my lips. I lick it off and groan.

"Hurry up," she says, her voice husky. "I need to come now."

"Your wish is my command."

I thrust my tongue out to coil it around her clit, over and over, breathing harder just from hearing her moans and gasps. She rocks her hips into me, and I seize the chance to dive my tongue inside her opening, licking furiously to devour every bit of her cream that I can.

"Oh, God!" she shouts as she begins to rock her hips wildly, and she slaps her palms on the floor at either side of my head. "Hurry, Gabriel. Make me scream."

I capture her clit and suck it hard and fast, letting my chin rub against her folds to get her even more excited. Her breaths have become sharp gasps. A sound like nails on a chalkboard tells me she's scraping her fingernails on the stone floor, so close to orgasm that it won't take much to push her over the edge. I release her clit and frisk my tongue back and forth along her folds until she jerks and cries out, then I go for it. I pull her nub into my mouth and rasp my teeth over it while I suckle her clit.

Her body goes rigid, her nails scrape the floor even harder, and she comes. Her scream reverberates inside the cavernous room. I keep tormenting her clit until she's done and struggling to catch her breath.

After a moment, she crawls back down to my groin and sits back on my thighs. "Wow, you've got skills."

"Thanks, but I need you to fuck me now."

She grasps my dick and strokes it gently, which drives me even crazier than if she'd pumped me fiercely. I make a noise that's something between a groan and a shout. But Sarah isn't done with me. She crouches over my cock and holds it with one hand while she rocks her hips. The movement skates her cleft over me again and again, the pace erratic, not giving me a chance to get into the rhythm, and that's exactly what she wants. Keeping me guessing drives me insane.

Damn, she's amazing.

"Mm, I love how hard you are," she says. "But I want you even harder."

She lowers herself just enough to take the head of my cock into her opening, but she doesn't take me all the way. No, she pulls out, then pushes me inside her again, only a little farther than before. I try to bend my knees, but it's hard to do that when I'm bound at the ankles and knees. Can't really lift my hips either. And when she finally slams down onto my cock, burying me inside her, she just sits there, not moving a muscle.

Her hands glide up my belly, and she pinches my nipples.

The only sound I can make is a strangled shout.

She rises to her knees, leaving me unsatisfied. No, that's not quite right. I love what she's doing. Sex has never been this intense or exciting before. The thrill of never knowing what she might do or when she might let me come… It's incredible.

Her delicate fingers massage the hollows of my hips, like she'd done the last time we had sex—when I wouldn't let her tease me this way. No holding back now.

Sarah shimmies down my body to massage my inner thighs. While she does that, she leans forward to take my dick in her mouth and pump it. Her motions begin at a leisurely pace, but they speed up gradually in sync with her massage. I start gasping again, thrashing though I don't really want to break free. I feel myself teetering on the cusp of a precipice, caught in the second before free-fall, unable to tumble over the edge.

And then she stops.

I suddenly realize I have my eyes closed and open them. Sarah is on her knees again, towering over me. She fondles her tits, pinching the nipples, and moans as she slides her hands down her belly to her mound. Then she slips one finger between her folds and begins to pet herself, seemingly in no hurry. When she slips another finger in there, she rocks her hips in a slow and erotic rhythm, her gaze locked on mine while she licks her lips and adds a third finger, petting herself more vigorously.

The vixen is going to make me watch her pleasure herself.

"Order me to come," she says, her voice even huskier.

"Do it, Sarah. Fuck yourself until you come."

She freezes, moving only one finger to rub herself, and comes with a harsh scream. Then she slams down onto my cock and bucks her hips wildly.

And I explode inside her.

CHAPTER EIGHTEEN

Sarah

HIS RELEASE ERUPTS INSIDE ME MORE POWERFULLY THAN EVER BEFORE, and I cry out again from the bliss of feeling him inside me. Then it's over, and I collapse on top of him. I need a few minutes before I can recover my wits enough to remember I should untie him. I do that quickly, and he folds his arms around me. I love being tucked against his body, feeling his warmth and strength.

Will I get pregnant? I don't care if I do, because I know I want to spend the rest of my life with Gabriel.

He combs his fingers through my hair. "If we hadn't sealed our bond one hundred percent before this, we've definitely done it now."

"You gave yourself to me without hesitation."

"I gave myself to you, body and soul, and I don't regret it at all."

"When I surrendered my body to you, I didn't regret either. It felt right."

For a while, we just lie here in each other's arms and revel in the afterglow. Maybe I shouldn't feel this way when I haven't known him for long, but I refuse to second guess my emotions. I trust him, I want him, and I care what happens to him. We're still trapped in the Echo, but I know we can decipher Sefton's journal and uncover the last secrets of the apocalypse. Then, we will end the madness.

Gabriel hooks a finger under my chin, urging me to look at him. "I'm sorry for the way I acted early on, especially on the beach. I would never have hurt you. The things I said, that was fear talking. I'd just gotten dumped into the middle of an Echo creature gang war, then got ripped away from there to crash down on a beach. That's not an excuse, just what happened."

"I know that. You don't need to apologize for it again. Even on the beach, I knew deep down that you wouldn't hurt me. Having amnesia has forced me to trust my instincts."

He kisses my forehead, then sits up and stretches. He slaps my bottom. "Get up, Lady Godiva. We have more journal pages to explore."

At first, I thought his nickname for me was annoying. But when he says it now, with humor in his voice and a twinkle in his eyes, I love it. But I don't have a nickname for him.

"Do you like being called Gabe?" I ask.

"Not particularly. I prefer Gabriel."

Okay, no nickname for him.

I get up and stretch like he had, but I also yawn. Lying with Gabriel makes me feel relaxed and warm and content. But we still have work to do, so we both get dressed and resume our study of the journal. This time, we sit side by side on the floor as we flip the pages, discussing each one before we move on to the next. Eventually, we come to the drawing Grant had told me about—a rendering of *The Vitruvian Man*, as envisioned by Leonardo da Vinci.

"Grant told me about this drawing," I say. "Da Vinci was inspired by the writings of Vitruvius, a Roman scholar who talked about the perfect proportions for architecture and the human body."

Sefton's version of the Da Vinci drawing looks remarkably like the original, almost as if he traced it. Maybe he did. Sefton Stainthorpe had given himself teleportation powers before he set the alchemy of worlds in motion, and he admitted to Dax and Allison that he had teleported into the Getty museum to steal rare alchemical manuscripts. He might've stolen *The Vitruvian Man* too. But that drawing is so famous that someone would've missed it, surely.

Maybe he hid in the museum after hours to copy it.

Ugh, like it really matters how he managed to reproduce the drawing with such amazing accuracy.

I touch my fingertip to the journal page, following every line of the drawing. Something about it seems vital, like we need to uncover its secrets before we'll have any chance of taking over the Brain. But what then? I have no idea. Can we stop the apocalypse? Sever the Echo from Earth?

Tapping my finger on the drawing, I ask, "Once we control the Brain, what do we do then? There must be a purpose for taking command of the Brain, but we don't know what that is. Do we?"

"I don't know what it is, that's for sure."

"You know, I remember Grant and Erin talked about something called the Tria Prima. The way I understood it, that was the magics that kickstarted the alchemy of worlds. Sefton called it an alchemical reaction."

"He was obsessed with alchemy, right?"

"Yes. There were boxes in the cellar of Fallenmouth that Sefton had imbued with powerful magics to help drive the apocalypse. Allison used her Echo power to circumvent that."

Gabriel squints at the journal, almost like he's trying to divine answers from the page. "Do you know much about the Tria Prima?"

"No. But I think there's more information about it in the journal."

"Let's skip ahead to that." He hesitates, glancing at me. "Mind if I, uh, dog-ear this page?"

"Sure, go ahead. It's not my journal."

Gabriel folds over the page's upper corner, then flips through the journal in search of information about the Tria Prima. We both skim the pages, but it's pretty clear that most of the journal consists of the ramblings of a deranged mind. Very little of it makes sense. But then we finally stumble on to something meaningful.

"Tria Prima," Gabriel says, tapping a page. "Sefton wrote about it right here."

"What does he say?"

"I'll paraphrase, because he tends to ramble like a lunatic for some weird reason." Gabriel smirks at me. "Can't imagine why he would do that."

"Everybody knows he was insane. Just give me the gist of it."

"Okay." Gabriel skims the text. "Here we go. Sefton's obsession with alchemy seems to have led him to an even deeper obsession—with his brother and with Allison. He decided that the three of them were the Tria Prima. That's a reference to the three basal elements of alchemy that triggered the first transmutation and created everything in the universe. Sefton believed that by recreating the Tria Prima with himself, Dax, and Allison, he could generate enough power to tap into the quintessentia, the prime catalyst that created the universe."

"He needed that to start the alchemy of worlds?"

"I think so." Gabriel flips to the next page, his gaze narrowes as struggles to comprehend the text. "There's more rambling, then he talks about the Triangle, which is composed of the Tria Prima. He says the Triangle has the greatest power of all, and he worried that someone might try to appropriate that power from him."

"None of my friends mentioned that. But they don't tell me everything about the journal."

Gabriel lifts his gaze to mine. "Why not? Don't they trust you?"

"Of course they do. But they also treat me like I'm a lost child they've taken in. I understand why, but sometimes, I wish they'd let me in on their deepest secrets."

"Does everyone else in Sanctuary know that stuff?"

"I don't think so. There are some secrets they won't share with anyone outside the inner circle—Dax, Allison, Grant, and Erin."

Gabriel holds the open book out to me. "But they gave you the journal. That means they do trust you. Maybe they just worried all this crazy stuff in the journal would scare you."

"That's probably true. I'm not a badass like Erin, or a fighter like Allison. Nobody taught me self-defense. Erin was going to teach me how to use a bow and arrow, but we didn't get around to that."

"Your friends think you're weak."

I start to object, but then shut my mouth. Do they treat me that way? Maybe a little. I don't blame them. They did find me on the beach, washed ashore like garbage, with no memory of anything before that moment. Of course they want to shield me from the worst truths. I've been coddled, kind of, but not anymore. Coming to the Echo has changed me.

Meeting Gabriel has changed me.

But am I strong enough to handle whatever comes next? I've never fought in a battle or stopped a mad man. But my friends wouldn't have given me the journal if they didn't believe Gabriel and I could handle the secrets hidden within it.

"You mentioned someplace called Fallenmouth," Gabriel says. "The cellar held boxes full of magics."

"That's right. Fallenmouth was the estate where Dax and Sefton grew up, and it became Sefton's home base once he enacted his insane plan."

Gabriel sets the journal on his lap. "The boxes were at Fallenmouth. They contained the magics that Sefton needed to start the alchemical reaction, and apparently, to sustain it after the apocalypse got rolling."

"Yes. Does the journal talk about that?"

"Not in so many words. I read between the lines."

I glance down at the book. "The boxes are dead. That's what Erin and Grant said. They can't power anything anymore."

"Well, I guess that doesn't really matter. We're trying to figure out what the Brain does and why we need to power it up."

"Right. Let's get back to studying the journal."

We browse page after page but don't find anything of interest—until we reach a section of text near the end of the diary. Sefton mentions the Heart and the Lifeblood, two vital elements of the Echo. He believed the world he created from magics would not survive without a "pulsing heart" and "flowing blood," like any living thing must have.

"He cast an intense spell," Gabriel says, "to create those two elements and give them the power to keep the Echo alive. He had discovered a flaw in the alchemical reaction, which meant the new world he created would disintegrate in 'catastrophic fashion' unless he gave it the 'organs' it needed to survive."

"The spell he cast created the Heart and the Lifeblood."

"Exactly."

I chew on the inside of my lip as I stare at the journal and try to comprehend the scope of Sefton's master plan. He screwed it up, though, didn't he? The alchemy of worlds accidentally gave some humans magical abilities, what we call Echo power. That power let Allison stop the alchemy of worlds and destroy those boxes.

"Why didn't my friends know about this?" I ask, though I'm not expecting Gabriel to answer. I'm thinking out loud. "They had the journal for two months and studied it extensively."

"They clearly missed a few things."

"Did they? I wonder. I mean, we are talking about magic and transmutation." I lay my hand on the open journal. "What if the book is imbued with magics too? Maybe it can hide what it doesn't want anyone to see yet."

Gabriel scrunches up his face, like he wants to tell me that's crazy. But then he relaxes and sighs. "Who knows? Maybe you're right. That would explain why we found clues that nobody else noticed. And you did say you felt something strange when you closed your eyes while holding the book."

"Exactly. I think the journal protects its secrets until the right person comes along."

"You are the right person, Sarah."

I lay my hand over his on the book. "We are the right people. You and me together."

"What are we supposed to do? I don't even know where the Brain is, much less how to tap into it. We've searched this entire castle, including the dungeon, and there's nothing."

"But the journal hid pages until we held it in our hands. The Brain might've hidden itself too."

Gabriel slaps the journal shut and jumps up. A muscle in his jaw ticks while he grits his teeth hard. "I'm damn sick of all this cloak-and-dagger bullshit. We're here. We did what we were supposed to do, and still the damn Brain won't show itself."

I scramble to get up and rest my hands on his chest. "Calm down, Gabriel. We're making progress. And we will find the Brain, I know it."

He scrubs a hand over his mouth, and his shoulders sag. "Sorry. I'm getting frustrated. Who knows how many years have gone by while we've been browsing a book."

"Let's go back to the throne room. That seems like the kind of room where Sefton would have hidden his treasure—the Brain."

Gabriel marches toward the doorway, walking so fast that I need to run to catch up to him. When I grasp his hand, he doesn't take hold of mine. Not at first. But I keep my hand wrapped around his while we hustle down the corridor, until he finally gives up and laces his fingers with mine. We hurry into the throne room and halt a few feet from the throne itself.

"Now what?" I ask.

He shrugs.

The floor begins to vibrate, emitting a low rumble.

I grip his hand even more tightly and try not to fall down as the vibrations ramp up more and more. The rumbling becomes a deafening roar, and we both slap our hands over our ears to dull the racket. It makes my ears hurt, so I'm sure Gabriel is experiencing the same thing.

The entire dais sinks beneath the floor.

As the dais and throne vanish from sight, something else rises in its place—a gigantic wall of stone that has its own stone floor attached to it. The new dais consists of one large piece and has symbols carved into its wall. But that's not what has me gaping at the newly revealed dais. The center of the rear wall houses a metal contraption. It has an outer ring with multiple spokes inside it, as well as metal cuffs that seem to have been made to hold a human being in one of two positions—arms spread and slightly raised with legs spread, or arms raised straight out to the sides with legs together.

I've seen this before. Today. A little while ago.

This is the Vitruvian Man.

Gabriel takes a step toward the dais, but I seize his arm to stop him. He rotates his head to look at me, brows raised.

"Don't go any closer," I say. "Please. I have a bad feeling about this."

"But this must be the Brain."

"Maybe. Even if it is, we need to know more before we approach that contraption. Who knows what it might do to us?"

He stares at the machine like he longs to walk up to it and let the thing take him. Maybe it wouldn't hurt him. But who knows? The Brain sent an Echo beast to kidnap us, and it created super destructive lightning, not to mention fireballs. We need to know more before we even think about approaching the machine. The Heart and the Lifeblood were not mechanical, after all. They were Erin and Grant, two humans who took control of those elements of the Echo. Why would the Brain be technological?

A mechanical pulsating noise emanates from the machine.

No, I don't like this at all.

Chapter Nineteen

Gabriel

EVERY TIME THE MACHINE PULSATES, I FREEZE AND STARE AT IT. SARAH keeps tugging on my hand to drag me away from the thing, but I only manage to shuffle a few feet before it pulsates again and I fall into another semi-trance. That can't be good. Sarah was the one who seemed possessed when she touched the journal's pages. But now I've become entranced by the machine. What the hell is going on? We're supposed to take control of the Brain, not the other way around.

Sarah tugs on my arm again. "Come on, Gabriel. We need to get out of this room."

I can't move or speak.

She kicks my shin.

The burst of pain snaps me out of the trance, but I feel the machine's energy licking at my skin, enticing me to walk right up to it and let the device take me. Sarah doesn't seem to feel it. If we're both halves of the Brain, why does it only want me? Or is Sarah just stronger and better able to resist the seductive energies? If the magics push through her resistance…

I won't let the machine take her.

Sarah leads me down the corridor to the entryway, but she hesitates there.

"What's wrong?" I ask. "Are you feeling the pull of the machine too?"

"No. But I hear something. Don't you?"

I tip my head to the side and listen, letting my jaw fall open a little, just enough to enhance my hearing slightly. It's enough. I detect the sounds she must have heard, but I can't tell for sure what they are. It sounds like a combination of noises—grinding, dragging, groaning, huffing, and even shouting. Echo creatures? If so, I doubt they've come to wish us a happy trip back to Earth.

"Wait here," I tell Sarah. "Let me take a look out there first."

She hugs herself and nods.

I approach the big doors and ease one side open a few inches, just enough that I can peer outside. But it's dark now, and I have trouble spotting any creatures that might wait out there. I see writhing shadows, but that's hardly proof of an impending ambush. Damn, I wish I had a pair of night-vision goggles. But I don't, so I need to trust my instincts, and they warn me that something bad is going to happen.

Shutting the door, I try to think of a way to bar the entrance, but I have nothing that would accomplish that feat. The castle is full of empty rooms. Nothing in our backpacks would help either. I have a gun and extra ammo, but not enough to fend off Echo creatures. They're too strong and too vicious. Only a strike to the center of the heart will take them down for certain.

"Grant and Erin teleported themselves out of the dungeon," Sarah says. "Maybe we could use our powers to zip out of here."

"Do something we've never done while being stalked by vicious creatures in a creepy castle that wants to pull me into its web. Yeah, good plan."

"Got a better idea? We did bring our backpacks to us."

That's true. But for some reason, I don't want to try teleporting. No, I'd much rather walk into the throne room again and touch the machine.

Oh, shit. Its magics are still slithering around inside me.

Sarah grasps my face in her hands. "Snap out of it, Gabriel. Your eyes went glassy, and your jaw went slack. You're under the machine's spell again, aren't you? Fight it, Gabriel, fight it hard."

The vehemence in her voice does the trick. It severs the magics from me, at least for now. But we need to get the hell out of here fast.

"Better teleport quick," I say. "Don't think I can keep fighting the machine for much longer."

She throws her arms around me, her cheek against my neck, and holds me tight. We concentrate on transporting ourselves to another place, away from the castle, away from the influence of the machine. It seems to take forever, both of us concentrating on the task so hard that my head starts to hurt, and my jaw aches too. I'm clenching my teeth and fisting my hands, even though I have my arms lashed around her. I must be crushing her, but she doesn't complain. I feel like I need to glue myself to her to stop the machine from sneaking inside me again.

The castle interior vanishes, replaced by the comforting environment of the stronghold and the bedroom where Sarah and I had made love earlier today. The sheets are still rumpled, and the scent of sex fills the room.

My entire body goes slack, with Sarah's arms holding me up. At last, I'm free of the machine's influence.

But will that freedom last?

Our backpacks lie on the floor. Sarah rushes over to them and digs out the journal, flipping the pages in a rush.

Right before we teleported away, the journal had been on the floor in the machine room, where I vaguely remember dropping it when the mechanism powered up. Sarah must have willed it into her pack.

"We've already been through the journal," I say, sounding wearier than I should. I haven't done anything strenuous, like running from monsters or fucking Sarah. I shuffle to the bed and drop my ass onto it, then rub my forehead. "What are you looking for now?"

"More information about the Brain."

"There isn't anything more. It's useless to keep searching."

She stops in the middle of rifling through the journal, while kneeling on the floor, her wide eyes trained on me. "The machine must still be influencing you. Why else would you give up? That's not like you at all."

"You met me yesterday. Maybe I'm a coward at heart, and exactly the kind of jackass who would give up."

"No, Gabriel, that's not true. You're brave and strong and selfless. Giving up isn't your style, and that means the machine still has a hold on you."

"Let's have sex and see if that helps."

She walks over to the bed and sits down beside me, still holding the journal in her hand. "We need to take control of the Brain, so it can't seize control of you. Right now, I think it's still doing what Sefton wanted."

"Which is what?"

"To connect with its creator. Sefton is dead, though, and even his Echo is gone. The Brain must sense that you are part of it now, but it can't comprehend a woman joining with it. Sefton would've wanted to keep the power for himself."

"So, you think the Brain assumes I must be Sefton and that it wants me to command it again."

"Yes."

I rest my elbows on my thighs and let my face fall into my raised palms. "I don't want to become one with a machine that's pining for Sefton Stainthorpe. He was a whackjob."

"But you aren't. Still, it's too dangerous for either of us to meld with that machine until we understand what needs to be done to keep the worlds from imploding."

I raise my head. "When did that become an option? Nobody warned me the worlds might implode."

"No one understands what having no Brain is doing to the Echo or to Earth. We might have enjoyed two months of peace and quiet, but the fact that the Brain brought us into this world to save itself doesn't bode well."

She has a point—a damn good one. The Brain can't function on its own, so it's desperately trying to find a replacement for Sefton. And that's me. Perfect. I feel like I've fallen into a science fiction movie about evil machines taking over the world. But this machine only wants me.

"What should we do?" I ask. "Can the stronghold protect me?"

"No, it cannot."

The response did not come from Sarah. Aldith stands in the doorway, wringing her hands.

"I thought this was a safe place," I say. "Now you tell us it can't protect me from the Brain?"

She bows her head. "I regret that I can't foresee every eventuality, and I can't stop what is about to occur. But if I can help in any way at all, I will."

"It's not your fault, Aldith. Do you have any idea what might be coming?"

She starts to speak but freezes. Her gaze veers to the picture windows. "It is already here."

A black shape speeds past the window.

Oh no, it can't be.

The Echo flier speeds by again, this time squawking like an angry crow.

"I have fortified the windows with wards," Aldith says. "But the Brain is far more powerful than I am. If it has invested the creatures with magics on the level of Sefton Stainthorpe's powers…"

We're screwed. Yeah, I didn't need a diagram to show me that scenario.

Two bird-like creatures soar up from the ground, each hauling an earthbound beast on its back. The fliers aim straight for the windows, then swerve away at the last second. Their passengers slam into the windows, clinging to the outer sill.

And they bash their fists into the glass.

The magics protecting the windows begin to pulsate, just like the machine in the castle had done. But here, the pulsations are clearly aimed at breaking through the shield Aldith had erected. The creatures clinging to the windows pound their fists while still hanging on to the sill with one hand. The wards pulsate even more strongly, creating a sensation of pressure inside the room that makes my ears hurt.

The Echo fliers drop off more creatures, ones even bigger than the beasts currently pounding on the wards, and they join in the party. *Bam, bam, bam.* Big fists batter the windows. A variety of creatures have joined forces with the fliers—big brutes with gnarly skin, scaly beasts with snake-like tongues, fanged monsters, and more.

And all of them want me.

"They've surrounded the stronghold," Aldith says, and for the first time, she sounds panicked. "And the wards are faltering. We can't fight Sefton's magics."

How can a dead man cause this much chaos? The answer must lie within the machine he left behind, but we can't risk returning to the castle to find out. The machine's pull is way too strong for me to keep fighting it.

I grasp Sarah's shoulders. "Get out of here. You can't let those creatures take you."

"They don't want me. They want you."

"But they might use you as leverage. Please, go back to Sanctuary."

"You know I can't." She glances at the pulsating wards and the beasts battering them. "The gateway is closed."

Shit. I'd forgotten about that. My mind has grown fuzzy, and I feel dizzy. My pulse beats so hard and fast that I can't think straight anymore.

"Please, go hide somewhere," I tell Sarah. "Maybe if I merge with the machine, I can reopen the gateway. Then you could at least escape."

"I am not leaving you behind."

Bam, bam, bam. The entire building shudders with every concussion.

"Go, Sarah. Teleport yourself to someplace far away."

She just stands there, chin lifted. I would love her defiance if she weren't endangering herself with it.

I grip her upper arms and drag her closer. "Listen to me, you stupid girl. Do you want to be ripped to shreds by an Echo creature? They love to rape sweet little things like you."

My growling tone doesn't seem to have affected her at all. *Dammit.*

"You can't scare me away," she says. "We're in this together."

"Sarah—"

The obstinate woman throws her arms around me and whisks us away. We wind up in an area I recognize. It's a part of the Echo that lies furthest away from the Capital City and Sefton's castle. I imagine she wished for us to be somewhere far away, and her magics interpreted that literally. We've wound up on the opposite side of the world.

I notice Aldith stands nearby, arms lashed around herself, glancing around with a wary expression.

"You okay, Aldith?" I ask.

She nods.

We find ourselves in what looks like a small town, though I doubt anyone still lives here. Most of the buildings have been reduced to rubble, and the ones that still stand have suffered enough damage that nobody would want to take refuge in them. Burned-out vehicles and burned-out landscapes complete the picture. This is the definition of a post-apocalyptic wasteland.

But at least we're far away from the castle.

For a moment, I just hold Sarah and shut my eyes to enjoy the feel of her body tucked against me. She rests her cheek on my chest. I set my chin on top of her head. I pull in a deep breath and let it out slowly as the tension melts away.

Then the pull of the machine tugs at me again. *Shit.* Even from literally half a world away, that thing can still find me and infect me with its seductive magics. With every fiber of my being, I want to push Sarah away and transport myself straight to the throne room, which now holds the laboratory of a dead lunatic.

Sarah lifts her head, studying me with those beautiful eyes.

Worry taints them. Worry for me. But she should be more concerned with herself because I can't protect her anymore. I can't trust myself. Would I hurt her if that was the only way to get to the castle? Is merging with the machine now my only goal? I don't want to become a monster, but I know I can't fight it for much longer.

So I push away from Sarah. "You need to move on to another location, another city or town, even a cave will do. I don't care where you go, as long as I can't find you there."

"Running away isn't the answer."

"It's all I can do. You and Aldith need to hide."

Even now, I sense the machine reaching out to me. Its magics snake out in slithering tendrils, hunting, sniffing, seeking me out with all the power Sefton left behind. Resisting the call takes every ounce of willpower I have, but I feel it crumbling away bit by bit, more every second. Soon, I will succumb.

But I can't let that happen here. I have only one choice.

I pull Sarah close and kiss her. Then I stumble backward and stop fighting the pull. The magics snatch me away to the castle. As I disappear, I see the look on Sarah's face as she realizes what I've done. Shock gives way to confusion, and finally, grief.

She screams, "No!"

But I'm already gone.

I stand inside the throne room, near the doorway, though the stone chair has been replaced by the machine and its rock housing. The pressure eased the second I materialized inside this room. And I know what I must do. I walk halfway across the room, but pause when I hear odd noises in the corridor.

Even before I glance back, I know what I will see.

A small army of Echo creatures files into the room, taking up positions around the perimeter, avoiding the dais and the machine.

I face the mechanism.

The creatures begin to grunt in unison, as if they're acting out a ritual.

All the hairs at my nape and on my arms shiver and stiffen as awareness teases my senses. *Oh, no, no, no.* I spin around.

Sarah rushes up to me and pounds her fists on my chest. "I can teleport too, you moron. How dare you kiss me and then run away to get yourself killed or melded with a machine or who knows what."

Her eyes shimmer with gathering tears.

Why the fuck did she follow me? Why couldn't she do what I said this one time? I can feel wards lowering over the castle and the entire summit of the mountain. Magics even stronger than the ones that empowered the creatures to break the wards of the stronghold have encased us.

"Dammit, Sarah," I snarl. "You weren't supposed to be here."

"I can't let you do this. There must be another way."

The machine emits a low, growling sound that seems part mechanical and part magics. We both turn toward the dais. The spokes of the Vitruvian Man wheel begin to glow, and the deep, unearthly sound emanating from it grows louder and louder until it finally stops with a thump. The metal clamps that are clearly meant to hold a human body in position pop open.

A soft hum resonates through the room and faintly vibrates into my feet. The call of the machine tugs at me so strongly that I'm breathing hard from the effort of trying to stave it off.

"No, Gabriel, please."

Tears trickle down Sarah's cheeks. I brush them away with my thumbs and cup her face in my hands. "This is how it has to be. I'm sorry."

Chapter Twenty

Sarah

I'VE BECOME FROZEN IN PLACE AS I WATCH GABRIEL STRIDE UP THE STEPS onto the dais and approach the machine. The hum that fills the room throbs once, and the clamps begin to glow faintly. The creatures keep chanting, though I don't think they're speaking words. Or at least, not words in English. Is that Latin? I don't know, and I don't care. Gabriel is about to surrender himself to a machine created by a lunatic.

"No, stop!" I scream, as I fly up the steps to seize his arm. "This isn't right. Please, trust me, don't do this."

"I have no choice. Maybe if I do this, you won't be trapped in the Echo anymore. Maybe I can send you home."

"Maybe? That's your great plan?"

"Don't make this any harder than it already is."

Tears dribble down my cheeks. I don't want to cry. I need to be strong, but I can't control my emotions. The thought of losing Gabriel makes me hurt in ways I've never experienced before. Is this grief? I have no idea. If it is, I'd rather die than live without him, with nothing but the grief to remind me of him.

He turns around, facing away from the machine, and takes a step backward, now inches away from the thing that wants to absorb him or whatever the hell it intends to do to him.

I rush toward him.

A wall of magics blocks my way. I careen off it, falling down the steps and rolling across the floor.

The creatures begin to grunt in unison.

I peel my aching body off the floor, rising to all fours, and glance back at the dais.

Gabriel stands there motionless, expressionless, like he's been drugged. But it's not any kind of drug affecting him. It's the fucking machine.

His clothes vanish.

I clamber to my feet. "Gabriel!"

The machine's clamps reach out to grab him. He doesn't react at all, not even when the clamps snap shut and he's pulled into the machine in a spread-eagle position with his arms slightly raised.

I run up the dais but bump into the wards again. This time, I manage not to fall. My heart thrashes in my chest, and my ears have started to ring. "Gabriel, talk to me, please. Are you okay?"

He blinks slowly, like he's just coming out of a trance. "Sarah?"

"Yes, it's me. I'm here. Are you okay?" I don't see how he could be, when a machine has taken control of his body.

"I'm okay. It doesn't hurt."

But he still sounds weird, like he's half asleep or drugged.

"Please go," he says. "Not safe here. For you."

"No, I will not leave."

The machine emits a series of bizarre thunking and cranking noises that make my skin crawl. What is that thing trying to do?

Meanwhile, the creatures increase the pace of their grunting, growing almost manic.

"It doesn't want you here," Gabriel says, his voice almost a whisper. "If you stay, it will hurt you."

"The machine?"

He nods.

A chill shimmies up my spine. The machine doesn't want me here and will hurt me if I stay. That suggests it's desperate, and in turn suggests I have more power than it does. But I couldn't even save Gabriel from the damn machine.

It blares a long, discordant sound that makes my eardrums vibrate painfully.

Then an invisible force drags me out of the throne room, down the corridor, and through the doors into the courtyard. I struggle against the magics, but they sweep me through the castle gates anyway.

And hurl me off the cliff.

I scream as I hurtle through the air, spinning and spinning.

A giant hand catches me.

While my head keeps spinning, since it hasn't gotten the memo yet that I'm not plummeting to my death anymore, I gaze up at the metal-and-flesh face of the golem. I'm lying on my back in his palm. Jarek looks at me and tips his head to the side, seeming for the life of me like he's worried.

"I'm okay," I tell him, once I can sit up without feeling like I might vomit. "Thank you for saving me."

He nods. Then he glances up at the cliff top.

"We can't help Gabriel right now," I say. "I need to escape the Echo so I can get help from my friends on Earth. Do you know of any way I can force the gateway to open?"

He squints his eyes as if he's considering the problem. Jarek starts walking, away from the castle, carrying me gently in his palm. What about Aldith? Should we find her? Maybe she's safer where she is.

I assume Jarek is taking me to the gateway, and I use this time to think about what to do next. Now that the Brain has taken Gabriel, does it still want to keep the gateway sealed? Since it clearly doesn't want me around, I wonder if it will allow me to leave the Echo now.

Jarek approaches the gateway and halts. He shrugs his shoulders, as if he's letting me know he doesn't know how to get me back to Earth. But it turns out I was right. The gateway spirals open for me. Jarek thrusts his arm through the opening and gently sets me down on the street of a city.

The gateway closes. I am alone in the dark, and nowhere near Sanctuary. I stand on an empty street that shows definite signs of the apocalypse—smashed pavement, wrecked buildings, bent street signs, and piles of rubble. But it's the growling noises emanating from somewhere in the darkness that cranks up my anxiety. Echo creatures make sounds like that.

I teleported myself to Gabriel in the Echo. Maybe I can whisk myself to Sanctuary now. So I close my eyes and wish I were there, wish it with every iota of mental strength I have left in me.

A breeze tickles my arms.

I open my eyes and smile, though it's a faint expression. I'm at the edge of the woods. The light of a bonfire glows in the area between the circle of tents that form our camp. I hear laughter too. My throat goes thick as I run toward Sanctuary, and tears pour down my cheeks until I can barely see where I'm going. Instinct guides me now, and I race up to the bonfire, knowing my friends will be there.

"Sarah!" someone shouts.

I wipe the tears away, sniffling, and see familiar faces heading my way. Erin, Grant, Dax, and Allison hurry over to me. Willow catches up a moment later.

Allison slings an arm around my shoulders. "What happened, sweetie? Where's Gabriel?"

"He's gone." I try not to cry, but a tiny sob bursts out of me. "The machine took him."

"Machine?"

"We can talk about that later," Erin says. "You were gone for three weeks. What happened?"

Three weeks? No, it wasn't that long. But time can move differently in the Echo. Gabriel had been trapped there for three years, though only eight months passed here.

Gabriel. Just thinking his name makes me start crying again.

"Let's get inside," Erin says. "Our tent is closest."

"Yeah," Grant agrees. "We'll take you there."

I let them lead me to Grant and Erin's tent, with Dax, Allison, and Willow following us. But I know they'll want details about what happened, and I don't think I can talk about it yet. I'm exhausted and dehydrated, hungry too. My friends insist I lie down on the cot in Erin and Grant's tent, just until I feel up to walking back to my own place.

Three hours later, I wake up. I hadn't realized I fell asleep, and I feel awful for wasting time while Gabriel is trapped in the Echo, in that machine.

I go to my tent to put on fresh clothes, then look for my friends. I find them all in Dax and Allison's tent. I can tell they've been talking about me, since they abruptly fall silent when I jingle the doorbell, and they stare at me when I walk into the tent.

"How are you feeling?" Allison asks. "We've been so worried about you."

"But not Gabriel. You all think he's evil."

"No, we don't. You know him better than we do." Allison pats the cot she's seated on. "Sit down, Sarah. We'd like to hear what happened. And I'd like to know if you're okay. You look the way I felt when Sefton cast Dax out of Fallenmouth and I had no idea if he was alive or dead."

"I'm okay, physically." I settle onto the cot beside her, but I can't look at my friends. Instead, I gaze down at my hands, which I'm wringing. "I lost Gabriel. Sefton's machine took him."

"Sefton's machine? What are you talking about?"

"When Gabriel and I looked at Sefton's journal, we found that the contents had changed. It showed us different information than what you guys know about."

"I guess that's not surprising," Grant says. "The Echo is a world of magic, and Sefton was its creator. For the journal itself to change based on who looks at it makes a kind of sense."

"None of this makes sense." I clasp my hands tightly to stop myself from wringing them anymore. "The only thing I understand is that Gabriel and I got sucked into the Echo and we couldn't leave. Then we found the machine and…" I wipe at my eyes, but the tears trickle from them anyway. "And now he's gone, trapped in that castle, in that mechanism. The Brain took him and won't let me join him."

I can feel them studying me, but I still can't make myself look at my friends.

"How long were you in the Echo?" Dax asks. "For us, it's been three weeks since we saw either you or Gabriel. We searched the beach and the forest, then went to Fort Worth to search for you more. But we never found even a small clue to your whereabouts."

"It was only two days for us. But it felt like much longer, like we'd known each other forever."

Allison settles her hand over both of mine. "You love him, don't you?"

"Yes. I know it's crazy, but I'm sure of what I feel. I never got to tell him."

"Tell us about this machine."

I take a moment to sort out my memories of my time in the Echo with Gabriel, then I share all of it with my friends. Well, I leave out the stuff about us having sex. But after I'm done, and everyone is digesting what I've told them, I realize I should share everything with them, including the personal parts. My friends don't need the details about our sexual encounters, just the facts about how those experiences changed us both and seemed to change the Echo too.

"There's something else," I say. "It's kind of embarrassing, but I feel like you guys need to know. You have more experience with the Echo than I do, so maybe the information will be useful. It's about me and Gabriel, our relationship."

Jeez, that sounded stupid. I practically stammered when I said the words.

Allison glances at Dax, and her husband nods. She turns to me. "It's about sex, isn't it? You and Gabriel made love, and the Echo responded to that. We've all experienced the phenomenon, though in different ways. Only recently did the four of us talk openly with each other about that stuff. We were uncomfortable discussing the topic."

"I am too. But I realized just now that it might be important, especially for getting Gabriel back."

"When Dax and I had sex for the first time, it amped up my Echo power. And the next time we made love, we both felt something indescribable had changed between us."

"That's what happened with me and Gabriel too. But then the machine got hold of him, and my powers weren't enough to save him."

"Tell us about this machine," Dax says. "My brother never mentioned that to me or to Allison."

"We never heard of it either," Erin says. "Grant and I were in the Echo for a while. Guess that contraption was waiting for Gabriel."

"For both of us, I think. Aldith said the Echo has a Brain, and that it's been adrift without Sefton. He was controlling it. Aldith believed the Brain wanted me and Gabriel to merge with it and take control of it. But if that's true, why did the Brain take Gabriel and kick me out of the Echo?"

Dax rises from his chair and paces the width of the tent. "Perhaps a remnant of Sefton—a ghost, if you will—lingers inside the Brain. It must be cast out before you two will be allowed to assume control."

"But why take Gabriel? I don't understand."

Grant exchanges a glance with Dax, then tells me, "We're all treading on unfamiliar ground here. You said the Brain has two hemispheres, and that it needs both you and Gabriel."

"That's what Aldith said. But maybe she was wrong."

"It's unlikely. She's tapped into the Echo like nobody else in either world. But it's possible the Brain shielded her from seeing that a remnant of Sefton was still in there."

"Yes, that could be," Allison says. "Sefton employed quantum entanglement to link me, Dax, and himself. I severed his links to us when I stopped the alchemy of worlds, but maybe he was also entangled with the Echo. So when he died, something of him survived."

This discussion is reviving more of my memories of the journal. I left it in my pack, and that's still in the Echo. But the more we all talk about these issues, the more I remember. "The machine is modeled after Da Vinci's Vitruvian Man. But Sefton recreated it exactly, with the two sets of arms and legs. If he meant for only one person to enter the machine, why have spaces for more limbs? Aldith must be right that it's designed to accommodate two people."

"But the Echo has become corrupted by the remnants of Sefton," Allison says. "It's interfering with the machine's intended purposed."

Dax halts his pacing and looks sideways at his wife. "Sefton planned to kill me and marry you. He probably wanted you to become the other half of the Brain."

"Yes, that would make sense."

I raise my hand, which is a silly thing to do. "The journal isn't the same as it was before Gabriel and I went into the Echo. I told you the text had changed. But I also felt something strange when I closed my eyes while reading it. I could feel the text, like it was a part of me."

"A part of both you and Gabriel, I'm sure," Grant says. "The way the Heart and the Lifeblood joined me and Erin."

"Can I use that connection to get back to Gabriel and free him from the machine?"

Grant shrugs.

A growling noise erupts outside, growing louder every moment and originating high above us in the sky. We rush outside to see what's happening, but everything looks the same. Something inside that growling sound triggers a memory. The machine made a noise like that.

"What is it, Sarah?" Erin asks.

"It's the machine. It made that noise right before it took Gabriel."

"But it's not here. The noise must be something else. The machine is still inside the Echo."

"Is it? How do we know? It might be interdimensional. I mean, if the Echo can cause lightning in this world, why can't the machine affect Earth too? The worlds are connected, right?"

"Yes, they are." Erin winces as the growling grows even louder, and we need to shout to hear each other. "Got any ideas about how to stop it?"

"Sorry, no."

The racket abruptly stops.

My ears ring, and I keep staring up at the sky, waiting for an Echo flier to swoop down and take me. But I think the machine only let me go with Gabriel because it knew he needed to have sex with me to get primed for melding with the machine. What does that thing want now?

I don't know. But I have no doubts we'll find out soon.

Chapter Twenty-One

Gabriel

THE METAL CLAMPS THAT HOLD ME IN POSITION FEEL STRANGELY WARM and silky. Energy buzzes through my entire body, though not enough to hurt. It makes every fine hair on my body stiffen, like an electrical current runs through them. Maybe it is mundane electricity, but I kind of doubt that. Echo power zings through the metal, through me, building up to something I'd rather not think about at all.

What does the Brain want from me? I can't merge with the ghost of a dead maniac. Or can I? Not sure which option is the most disturbing.

I can't even move my head. One big clamp holds it in place.

The gang of Echo beasts hasn't moved since they marched into the room and encircled the perimeter. They've stopped growling, just standing there, silent and motionless. Echo creatures never hang out. They rampage. I think they're in a trance of some sort, waiting for instructions. But from who? Sefton is gone. His doppelgänger is gone too.

I shut my eyes and try to think of a way out of this.

"Afraid there's no time to rest. Wake up, Gabriel."

That voice sounded British.

I open my eyes and blink several times to clear my vision. A blonde man stands several yards away at the edge of the dais. He wears a suit that looks bespoke, though I'm hardly a fashion expert, and his features remind me of someone I sort of know. He reminds me of Dax, though less muscular and without the growling tone in his voice.

"Who are you?" I ask. "Did you bring me here? What did you do with Sarah?"

"That is a long string of queries." He ambles closer, now an arm's length from me and the machine. "Give me time, and I will answer all your questions."

"Start with where Sarah is."

"Gone. She is no longer necessary."

Not necessary? I struggle against my bindings, but the clamps make it hard to wiggle my big toes, much less break free. "What happened to Sarah? You tossed her off a cliff, didn't you?"

"Yes. But unfortunately, she survived. That bloody golem saved her."

Way to go, Jarek. I'll give that golem a big wet kiss the next time I see him. At least I know Sarah is alive.

"I permitted her to leave the Echo," the stranger says. "She will never be allowed to return, and you will never leave. Might as well forget about her."

Never. But telling him that would be monumentally stupid. "Who are you?"

The man smiles, but it's not a friendly expression. "I am Sefton Stainthorpe."

"He's dead."

"Indeed he is. But I am the remnant of his master plan, the entangled Echo of his quantum self."

Yeah, that statement made perfect sense. I should've gotten a degree in quantum physics instead of computer programming.

"How are you a remnant of a dead man?" I ask. "Sefton died months ago."

The pseudo-Sefton sighs with irritation and shakes his head. "You might be the best candidate to fuel the Brain, but you are shockingly ignorant."

"Yeah, I really care what you think of me."

He tips his head to the side, studying me. "I control you. So perhaps you should try being more submissive."

"Wrong. You don't control me, you need me. The Brain doesn't work without me, does it? That's why you needed to use magics to get me here."

A furrow forms just above Sefton's nose, like he doesn't understand what I just said. I'm sure he does. It's more likely that he refuses to accept it.

"You don't have the thought capacity to understand," he says. "Soon, you will be entangled with the machine, and you won't care about petty concerns any longer."

"Why don't you just tell me your evil plan and get it over with?" I'm getting sick of listening to his insults and arrogance. From what I've heard, the real Sefton behaved the same way. So I guess this version of him inherited all the characteristics of his whackjob original.

Entangled Sefton only matters to me because he seems to have control over my body. Once I find a way to break free, I'll scatter his quantum ass into the galactic void. I have no idea if such a thing exists, but I don't care. Screw the scientific terminology. I refuse to become the human puppet of a mad man's ghost.

But I am his puppet right now. Not for long, though.

Sarah and I used our shared Echo power to do a lot of things, like reading the hidden messages in the journal and teleporting our backpacks to us. She managed to teleport both of us and Aldith too. If I can tap into that shared power, maybe I can break free of the machine.

Or at least control it.

Sefton glances at my body and winces. "I wish the machine would allow you to be covered. I dislike seeing unclothed humans."

"You'd be cool with unclothed Echo creatures, then, eh?"

He scowls. "No."

I wonder if the real Sefton had a hang-up about nudity, but that's not important right now. "Go on, tell me your evil plan. I know you're dying to share."

"There is no 'evil' plan. I intend to fulfill Sefton's wishes. He orchestrated the entire plan to create the Echo and initiate the apocalypse, but Dax and Allison circumvented the final chapter. Now that I have the energy provided by your flesh and mind, I may restart the terminal phase."

"You mean the alchemy of souls."

"How does a brute like you know about that? It's beyond the scope of your puny mind to understand it."

Yeah, I can see why Dax snapped his brother's neck. Even the quantum shadow of Sefton is damn annoying and arrogant as hell. Of course, Dax didn't kill his brother for that reason. He did it because Sefton murdered Allison. Thank goodness that girl Willow was able to bring her back. If anything like that happened to Sarah...

I'd rip the throats out of every Echo creature in this room, then I'd find a way to destroy quantum Sefton—and make it hurt like hell.

The only reason I'm listening to him is so I can figure out what he intends to do and how I can stop him.

"Don't you want to tell me all about your grand plan?" I ask. "You know, so I can be awed by your genius."

"Be as sarcastic as you like. It won't save you."

"I'm serious about wanting to hear your plan. If I'm a part of it, I'd like to know what to expect." I try to push against my bindings, but I can't move even one millimeter. "See? I can't escape. Might as well share your ideas. Not like I can tell anybody about it."

"Surprisingly, you've made a good point. Perhaps I will share my plans with you. Saying it out loud is a fine way to hash out a plan."

I didn't really expect him to agree with me, so yeah, I'm feeling proud of myself for tricking him that way. But since I'm still glued to a machine, maybe I shouldn't congratulate myself yet.

Sefton freezes, like a computer that just got unplugged. He doesn't breathe, doesn't move, doesn't blink. Then he abruptly comes back to life. "I am afraid I can't explain right now. I need to deal with another issue first."

He vanishes.

The creatures positioned around the perimeter of the room remain perfectly still, though not as immobile as Sefton had been a moment ago. They make tiny movements, like blinking or minutely twitching a finger, while Sefton seemed as immobile as a statue. That suggests to me that he isn't a living being, but some sort of magical construct designed to act out the desires of the Brain and its machine. Is the Brain separate from the machine? I wish Sarah were here to talk about this with me. I think better when she's beside me.

Yeah, we're a good team. More than a team, actually. We fit together like we were designed for each other. Or maybe destined. I never used to believe in that shit, but now I know it's true.

I wonder if I could summon Sarah here.

No, I won't do that, even if I knew how. She's safer in the normal world than here in the Echo. I'd rather die strapped to this fucking machine than endanger her. But I've still got magics, right? I need to figure out a way to use that to stop the machine.

The creatures begin to moan and grunt, but they still don't move.

A figure appears in front of me.

My heart stutters. "Sarah? How—"

"Don't worry about how. I'm not sure if I have much time, since I can feel the Echo fighting me. It wants me gone."

"Are you really here? Or am I hallucinating?"

She lays a hand on my cheek. "I'm real, Gabriel."

The feel of her palm on my skin makes me almost lightheaded, as relief floods through me. She's here. She's real. I want to touch her, but I can't, so I'll settle for sucking in a big breath to inhale the scent of her. She smells like grass and earth, but I don't care. *She's here.*

"Have you been rolling around on the ground?" I ask. Then I realize what a stupid thing that was to say.

She smiles sweetly. "I tripped and fell down on the grass. Before you panic, I'm fine."

"But I see dirt and grass stains on your clothes. There's something you aren't telling me."

"I was getting there. But I need to do this first."

She rises onto her tiptoes, takes my face in her hands, and kisses me. I relax even more, because the feel of her soft lips and her breaths tickling my skin proves to me that she is real. When she pulls away, she rubs her nose against mine. "I love you, Gabriel."

"I love you too." Maybe I shouldn't, not yet, but life in the Echo taught me the importance of seizing the moment. I should've told Sarah how I feel before the machine took me. I knew it even then. "You shouldn't be here, Sarah. Sefton might come back any second."

"Sefton?"

"Well, not literally him. It's more like a quantum ghost of Sefton Stainthorpe, left behind after the man himself was killed. The being I've met is the entangled Echo of Sefton, and he's somehow infused with the machine."

"That would make sense. I went back to Sanctuary and talked to the others about what's going on. We also wondered if there might be some remnant of Sefton left behind."

"I can confirm that. I've seen him and talked to him."

Sarah still has her hands on my cheeks, as if she can't bear to let go. "I want to try to free you from the machine."

"No, don't do it. Not yet."

"What? Who knows how that machine is affecting you. We need to get you out of there."

"No. Just leave, Sarah. It's too dangerous to try to free me."

She bites her lip and hugs herself. "Gabriel, things aren't going well on the Earth side of things. Something's happening, and I don't think it's good. I have grass and dirt on me because I fell down during an earthquake. Tents were knocked down, and small trees fell too. Then there was the noise in the sky. It reminds me of the sound the machine made when it first activated."

My skin goes cold, and the deep freeze penetrates beneath the surface to chill me to the core. "You heard the machine on Earth?"

"Yes."

"Shit. You need to go home and find out what's going on."

"No. I need to be here with you."

I open my mouth, but I don't get a chance to speak. Someone else does.

"You can't stop what's coming next," Sefton announces as he reappears beside Sarah. "The new alchemy of worlds will begin soon, now that I have you to serve as the power cell. The alchemy of souls won't be far behind."

"You're nothing but a ghost in the machine."

Sefton chuckles. "Don't tax your small mind trying to understand the grandness of my scheme. You don't need to think at all. You are nothing more than a power cell."

"Bullshit. You need me, or you wouldn't be spending so much time trying to convince you're a genius."

"Gabriel? Who are you talking to?"

I rotate my eyes toward Sarah. "You can't see him, can you? It's the quantum ghost of Sefton. He wants to restart the—"

A jolt of electrical energy rips through me, rending a shout from my throat. Spasms rack my muscles, and I feel as if they'll tear me apart. I grit my teeth against the pain, blustering breaths out through my nostrils, until the agony finally subsides.

Sarah tries to touch me, but the last fingers of electricity leap from my skin to zap her. She yelps and stumbles backward. "What was that?"

"The machine doesn't want me to tell you about Sefton's plan."

Sefton laughs. "Of course I don't. Am I a moron? No, that's what you are."

"I can see why your brother snapped your neck," I snarl. "And I'm going to find a way to destroy your quantum ghost too."

"You have neither the power nor the wherewithal."

I want to wring his neck so badly, but even if I could break free of the machine, I can't grab onto a ghost.

"Go," I tell Sarah. "Please. I need to know you're far away from here with people you can trust."

She takes half a step toward me, then stops. Her gaze shimmers with growing tears, but she blinks them away. "This isn't over yet."

The woman I love disappears.

And I'm stuck here with a cadre of monsters and the remnants of a dead man.

Sefton strolls back and forth across the dais in front of me, hands clasped behind his back, a smug smile curling his lips. "You are as stubborn as Dax, but not nearly as strong. I molded him into the perfect monster. He was meant to remain in the Echo, but being a bloody stupid wanker, he just had to leap through the gateway along with the other beasts."

"I bet he's awfully sorry about messing up your plans."

He halts and swivels his head toward me, glaring with all the fire of a mad man. "Do not patronize me. I'm giving you the most incredible gift in the universe."

"Being your Energizer bunny doesn't appeal to me."

"What you want is irrelevant. Together, you and I will restart the alchemy of worlds. It's only the first phase, but I doubt your sweet girl will survive it."

Sarah is much stronger than he thinks. I misunderstood her true nature at first too. But amnesia doesn't make her weak. She's amazing and strong and loyal to the people she loves. The real Sefton Stainthorpe had lacked all those qualities, and his ghost is no different.

If Sarah could teleport into this room, crossing through the gateway despite the Echo not wanting her here, maybe I can summon enough power to shut down this machine.

"No more dillydallying," Sefton says. "It's time to initiate the alchemy of worlds again. And that begins with the quantum entanglement of you and the machine, an unbreakable bond even your friends can't sever."

He vanishes.

And the machine ramps up, grinding and groaning, vibrating the entire room. The creatures begin to chant in grunting, wordless exclamations. Magics inundate the room, invisible yet palpable, nipping at my skin and stinging me like unseen bees. I wince and grit my teeth, but I refuse to give this machine the satisfaction of making me vocalize the pain.

Screw you, Sefton. Not even a remnant of you will fulfill your evil plan.

Because this machine is going down.

Chapter Twenty-Two

Sarah

LEAVING GABRIEL THERE IN THAT CREEPY CASTLE WITH ALL THOSE CREA-tures and the entangled Echo of Sefton Stainthorpe had been the hardest thing I've ever done. I love him, and he loves me. But that's not enough to save him. We need more than our connection to defeat the machine. We need allies, but not just any allies. Only four other people on Earth understand what it takes to stop the alchemy of worlds and the ghost of its architect.

Sefton let me leave on my own this time, instead of casting me out. He must've hoped I would crash to the ground and die. He no longer seems to view me as any kind of threat, which seems like a bad sign. He believes he holds all the cards, but I will show him how wrong he is. But first, my friends need to know what I've done.

I landed at the edge of the woods and now march across the field to the encampment that is Sanctuary. They haven't lit a bonfire or started up the barbecue grill. It will take time to undo the damage caused by the Echo storm that ravaged our camp. Now that I know for sure the machine is behind the chaos, I also know exactly what needs to be done. I'd had an epiphany while standing in front of that machine, the thing that's holding Gabriel hostage. I felt what he couldn't say, because Sefton was nearby. Gabriel believes I need to stay out of the line of fire, but I know he's wrong. We are stronger together.

Most of the tents have been erected again, so I head straight for Dax and Allison's quarters. When I march inside without even bothering to ring the doorbell, I discover Grant and Erin are there too.

"How did it go?" Grant asks. "Did you see Gabriel?"

"Yes. He's alive and basically okay. But things are about to get much worse for both worlds."

"Tell us everything."

I explain what I learned during my brief visit to the castle. But that's only the beginning. I need to share my plan for stopping the regeneration of the apocalypse, but Dax has a few questions first.

"If you couldn't see Sefton," he says, "how do you know Gabriel wasn't hallucinating? He is trapped inside an Echo machine."

"Can't give you a concrete reason. I trust Gabriel, and I know he actually saw Sefton's quantum ghost."

Dax nods. "Good enough for me."

I hesitate, but only for a few seconds, before I suck it up and tell them the rest. "Any moment, the machine will ramp up and restart the alchemy of worlds. We don't have much time to prepare, but I know what we need to do."

Allison, who had been relaxing on a cot, suddenly springs forward, her gaze pinned to me. "You have a plan?"

"Yes. It will probably sound one hundred percent insane, but please hear me out before knocking it down or duct-taping me to a chair."

"We only duct tape men to chairs," Grant says. "The ones who act like jerks."

Allison rolls her eyes at Grant, then looks at me. "Go on, sweetie. Tell us your plan."

"Here's the short version." I square my shoulders and lift my chin. "We invoke the Tria Prima to take control of the machine and the Echo."

A furrow forms over Allison's nose. "The Tria Prima doesn't exist anymore. It consisted of me, Dax, and Sefton. But I severed our quantum entanglement on the day Sefton died."

"You three were the original Tria Prima. I'm talking about forming a new, stronger version that doesn't involve a wacko who loves dark magics."

"That's interesting," Dax says. "But even a new Tria Prima would only involve three people."

Standing my ground before these four people, my friends, takes all the gumption I've got. For months, I've let everyone else do the hard jobs. I was treated like a delicate princess. But that ends now.

"The new Tria Prima," I say, "includes three couples. The triangle will be formed by those groups, not individuals."

"Couples?" Erin says. "You can't mean..."

"Us. You and Grant, Dax and Allison, and me and Gabriel. We are the real Tria Prima."

Dax gives me a skeptical look. "But the triangle that initiated the apocalypse was three individuals. What makes you think three couples can initiate a new Tria Prima? Especially when Gabriel is being held hostage by a machine."

"You let me worry about Gabriel." If I told them how I intend to ensure our side of the triangle holds up, they would never let me do it. But I'm a grown woman, not a child, and I make my own decisions. "What I need from you guys is your total commitment to this plan. If you don't believe in the Tria Prima, it will never work."

Erin approaches me and lays a hand on my shoulder. "Tell us more about it. Knowing how you came to this conclusion will help us understand."

"Okay." I realize I've been clenching my hands, and I force myself to relax them. "I came to the conclusion that we need a new Tria Prima because I had a revelation while I was studying the journal. Remember I said I could feel the text on the pages? Well, I believe the journal was giving me subconscious clues. Once I understood that, I could more easily see what the Echo needs me to do."

"But the Echo kicked you to the curb, sweetie. Why would it give you clues that might help you destroy it?"

That's another part of my plan that I'd intended to share after I convince them to participate in the most important part. "Let me finish telling you about the Tria Prima first, okay?"

"Sure. I'll zip it." Erin smiles with her lips closed and makes a zipper motion across them. Then she winks and returns to Grant, where they both sit on chairs.

Dax rarely sits down during these kinds of discussions. He prefers to stand behind the others with his arms folded over his massive chest. And that's what he's doing right now.

"To form the new Tria Prima," I say, "we all need to be on board. I know this is a big ask, but let me lay out the scene for you. Dax and Allison were, and as far as any of us know still are, the Anchor and the Catalyst. Erin and Grant are the Lifeblood and the Heart of the Echo, while Gabriel and I are two halves of the Brain. Don't you see? The Echo laid out this plan before we ever set foot in the other world."

Dax seems about to speak—and disagree, no doubt—but I raise a hand to stop him. He smirks a touch but doesn't say anything.

"I believe, though I have no concrete evidence to support the theory, that the Echo is not entirely Sefton Stainthorpe's construct." I wait a couple of seconds, strictly to let that statement sink into their minds. "He created it, yes. But Dax and Allison were integral to the spells that crafted the Echo world itself and the magics that control it."

"Which means what?" Dax asks.

"That you and Allison are a part of the Echo, just as much if not more than Sefton was. Now Grant and Erin have become an integral element too. We have our new Tria Prima, which I believe will be far stronger than the original."

Grant smiles and nods. "I knew you were a genius in disguise, Sarah. Glad you finally let your wings unfurl."

"You don't think I'm insane?"

"No. I think you're amazing."

I can't help blushing a little. Only Gabriel has ever given me a compliment like that.

Dax clears his throat. "I'll reserve my judgment for after Sarah explains the rest of her plan."

And this is the part that will probably convince them I am insane after all. Here we go…

I resist the impulse to bite my lip and glance at each of my friends in turn. "We are going to sever the Echo from the Earth, leaving it as a completely separate world that, I believe, exists only in a parallel universe of magics."

Dax lifts one brow. "That would strand all the Echo creatures who have invaded this world. They will have free rein to wreak havoc on Earth."

"Like they don't already?" Erin says. She shakes her head. "But I'm sure Sarah has more to tell us."

"Yes. That's not my whole plan," I say. "We will also send all the bad creatures back into the Echo just before we sever it from Earth. Good creatures will be allowed to stay here."

Grant raises both his brows. "Are you talking about only Aldith and Jarek? Or other creatures too?"

"All the good ones."

"How are you going to separate the good ones from the demons?"

"With the power of the Echo's Brain, once Gabriel and I take command of it."

"Allison will not enter the Echo," Dax states, his tone fierce. "We will not risk our child's life on a mad scheme like this one."

"I never intended for Allison to go into the Echo. None of you will. I need you here on Earth."

They all stare at me like I've suggested I want them to strip naked and dance in circles around a bonfire.

"Can you guys trust me or not?" I ask. "Because everything depends on you four. No matter what Gabriel and I do, it means nothing without our allies."

"Will you bring Aldith and Jarek in on this?" Grant asks.

"Yes. But I wanted to make sure you guys are in before I tell them." I can't deny I'm a little depressed by their reticence about my plan. But I'd known the moment I conceived it that this would take some serious convincing. "Here's what I need from you guys. Dax and Allison will go to the epicenter of the apocalypse on Earth. That means Fort Worth, Texas. Grant and Erin will go to the point on the planet that is equidistant from Fort Worth."

"Allison cannot go to Texas," Dax snarls. "She's eight months pregnant, and Fort Worth is still a dangerous place."

"I know. But I have a plan for that too."

He sharpens his gaze on me. "It had better be good."

"We will pool our Echo powers to cast a protection spell on Allison. No creatures will be able to touch her."

"Suddenly, you're an expert on magics. That's bollocks."

"No, it isn't." I take a breath and exhale out my frustration. I understand Dax's concerns, and I would never want to put Allison in danger. But I can't figure out how to explain this in a way that will convince Dax. If he says no, my entire scheme falls apart. "You don't know what happened in the castle, while Gabriel and I were there together. Before the quantum ghost of Sefton appeared. We shared more than sex. We forged a bond so deep that I can't even describe it. We met a few days ago, yet I feel closer to him than to anyone else in the world. I know our connection will provide the power we need to complete the mission."

"We're meant to rely on what a book told you to do."

"No, Dax, that's not what I'm saying. Gabriel and I activated the journal, unknowingly, and that's why it provided information to us that no one else had seen."

Erin is watching me with a tight expression. "Don't mean to rain on your parade, Sarah, but we have solid reasons for being skeptical. You have amnesia. That means you don't remember the alchemy of worlds and all the horrific things that happened in the days after the apocalypse began. We do. This world is full of Echo creatures who poured out of the gateway and swarmed the Earth. We fought them. We lost loved ones because of them. Every single person in Sanctuary has experienced the horrors of the apocalypse—except for you."

She's not being nasty or insulting me. I expected this reaction, but I can't deny that I feel completely deflated by having the truth thrust in my face like a pin popping a balloon. But I can't let that stop me. The stakes are too high. So it's time to reveal my biggest revelation.

"While I was inside that castle earlier, with Gabriel pinned to that machine, I experienced what you might call an epiphany." I feel my fingers wanting to curl into my palms, but I order them not to do that. "I believe my amnesia is not a fluke. It's part of a plan so vast and incredible that I don't know how to describe it. The best word would be fate. I remember men trying to protect me when the alchemy of worlds started, and I believe they somehow realized I would become an important link in the chain of saving the world."

My friends exchange surprised looks. But are they surprised by how bonkers I am? Or by how much they believe what I said?

"My amnesia gives me a different perspective," I say. "You might say I have a clean slate on which to draw my conclusions. I'm not riddled with pain and guilt over loved ones I've lost. My opinions and actions aren't colored by experiences during the alchemy of worlds and everything that came later. Maybe I'm the one who thought of this plan because I have no memories of the first days of the apocalypse. And I'm not hindered by constant worry about what happened to my family and friends, if I have any of those."

They all stare at me again. But I think I see a glimmer of understanding in their eyes, and maybe, just maybe, the beginnings of acceptance.

A horrendous racket erupts in the sky, and the ground shudders violently.

I stumble sideways. Dax tries to reach Allison, but trips and tumbles to the ground. Allison slides off her cot to huddle beside her husband. Erin and Grant cling to each other, until they see me struggling to stay on my feet. Then they both rush over to me, and we huddle together while the most bizarre mechanical noises I've ever heard rattle and screech and scrape in the air. The noises are so loud that I wince and squeeze my eyes shut.

Whump. Whump. Whump.

The concussions vibrate through my entire body. As the mechanical noises fade away, screams pierce the air.

Whump. Whump.

The roars of Echo creatures resound everywhere, and the first slashes of Echo lightning stab into the ground. But unlike before, the lightning sizzles and buzzes like electricity racing through a high-tension line.

"Stay here with Allison," Dax tells me. "The rest of us will see what's going on."

"The machine is angry, that's what," I say. "It wants to destroy both worlds."

"Remain here. We will inspect the situation."

Dax, Erin, and Grant rush outside.

I should be out there with them, since I know about the machine and they don't. But I won't leave Allison alone.

Explosions detonate outside, too close and too powerful. They make the ground shudder like an earthquake.

Crack. The sound reverberates in the clearing that surrounds the camp. I've heard that sound before.

A falling tree splits the tent open and smacks down.

Chapter Twenty-Three

Gabriel

THE MACHINE HUMS AND WHIRS AND EMITS A HARSH RATCHETING noise, while the creatures begin to chant again, though I still can't recognize any words in the sounds they make. Energy crackles through my bindings, pinching and biting at my skin. I grit my teeth against the pain and try to focus on a way to escape, or at least halt, the machine's actions.

What is it doing? How many people will it mow down in its determination to complete its task?

The ghost of Sefton appears in front of me. He smiles just like the Cheshire cat, so smug and hungry for blood. "It has begun. Stop trying to find a weakness in the machine. There is none. Once the process has completed, I will no longer require you."

"Bullshit. You don't have the power to keep the alchemical reaction going. Or have you forgotten what happened after Allison shut it down? Fallenmouth was devoured, but the rest of the world went into a kind of stasis."

How do I know that? Through my connection with Sarah, I think.

Sefton lifts his chin. "This time is different."

"Delude yourself all you want. But if you kill me, in six months you'll regret it."

Will he? No idea. I'm snowing him to buy time.

But I don't believe what he said. *It has begun.* I don't think so. The machine has been making all kinds of noises, but I don't feel anything different, certainly not the kind of magics that restarting the alchemy of worlds would require. He'll need me and Sarah for that. But that bastard will never get his hands on her. She's tougher, smarter, and stronger than he thinks.

He clearly has turned the machine up to a higher setting, one that probably uses more energy. Maybe I can leverage that. If it's struggling, why can't I make its job even harder?

I close my eyes and focus all my thoughts on the clamps that hold me in place, funneling every bit of supernatural energy inside me on the task of loosening the bindings. Nothing happens. I keep trying. Slow, deep breaths. Relax my muscles. I need to stop consciously trying to affect the machine and let instinct take over. The energies grow inside me, spreading outward from my chest, into my arms and legs. The magics rush up into my head, buzzing in my brain.

The strength of the magics makes my heart pound and sweat break out on my brow. I struggle to take normal breaths, but I will not give up no matter how hard the energies hit me.

A loud thunk echoes inside the throne room, and the machine winds down. I'm still trapped inside it, but at least the thing has lost power. For how long? At least I can relax, for now, while I consider what my next move is. I let my lids fall shut and sag against my bindings.

"Gabriel? Are you hurt?"

My lids fly open, and I gape at the woman standing a few yards away on the dais.

Aldith has her hands clasped in front of her, as always, but she's wringing them so hard that I wonder if she's abrading her own skin.

"What's up, Aldith?" I ask. "You should be hiding."

"I couldn't stay where you and Sarah left me. Jarek came for me, and I learned that the machine is on the verge of reaching its full capacity." She meets my gaze briefly, then winces. "You are its full capacity."

"No, I'm half of it. As long as Sarah doesn't come back here, the machine will never get what it wants."

"Buy you cannot take control of it without her."

I just manage to stifle a growl. "Yeah, go on and shout that a little louder, would you? Not sure Sefton's quantum ghost heard you."

She tips her head to the side. "I am trying to help you, Gabriel."

"Yeah, I know. I'm sorry, Aldith. It's not your fault I can't stop this machine from destroying both worlds."

"The only way Sefton wins is if you give up. His mortal self wrought untold devastation on two worlds, and now a remnant of his magics may do the same thing. You must keep fighting, please."

She sounds worried. No, more than worried. I think Aldith is terrified of what might happen if the Brain succeeds in recreating the alchemy of worlds. Maybe it already has. I hear explosions outside. Since this room has no windows, I can't see the lightning bolts and fireballs, but I have no doubts they're out there.

"You must find Sarah," Aldith says. "This time, the apocalypse has no boundaries, because no one has control of it."

"I get it, we're in deep shit. Don't need to keep harping on the issue."

She glances around as if she's looking for something—maybe the ghost of Sefton Stainthorpe. "I must go. But please, Gabriel, never stop fighting. Both worlds need you."

Aldith vanishes.

I've never seen another Echo creature do that. Of course, I hadn't seen a human do that until I met Sarah. I suppose Aldith is different from other Echo beings, and that's why she protects the stronghold.

Now what? I shut down the machine, but it still has a hold on me. I stand here, held in place by metal clamps and plates, and listen while the apocalyptic sounds outside draw closer and closer to the castle. The floor begins to vibrate with every concussion. The machine vibrates too, only a little at first, then growing stronger as the lightning and fireballs continue to assault the ground.

What are the odds that Sefton cast a protection spell around this building to spare it from the apocalypse? If he didn't, I won't need to worry about how to get out of this machine. I'll die when the monstrous thing crashes down on me.

The creatures become restless, milling around like they don't know what to do. They begin to grunt, louder than before, and jostle each other as they move around, apparently without any idea what they're doing.

Great. Disturbed creatures are exactly what I need right now.

The room around me shifts and fades away, replaced by a dark void with a single ray of light emanating from above. But when I glance up, I can't see the source, only the diffuse glow.

Five figures appear in a circle that includes me.

"How did you guys get here?" I ask. "And how did I get here?"

Sarah clasps my hand. "We needed a safe place to talk about our plans, and we needed you to be here with us. Since we couldn't risk Sefton hearing what we say, the five of us managed to create a bubble of magic that exists outside the realm of reality."

"Uh, sure, whatever you say." I must be hallucinating. Magic bubbles? Come on.

"I know it sounds crazy." Sarah leans against me, lifting her head to meet my gaze. "But you know what I can do. I teleported myself straight into the castle from Earth. And with four friends to help, it shouldn't be a surprise that we could create this bubble. We're more powerful together."

"You're right, I know. So just tell me what this is all about."

"It's happened. Sefton's quantum remnant has restarted the alchemy of worlds. We need to stop it, once and for all, so neither world will be subject to a mad man's whims ever again."

"Okay, good plan. But how do we implement it?"

Dax steps forward. "We are going to tap into the power of the Tria Prima."

"I thought the Tria Prima was you, Allison, and Sefton."

"Yes, it was. Sarah pointed out that we have a new version of the Tria Prima that may prove even stronger than the original." He hooks an arm around Allison, tugging her close. "The six of us represent the new Tria Prima, the power that can stop the alchemy of worlds. This was all Sarah's idea, and we believe she's right."

"Six of us?"

"That's right," Sarah says. "Three couples whose undying love and strength might be the key to ending the apocalypse forever—Dax and Allison, Grant and Erin, and you and me."

A chill rushes over my skin, but I'm not afraid. This is a shiver of excitement. When Sarah spoke those words, telling me about the New Tria Prima, I felt something indescribable, something so deep and immutable that I know everything she said is true. Three couples. Of course the way to end the apocalypse is for the six of us to flip Sefton's idea on its head. Not one group of three, but three distinct groups that together possess more power than even the original Sefton Stainthorpe.

This might just work.

"How do we do this?" I ask. "You said you have a plan."

Sarah ducks under my arm to slide hers around my waist, and I instinctively wrap my arm around her. "It begins with the two of us seizing control of the machine to shut down the alchemy of worlds."

"How, exactly?"

"Through the power of the Tria Prima. Dax and Allison will go to Fort Worth, which is the epicenter of the apocalypse. Then Erin and Grant will travel to a spot on the other side of the world that's equidistant from Fort Worth. At the same time, you and I will be inside the castle in the Echo, since that seems to be the epicenter of everything in that world."

She really has thought about this. The journal ignited something inside her, and she is no longer just a girl with amnesia. Sarah has become a powerful woman.

I could kiss her right now.

"How do we shut down the apocalypse?" I ask. "I've tried to stop the machine, but the most I could do was shut it down for a while. I can feel it ramping up again even now."

"You haven't been able to shut it down completely because you didn't have me. We're one corner of the Tria Prima triangle, remember? You and I need to stop the machine together."

"Have you found a way to get me out of the machine? Can't see any other way that we can both shut it down."

"I think it's best if I show you what I mean."

Dax chuckles. "Why be shy about it now? We had a group discussion on the subject back in the tent, before everything went to hell—again."

I squint at Sarah. "What is he talking about?"

"The alchemy of worlds has started up again."

"Yeah, I know that. But Dax just said you guys had a group discussion about something that you don't want to tell me."

"I was going to tell you. Just not in front of the others."

Dax is smirking. Allison seems amused. Grant wears a calm expression, while Erin seems to be trying not to smile.

"Somebody tell me what the hell is going on," I say. "We don't have time to dance around whatever it is."

"You're right," Sarah says. "We've realized that sex is a vital component of stopping the apocalypse."

I stare at her. Is my mouth hanging open? I think it might be. For a moment, I can't think, much less come up with words. Sarah just announced that to save the world, we need to fuck. Yeah, I'm pretty sure that's what she meant. Not that I mind. But come on, we can't talk about sex in front of the others.

"We felt weird about it too, at first," Grant says. "But then we realized Sarah is right—and she's a genius."

"I knew that already," I say. "But how does getting naked save the worlds?"

Sarah rests her chin on my chest. "The first time Dax and Allison made love, it increased her Echo power. Erin and Grant experienced the same thing. You and I felt the same thing. Didn't we?"

"Well, yeah. But I don't know if I can, uh, get in the right frame of mind to do that right now. Besides, I'm still trapped in the machine."

"Don't worry about that."

"How do you plan to get around it? Having sex kind of requires physical contact."

She pats my chest. "Let me worry about that. You trust me, don't you?"

"Of course I do."

"Then trust me on this."

How can I say no to her? She's amazing, and I will do whatever she says we need to do. The fact that I love screwing her has nothing to do with my decision.

But I suddenly remember something. "Allison is very pregnant. We can't risk sending her to the epicenter of the apocalypse."

"We've taken care of that," Sarah says. "Using our combined Echo powers, we cast a protection spell around Allison."

"Can't we all get one of those?"

"We didn't want to deplete our magics when we still need to implement the plan. Allison needed the most protection. The rest of us can take care of ourselves."

She's right. We shouldn't waste energy. Because I have a feeling that we'll need every iota we have to defeat Sefton's quantum ghost and end the chaos.

"Okay," I tell Sarah. "Let's get this train rolling."

"There's one more thing we all need to discuss." She glances at each of our friends, then lifts her gaze to mine. "I believe we can restore the Earth to the way it was before the apocalypse, but there's a caveat."

"What is it?"

"I can't guarantee we will remember who we are now. The spell might erase our memories of everything before the Echo, and then we wouldn't know we ever loved each other." She glances at our friends again. "Or that we became a family."

We all just stand here, frozen and silent, as we digest what Sarah said. Forget her? Never. But we're talking about magics, and nothing is ever certain with that stuff. My life before the apocalypse had been dull and lonely. Then I got thrown into the hell of the Echo and became someone I never imagined I could become. The computer programmer turned into a fighter.

I'd love to say adios to the alchemy of worlds and see the Earth returned to its natural state. But I never want to give up the best thing that ever happened to me—finding Sarah. She taught me more than I could ever explain and changed me in all the best ways.

To lose her love… I'd rather die than forget about her.

Dax pulls Allison into his arms. "That's a hefty price to pay for saving the world. But we don't have a choice, do we? And you said you don't know for certain that we will lose our memories of knowing each other."

"That's right," Sarah says. "I believe with all my heart that we won't forget each other. But I won't swear it's a certainty. You need to know the risks."

Dax and Allison gaze into each other's eyes, and he brushes his fingers over his wife's cheek. "We must risk it."

She nods, as tears brim in her eyes.

Erin throws her arms around Grant's neck and whispers into his ear. He nods, and they both seem to be choked up. Grant sounds that way when he says, "We're on board, whatever might happen. Bringing back the world everyone used to know is worth the risk. And I believe, like Sarah does, that we won't forget each other."

I pull Sarah close and kiss her. "Whatever comes next, remember one thing. I will love you until the day I die and beyond, until the universe explodes and there's nothing left. I'll love you forever, and nothing can erase that."

She flings her arms around my neck and rises onto her tiptoes to whisper, "Destiny brought us together, and that's how I know we will survive—and remember."

But we all understand what we're risking and how it might all go sideways.

"It's time to go our separate ways," Sarah says. "Go to your assigned locations, while I find a way to reach Gabriel."

"You're going in well-prepared," Dax tells her. "And we all know you can do this."

The others disappear, leaving me and Sarah alone in this bubble of magic.

She gives me a small smile. "See you soon."

Then she's gone.

And I'm back inside the machine.

CHAPTER TWENTY-FOUR

Sarah

WE RETURN FROM OUR TRIP INTO THE BUBBLE AND DISCOVER THAT the world has gone insane in the meantime. Not only do fireballs and lightning slam into the earth, but Echo creatures attack every human they see. Everyone in Sanctuary has learned how to fight, and they wield all sorts of weapons to fight off the beasts. Flying creatures keep swooping down in their attempts to snag a meal.

Yes, everyone here can fight—except for me. My friends thought I needed to be protected. But now, I need to breach Sefton's castle, without having any idea what I'll do if I can't simply teleport into the throne room. I don't have training in how to defend myself, but it can't be that hard to stab a monster with a sword.

"I need a weapon," I say. "In case I have to fight my way into the castle. The machine doesn't want me there."

"Okay," Grant says. We're shouting to be heard above the din. "But I think you'd be better off locating a weapon inside the Echo. I can tell you where to find a sporting goods store that has firearms and lots of other stuff."

"That's a good idea," Erin says. "But we should give her a crash course on how to operate a gun."

Dax has his big body wrapped around Allison, shielding her from the melee. "We will head to Fort Worth and find a place to hide that's near the gateway. Let's agree to enact the plan in thirty minutes."

We all agree, and Dax whisks his wife away. I know that they, along with Grant and Erin, have been keeping their watches synchronized just in case something like this happened and we needed to find each other. I also know they had agreed that, if the worst happened, they would teleport to search for each other once every hour.

But I don't have a watch.

Grant and Erin shepherd me into the woods, where the creatures haven't yet decided to hunt. They will soon, I'm sure. The melee is a bit quieter here, the noises dulled by the trees.

"I need a watch," I say. "Otherwise, we won't be synchronized."

"Take mine," Erin says. "I'll be with Grant, so we can share his watch. But time can move differently in the Echo, so we might end up not synchronized after all."

"No choice. This is the best we can do."

For the next ten minutes, my friends give me that crash course Erin had mentioned. It sounds like operating an automatic machine gun isn't that difficult. Of course, hearing about it isn't the same as actually handling such a weapon.

Erin and Grant both hug me, then teleport to their assigned location.

And I transport myself directly into the Echo. The machine didn't try to stop me. Maybe quantum Sefton is distracted by orchestrating mayhem. I can't assume that will keep him occupied for much longer, so I teleport to the shop Erin and Grant had mentioned. I find the items they recommended—a machine gun, extra magazines for it, and a machete. That's a long, wicked-looking knife. Maybe I was a badass in my life before amnesia, because I don't feel weird at all about fighting my way into the castle.

Erin had also recommended a few more items. Grenades are pretty straightforward to use. Pull the pin and throw the grenade. I dump the grenades and the extra magazines of ammo into a canvas bag and sling that over my shoulder.

Then I zip myself to the castle.

But I wind up at the base of the mountain on which the castle rests. It would take forever for me to climb up the steep cliff. I try again to teleport, but the wards around the mountain prevent it.

I hear so much chaos throughout the Capital City that I can't sort out which noises indicate what type of danger. The sky has become crimson. The stench of rotting flesh and blood fills the air.

Oh God, is it this bad in Fort Worth?

I refuse to look back. There's no point. I need to focus on finding a way up the cliff. Only by stopping the apocalypse can I save any innocent Echo beings that still live here.

The ground shudders.

Probably fireballs punching into the earth.

I try to climb the cliff, but I can't even get a hand-hold. The wards prevent it.

A large hand scoops me up, lifting me to the height of the cliff top.

I glance over my shoulder and realize I'm cradled in Jarek's enormous palm. He can give me a lift to the top of the mountain, but I still have the wards to deal with before I can get anywhere near the castle.

But I can feel Gabriel in there, reaching out to me.

Jarek fists his other hand, pulls it back, and slams his fist into the wards. They crackle and shimmer but remain in place.

"Do that again," I say. "And I'll focus on tapping into my connection with Gabriel."

The second I attempt to reach him, I sense the warmth and love and passion he feels for me coming down through our connection, feeding into my passion for him. I suck in a breath, stunned by the ferocity of our shared emotions and desires.

Jarek rams his fist into the wards.

They shatter with a sound like breaking glass and a rush of released magics. But I have no time to waste. I leap off Jarek's palm, shout "thank you" to him, and race toward the castle gates.

A figure appears there just as I reach the gates. Aldith wears an expression I've never seen from her before—resolute determination. "If you have a weapon to spare, I would like to fight with you."

"I'd be grateful for the help. Would you prefer a gun or a machete?"

"Whichever is easiest to use. I have no training in weaponry."

"Neither do I, but my friends gave me a crash course." I dig inside my bag and bring out the machine gun. "Try this. You pull the trigger and it shoots a volley of bullets. I have extra ammunition too."

I get out the extra clips and show her how to switch them out, something I learned less than half an hour ago from my friends. Was I in the military before the apocalypse? Doesn't matter. Today, I have become a warrior—and so has Aldith.

When I check my watch, I see that we have seventeen minutes to break into the castle and enact the plan my friends and I devised. My heart rate spikes, and I feel a strange mix of excitement and fear. What we're about to do... It's beyond epic. If we survive, this will be the most incredible feat in the history of the world.

The castle gates are closed. When Aldith and I try to open them, we can't do it. The wooden barrier is too thick and strong.

A large metal-and-flesh hand reaches around us to tap the gates. They fly open.

"Thank you, Jarek," I shout to the golem.

Aldith and I storm the castle.

But we find only an empty courtyard and an empty entryway. The Echo creatures who guard Gabriel haven't sent any of their brethren to protect the rest of the building. They must assume that no one can breach the castle. We slow down as we approach the doorway to the throne room, which has become the machine room, and we hear a strange humming that does not sound mechanical.

I recognize the sound. It's the creatures who are guarding Gabriel.

Aldith and I stop in the corridor, sidling up to the wall beside the doorway. My watch tells me we have ten minutes left.

I whisper to Aldith, "Get your gun ready. We're going in there, and those creatures won't be happy about it. If you need to run, do it."

"No, I will not leave you."

"Please, Aldith. If the creatures try to swarm you, just run. Teleport away if you can. Getting yourself killed won't help anybody."

"All right."

She doesn't sound happy about what I told her, but I know she will do as I asked.

Now, it's time to storm the throne room.

But we don't burst in, surrounded by a hail of bullets. No, I have a different plan, and it depends on the creatures behaving the way they have since the moment the machine revealed itself.

Aldith stays huddled just out of sight, at the threshold.

I walk into the room, working hard to stop myself from seeming anxious, and casually pass by the creatures who are arrayed around the periphery of the room, including at either side of the doorway. Though my pulse kicks up a couple of extra notches, I remain outwardly calm. The creatures don't seem to notice me, not yet. They're chanting wordlessly while rocking side to side.

Gabriel watches me.

He probably wants to tell me to go away, but he knows as well as I do that any sound might set off the creatures. I hold my machete in one hand, while I have the canvas bag over my opposite shoulder. The grenades are in there. I hope I don't need them, but I won't hesitate if they threaten me or Gabriel.

A shiver sweeps over my skin from head to toe, raising every hair on my body.

I glance around, but the creatures still seem entranced and unaware of my presence. But my intuition warned me to watch out. That's what the shiver meant. Something is about to happen, and I need to be hyper-aware of my surroundings.

Halfway across the room, I stop. Another shiver, much colder than the first, tingles over my skin. I look around but can't see anything. That doesn't mean nothing is going to happen. If my intuition needs to warn me about something, I'll pay attention.

But I won't stop. I can't.

So I start walking again.

Gabriel mouths, "No."

He doesn't really expect me to stop. He knows me too well to believe I'll do that.

A shimmering curtain of magics drops down at the foot of the steps, enveloping the entire dais and the machine. Wards? If quantum Sefton wants a fight, he's about to get one.

I approach the invisible barrier and speak in a calm tone. "Come out, Sefton, and let me see you. Or are you afraid of me?"

"Afraid? Hardly." The ghost of Sefton has appeared on the dais, between me and Gabriel. "You are a foolish child, coming here alone."

He doesn't realize Aldith is in the corridor. Guess he's not all-knowing.

"Why didn't you let me see you last time?" I ask. "If you aren't afraid, you had no reason to hide from me."

"I simply had no desire or need to speak to you."

The sounds of the apocalypse in full swing continue outside, though the ruckus became a background noise the moment Aldith and I entered the castle. I suppose the real Sefton didn't want to hear the agony and suffering of living beings and made sure to dull the noise in his cliff-top hideaway.

"I want to talk to Gabriel," I tell Sefton. "Take down your wards and let me approach the machine so I can speak to him. Please."

Might as well try politeness first.

He glances down at the machete in my hand, then raises his brows. "Why on earth would I do that? You mean to murder me. Not that you will succeed. I have no physical form."

"I know that. This weapon is for your minions, in case they get a little too frisky."

A quick glance at my watch warns me I have only six minutes to complete my task. Screw this. If the ghost of Sefton Stainthorpe won't get out of my way, I'll move him myself.

I shift slightly to the side, where I can see Gabriel, and tap into the connection between us, which makes his eyes flare wide for a split second. Then he reverts to the neutral expression he's worn ever since I entered the room. The power we share sizzles inside me, enlivening my skin and diving deep beneath it to awaken the most sensual parts of me. My nipples tighten. I grow slick between my thighs. The nature of our shared magics has always been erotic, and I no longer worry about why.

I revel in it.

We gaze into each other's eyes, and I feel the Echo energies gathering inside us both.

"Stop that," Sefton snarls. "Stop it now, or I'll have my disciples do it for you."

I ignore him and focus on Gabriel as the energies infiltrate my body, rushing through every part of me and down to my bones too.

"Kill her!" Sefton shouts.

The creatures rouse from their stupor and run toward me.

Automatic gunfire erupts from the doorway, but I don't have time to worry about Aldith or the creatures. The power inside me and Gabriel has reached critical mass, and it's time to unleash it. A ball of sizzling white energy appears between us.

I hurl it at the wards.

They don't shatter, because I don't want them to do that. Instead, the wards let me slip through them, then they seal behind me. Sefton has been ejected from the dais and now lies sprawled on the floor.

"No, Sarah," Gabriel says as I approach the machine. "Please, don't—"

"We've all agreed. This is the only way. You can't back out now, or both worlds will be destroyed."

He shuts his eyes briefly. "I know this is the only way, but I worry about what the magics will do to you."

I clasp his face in my hands. "Stop thinking. It's time to let our instincts take over."

Gabriel's brows knit together, but he seems to be looking at something behind me. I turn to look. Aldith is knocking down Echo creatures like they were bowling balls, though all the bullets in the universe probably can't kill those monsters. But she's buying us time, and that's all I needed her to do.

"Run, Aldith," I shout. "Find a place to hide."

Sefton leaps to his feet and races toward Aldith with his teeth bared, screaming like an enraged animal.

I drop the machete and my bag, then strip off my clothes.

Gabriel's dick is hardening. That's exactly what needs to happen right now. His breathing grows heavier, and he licks his lips as he watches me walk up to the Vitruvian Man device. He shakes his head. "We can't. I'm stuck in this machine and—"

"Let me handle this."

I kneel before him and take his cock in my mouth, pumping the base with one hand while I lick and tease the head. He sucks in a breath. I keep working him with my mouth and hand until I can feel he's on the verge of orgasm. Then I stand up.

"Sarah…" His voice trails off, but the rough tone makes my clit throb.

I climb onto the machine, setting my feet on top of his, then shift my soles onto the inner set of clamps while I place my arms in the second set of clamps that lie just below where his arms are locked in position. The machine wakes up, buzzing and thunking and whirring. The clamps snap into place around my arms, and the action lifts my feet onto my toes. Now I'm attached to the machine in the same way he is. But the fact that I'm shorter than he is means that his cock rubs against me but I can't get him nestled between my folds. The vibrations of the machine increase my arousal, and I've become so wet that the slickness dribbles down my inner thighs.

"Unhook us from the machine," I say, my voice huskier and laden with desire. "We can do it together."

The desire that keeps mounting inside me has stolen my breath. I want him more than I ever have before, and I can tell from the darkening of his eyes and the way his cock jerks against me that Gabriel is experiencing the same intense need.

The machine ramps up, its power vibrating through the floor and into our bodies, as if it's giving us whatever we need to accomplish our task. Only one thing remains.

A surge of power rushes out of the machine and into us. The man-size wheel pops free and falls to the floor face-down. I'm crushed under Gabriel, but I'm not injured. The clamps loosen enough that I can wriggle upward to get his cock into position and slide it inside me.

"Fuck me, Gabriel," I say. "Fuck me now."

Chapter Twenty-Five

Gabriel

I HAVE NO CONTROL OVER MY BODY, AND I DON'T CARE. THE POWER WE share has taken command. The feel of Sarah's body wrapped around my cock steals any thoughts I might've had, and I relinquish myself to her. Even the machine seems to want her, the way it molded itself to her body the instant she stepped into it, then tipped the wheel over to give us the perfect position. So what if we're trapped under the machine? It's feeding us the energy we need. I have just enough leeway to thrust into her, over and over, helpless to stop. Not that I want to stop. Making love to Sarah to save the world is one order I'm happy to comply with, again and again.

The wards around the machine have turned opaque, almost like the Echo wants to give us privacy for this.

She moans when I rock my hips with more vigor and the energies that surround us begin to cling to our skin and sink beneath it. I've never felt anything like it. My ears have started to ring, and black spots appear in my vision, but still, I need to keep fucking her.

The machine is vibrating and shaking, and I can see quantum Sefton standing at the edge of the dais, holding his head in his hands while shrieking in agony.

Don't care. I need to make Sarah come, and nothing else matters. She has her face mashed to my chest, and my flesh muffles her screams, though she hasn't hit that peak yet. I thrust deeper and harder, straining the clamps with the force of my movements, desperate to break free. The pressure inside me intensifies, and my dick feels like it might explode if I can't give her what she needs.

I shift the angle of my thrusts minutely, but it's enough. Now I'm rubbing against her clit with every movement, no longer trying to get as deep inside her as possible, only caring that she needs to climax right now. Faster, faster, I scrape her nub.

Sarah squeezes her eyes shut and screams.

I thrust deep and hold that position, while her body clenches me, her cries become hoarse, and her eyes roll back in her head.

The clamps pop open.

We tumble to the floor, still entangled, and the wheel swings back up into the machine. I lock my hands around Sarah's wrists to hold them above her head.

"Don't stop," she pleads. "Please, don't stop."

No way in hell I'll give up now. Lying sprawled on top of her, I keep pumping into her wildly, grunting and shouting, gazing into her eyes the entire time. Fire scorches down my spine and straight into my cock, like nothing I've ever experienced before. My back bows up, and I explode inside her.

Sarah screams and comes again. Her body milks me while I keep coming, buried so deep inside her that it seems impossible. By the time it's over, we're both boneless and stunned, incapable of moving or speaking. Taking a breath seems like a Herculean task. My head rests over Sarah's heart, every beat thumping in time with mine. After a few minutes—or maybe a few hours, who knows—I slide off her and pull Sarah into my arms.

"Do you hear that?" she asks.

"Hear what?"

"The silence."

I freeze, listening for any sound. But I hear only my own heartbeat and the soft sound of her breaths. The wards have disintegrated, I can tell that much. The machine has shut down. I should hear noises from outside, shouldn't I? And the creatures who guarded the machine ought to be making noises too.

"Did we do it?" I ask. "Did we stop the alchemy of worlds?"

"Seems like it."

I sit up and look around, surprised to find all the Echo creatures lying dead on the floor.

Aldith stands near the doorway, biting her lip.

"Did you do that?" I ask. "You're holding a machine gun, so I figured..."

Aldith nods. "I didn't mean to shoot them all, but they kept coming at me."

"You did what you had to do. They were lunatics." I glance at Sarah, who lies huddled on the floor, as if she's cold. "Better get dressed. Our work isn't done yet."

While she finds her clothes and pulls them on, I stand up and search for my stuff. My clothes kind of just disappeared, so I don't know if I can find it again. Every time I glance at Aldith, she swerves her gaze away from me, then covertly peeks. Maybe she's never seen a naked man before. She did live in the stronghold, all alone.

Sarah squints and flattens her lips.

My clothes appear in her arms. "Better cover up that sexy body. Don't think Aldith knows how to deal with nudity."

I pull on my clothes, then lead the ladies out of the throne room. We bump into a few creatures, but they seem dazed and uninterested in causing trouble. Outside, we find Jarek waiting to give us and Aldith a ride to the gateway. Our job isn't done yet. The most daunting task still lies ahead of us.

Reversing the damage to both worlds.

When we reach the gateway, we discover it's wide open—wider than usual, in fact. The opening stretches across the horizon, though it still hangs high above the ground. Jarek could easily walk through it, but instead of doing that, he hesitates and looks at us.

"Go on through," Sarah says. "You're coming with us. Once all the good Echo beings have escaped, all the bad ones will be locked inside that world. You need to leave now."

A distant rumbling draws all our attention to the city behind us. The castle is crumbling and sliding off the steep sides of the mountain.

Good riddance, I say.

Jarek steps through the gateway.

Echo creatures who had loitered nearby—in hopes of catching someone to eat, no doubt—now turn and run away from the golem. We'll catch them later. Right now, we need to find our friends. Jarek crouches to set us down on the wrecked street.

We're in Fort Worth. The apocalypse began here, and it's only fitting that it should end here too. The nightmare Sefton Stainthorpe crafted will vanish, replaced by the beautiful, imperfect world we'd known before the alchemy of worlds. Sefton tried to transmute the Earth into his vision of perfection, and it cost the lives of countless humans and Echo beings, not to mention his own life. Was it worth it? Only Sefton knows if he was satisfied with the result.

Two figures emerge from the shadows in an alley, striding toward us. As they draw closer, I realize it's Dax and Allison.

"How did it go?" Allison asks. "On our end, it seemed to work."

"Yeah, it worked," I say. "The machine and the castle are gone. The Echo will be just a normal planet now, in a parallel universe, and the beings left inside it will need to teach themselves how to live without magics."

"What about the Heart and the Lifeblood?"

Erin and Grant appear in front of us.

Sarah grins at them. "You're back."

"We heard you guys talking about us," Erin says. "Or rather, we sensed you talking about us. Were you guys discussing the Heart and Lifeblood? Felt like you were."

"Yeah, were," I say. "The Echo doesn't need those elements any-more. The Brain, the Lifeblood, and the Heart were simply magical constructs to keep the Echo from crumbling into chaos that would destroy both worlds."

Dax gives me a skeptical look. "How do you know so much about that rubbish?"

"I was connected to the machine. Everything it knew, I knew." I glance up at Jarek, then look at our friends. "We need to bring all the good Echo refugees here, and toss all the bad ones back into the other world. Once we've unbound the Echo and Earth, we'll reverse the damage done to both worlds."

Growling and grunting noises originate from across the street, and I spot figures moving around in the alley.

Jarek lights up his fiery red eyes and bends his knees, like he's about to pounce on those creatures.

They turn around and run away.

But they won't be able to run once we get started on the next part of our plan.

I smirk at our friends. "So, did everybody have a good time during phase one?"

Dax and Erin smirk right back at me, but Allison bites her lip and bows her head, while Grant scratches the back of his neck and glances sideways at Erin. His lips kink up at one corner.

I take that to mean yes, they had a very good time.

"Please tell me," Dax says, "that phase two does not involve sex. I will not participate in an orgy."

"No sex. Though we will need to hold hands." When Dax compresses his lips and squints at me, I raise a palm. "Calm down, Bigfoot. You'll be holding hands with Allison and Erin."

He relaxes and stops giving me the deadly squint.

I've seen way worse nasty looks. His does not impress me.

"Jarek, stay here," I say. "You too, Aldith. We're about to send all the murderous creatures back into the Echo, and we don't want you guys to get sucked in accidentally."

Sarah and I lead the gang back to the gateway, which has expanded, so it reaches all the way to the ground. We link hands one by one until we've formed a circle, then summon all the Echo power we have inside us, the combined strength of six individuals and three couples—the ultimate Tria Prima. Energies begin to swirl in the air around us, and wind erupts, whirling with tornadic strength. We grip each other's hands harder as the magics grow inside us, and a glittering curtain of golden Echo power forms around our group.

Screams. Far away. Coming closer.

Through the curtain of magics, I spot Echo creatures flying through the air toward the gateway. It sucks them in while they keep thrashing in a desperate attempt to escape. Only the evil creatures will be consigned to the Echo forever, and I have no sympathy for them. They chose to become monsters.

They won't die, anyway. They'll have their own world, and it's up to them how they use it.

Shape after shape gets whisked into the Echo, until finally, the last one flies through the gateway. And it telescopes shut, vanishing from sight.

We keep holding hands, because the most arduous and dangerous part of our plan comes next.

"Time to sever the worlds," I say. "And reverse the damage to them."

Sarah grips my hand harder. "We'll remember each other when this is over. I know we will."

Dax glances at Allison. "Everyone will remember the apocalypse, and each other, but we'll be free of the Echo forever."

I swear I can feel the anxiety inside our circle, like a palpable force that might knock our final blast of magics out of whack and wreck what we're trying to do. "Come on, guys, no wistful gazes or repressed anxiety. I spent enough time in that machine to know the Echo feeds on negative emotions. We all have to believe we can do this, or it will go sideways."

"You're right," Grant says. "No worries. I know we can do this."

"That's better."

Dax touches his forehead to Allison's. "I want our child to grow up in a beautiful world. We can do this—for our baby."

She touches her lips to his. "Me too. Let's make it happen."

I glance at Sarah. "No turning back now."

"We don't want to go back. Everyone on Earth needs to move forward, and what we're about to do will make sure that can happen."

While Aldith and Jarek observe from a distance, we begin the new alchemy of worlds, gathering magics from both worlds and transmuting them from bad to good, weaving a spell of such magnitude that I doubt anyone else in any universe has ever attempted something like this. The power once housed in the Echo, in the castle built by Sefton, reels out of that world and into us, whirling around our group like a hurricane wind. We cling to each other's hands to keep from falling down.

Whatever happens now, it's beyond our control.

A monstrous cracking sound originates overhead, from the place where the gateway to the Echo once hovered. The sky splits apart, but not in the same way as it had on that day when one man's fury and madness destroyed the Earth and unleashed hell on two worlds. The cracking gets louder and louder, and though I want to cover my ears, I keep hold of Sarah and Allison's hands, squeezing my eyes shut as the magics inside the Echo are sucked out of that world and dissipate into the air, gone forever.

Silence descends. The most profound silence I've ever experienced.

Then I begin to hear other sounds, things I haven't heard since before the apocalypse. Birds chirping. Leaves rustling. I open my eyes, and the sun blinds me for a moment. Then I realize we're standing on a grassy hill that overlooks a river and the City of Fort Worth.

"Look!" Allison shouts, grinning as she points toward something in the distance. "The library is back."

"You're excited about that?" I say. "What about the green grass and the wildflowers and the lack of a gaping hole in the sky?"

"That's awesome too," Allison says, still grinning as Dax folds an arm around her. "You don't understand. I used to work at the public library. Seeing it again, the way it used to look, is amazing."

Sarah stares at me, her eyes wide. "We did it. The worlds are unbound, Earth has been restored, and we remember everything."

"But do you remember your life before Sanctuary?"

Her face goes blank. Her gaze is aimed directly at me, but she just stands there as if she's turned to stone.

"Sarah?" I grasp her shoulders. "Are you okay?"

"Gabriel..."

She collapses in my arms.

Chapter Twenty-Six

Sarah

I ROUSE GRADUALLY, AT FIRST HEARING ONLY THE SOUND OF MY HEART-beats and my breaths, then noticing the breeze that tickles my face and the feel of strong arms wrapped around me. I smell the unique and indescribable scent of Gabriel, then realize the breeze I thought I'd felt is actually his breaths on my skin. My lids flutter open.

Gabriel hugs me to him even tighter and cradles my cheek in his hand as he gazes into my eyes. "You're awake. How do you feel? What happened?"

"Not sure. I got woozy, and then I must have passed out."

"I know that. But how do you feel?"

"Fine." I sweep my gaze over our surroundings, and I can't help smiling. "We did it, didn't we? The worlds are unbound and devoid of magics, and we haven't forgotten each other."

"You already said that, before you passed out."

"Oh. Sorry." I glance around, but stop as I feel something strange inside me. For a moment, I can't understand what I'm sensing. Then it hits me—so hard that I gasp and stumble into Gabriel, clutching his shirt. "Oh, my God. I remember everything."

"Do you have brain damage from all those magics? You keep repeating the same phrase."

"No, no, I'm not." I lift my face to his and grin. "I don't have amnesia anymore. My name is Sarah Delaney, and I was born in Olympia, Washington. My brother and parents were alive before the apocalypse, but I have no idea what happened to them after that. The rest of my memories are still pretty fuzzy."

"You'll get all your memories back, eventually."

I don't see how he could know that, but I realize Gabriel wants to make me feel better. He shouldn't bother. I feel amazing right now, just knowing we saved the world and that I do have a past.

Unfortunately, everyone who died during the apocalypse will stay dead. We couldn't bring them back. Something in the magics that Sefton Stainthorpe used to create the alchemy of worlds prevented that. But we have each other, we have a beautiful world to live in, and we have all the time we need to rebuild the Earth. All the infrastructure has been resurrected, but it might take decades to get everything working again.

"How will we get back to Sanctuary?" I ask. "We need to check on our friends, but we can't teleport anymore."

"Oh, don't worry about that," Erin says. "I can hot-wire any car you want. We'll return it to the original owner later on."

As we wander down the hill to the bridge that spans the river—the Paddock Viaduct, Allison tells us—we don't talk at all. I think we're in shock, still coming to terms with what we've done. We saved the freaking world. Grant will never have his wife and son back, and Erin will never see her sister again. But we've all forged new bonds that mean everything to us, as friends and as lovers.

Do I wish we could've brought back everyone who died? Of course I do. But we can't change the past. It's time to make a new future.

A few blocks past the viaduct, we find an abandoned vehicle that we can all just barely fit inside, but we can find something bigger as we travel. Erin hot-wires the car, and we get on the road.

We don't see anyone.

Maybe they're hiding, unsure of what has happened and whether they should trust it. It will take time for people to accept that the horrors have ended and they've been given a second chance. Still, it feels odd not to see anyone walking around. The city seems normal again, but vacant of human life.

Jarek follows us, loping along at an easy pace that lets him keep up with our car only because he's so enormous.

Allison, who sits up front with Erin, turns on the radio. Nothing but static. She flips through stations but finds none in operation. That's also no surprise.

While we traverse the city, I focus on what I do see rather than what I don't see. Though I had never visited Fort Worth before the apocalypse, I imagine it didn't look as pristine as it does today. Cities never are like that, at least not the ones I've visited. We pull over at the public library so Allison can take a peek inside. We all climb out to join her, mounting the steps to the portico and pushing through the unlocked doors.

While everyone else admires the restored library, which no longer bears the wounds of the apocalypse, I stand near the windows and stare out at nothing in particular.

Gabriel comes up behind me and loops his arms around my waist. "What's going on inside that amazing brain of yours?"

"This will sound weird."

"I'm on board for weird. I did make love to you inside an apocalypse machine, after all."

"Yeah, I know. But, um…" I glance back at our friends, who are laughing and smiling. "Maybe I should wait. Let everyone enjoy the remade world for a while first."

"You can tell me, Sarah. I can keep a secret, and I can handle whatever it is."

Of course he can. I know that. Gabriel is the most incredible person I've ever met.

So I decide to tell him. "I think we still have our Echo powers. Pretty sure nobody else does. Just the six of us."

"Not Aldith either?"

I shake my head.

"What about the creatures here and the ones we consigned to the Echo?"

I shake my head again. "Just us."

Our friends wander over to us, and they can clearly tell Gabriel and I have been engaged in a serious discussion. I can see it in their expressions.

"What's going on?" Allison asks.

I turn toward Gabriel, and he rubs his thumb over my chin. He wants me to share my revelation, and that makes me realize I should.

"We still have Echo powers," I say. "I just realized that a few minutes ago. No one else has them, just the six of us. Are you guys okay with that?"

Our four friends exchange glances and shrugs. Then Allison says, "It actually makes sense that we would keep our powers. Each of us played a vital role in the apocalypse and its reversal. We must be quantum entangled—with each other, at least."

"With the universe," I say. "That's what my intuition tells me."

"And we believe you. But this is one revelation that should never be shared with anyone outside our group."

"Does that mean we have to drive all the way back to Sanctuary?"

Erin grins. "Oh, yeah. But we'll do it in style."

When we leave the library, we find out what Erin meant. She had spotted a big RV in the parking lot across the street, and now she hot-wires it so we can travel in comfort. Jarek will follow on foot.

Our journey takes the better part of two days. The whole time, we debate whether anyone will be waiting for us in Sanctuary and whether that camp still exists. We have to leave our RV and travel the last bit on foot. But when we reach Sanctuary, it still looks like it had before the Brain destroyed it, and our friends are thrilled to see us. Willow races up to give all of us big hugs.

After our homecoming, we begin to take small groups of our Sanctuary friends on little excursions out into the wider world so they can see that the destruction brought on by the alchemy of worlds has indeed been reversed.

I wish we didn't have to tell everyone that their loved ones who died will never come back. I wish we'd been able to save them. But our friends understand.

A week after we reversed the apocalypse, I ask Gabriel to come with me on a private excursion. I've been having dreams about the day the alchemy of worlds began, and I have a hunch I can find more answers about my past by following the clues in my dreams. To make the journey faster, we teleport to Olympia, Washington, being as careful as we can to make sure no one sees us using magic.

We find the house where I'd lived, but nobody is home. Though I'd shared this home with a roommate, my intuition tells me she didn't survive the first wave of the apocalypse.

As we're walking out of the house, three men amble up the driveway.

Gabriel pulls out the revolver he had holstered under his jacket and aims it at the men. "Stop right there. Who are you and what do you want?"

One man holds up his hands. "Take it easy. We've been coming here every week for the past six months, hoping to find Sarah."

"Why?"

"To make sure she's okay. She took off so fast that we never had the chance to explain."

I sidle up to Gabriel but look at the stranger. "I saw you in my dreams. How do we know each other?"

"From the hospital." The man lowers his hands but does not try to approach us. "I was a doctor, and these guys were nurses. We took care of you during your coma."

"My what?"

"Six weeks before the apocalypse, you were in a car accident with your parents and your brother. Only you survived, but you were comatose. Until the day the world went crazy. Then you woke up and ran."

"I remember running. Creatures were chasing me." I inch toward the man but halt a couple of yards away. "You do seem familiar."

Gabriel grasps my arm. "Are you sure you recognize these men?"

"Yes." I freeze as I realize what the doctor said. "My parents and brother are dead?"

The man nods. "I'm sorry. We tried to find any other relatives you might have, but there wasn't anyone. We managed to catch you and protect you from the creatures, but you fell into another coma. Then two months later, you vanished."

I hug myself, suddenly feeling cold. Tears sting my eyes. My family is gone. A force I might never understand must have sent me to Sanctuary, so

Gabriel and I could save the worlds. I will grieve for my family, but I have a new home now and friends who mean everything to me.

Gabriel places a protective arm around me. "Thanks for letting us know about Sarah and her family. But I need to take her home right now."

"Of course. Good luck. It's a new world out there."

We return to Sanctuary, and life goes on. What else can we do? This new world presents many challenges, and we need to focus on the future. Over the next few weeks, we start to improve our camp—erecting permanent structures and bringing in generators to give us some electricity. It will be a long time until the power grid gets up and running again.

We travel around in our RV to meet other survivors and find out what's going on elsewhere, making friends along the way. It helps us feel less isolated and more like the world is gradually returning to normal.

Then the big day arrives. Allison goes into labor. Forty-six hours later, she gives birth to a beautiful baby boy. And three days after that, the camp hosts a double wedding—Erin and Grant, and me and Gabriel, with Willow as our flower girl. Life might not be exactly what it was before the apocalypse, but this new beginning gives everyone hope for the future.

To survivors of the alchemy of worlds, hope means everything.

ANNA DURAND IS A BESTSELLING, MULTI-AWARD-WINNING AUTHOR OF contemporary and paranormal romance. Her books have earned bestseller status on every major retailer and wonderful reviews from readers around the world. But that's the boring spiel. Here are some really cool things you want to know about Anna!

Born on Lackland Air Force Base in Texas, Anna grew up moving here, there, and everywhere thanks to her dad's job as an instructor pilot. She's lived in Texas (twice), Mississippi, California (twice), Michigan (twice), and Alaska—and now Ohio.

As for her writing, Anna has always made up stories in her head, but she didn't write them down until her teen years. Those first awful books went into the trash can a few years later, though she learned a lot from those stories. Eventually, she would pen her first romance novel, the paranormal romance *Willpower*, and she's never looked back since.

Want even more details about Anna? Get access to her extended bio when you subscribe to her newsletter and download the free bonus ebook, *Hot Scots Confidential*. You'll also get hot deleted scenes, character interviews, fun facts, and more!

VISIT ANNADURAND.COM TO SIGN UP.

www.ingramcontent.com/pod-product-compliance
Lightning Source LLC
Chambersburg PA
CBHW072134300726
48975CB00003B/1062